{ DELPHINE PUBLICATIONS PRESENTS }

INEVITABLE
ACT II

AN EROTIC ROMANCE BY

JOHNIE
Jay

IF I CANT HAVE YOU...

Inevitable Act II

Delphine Publications focuses on bringing a reality check to the genre urban literature. All stories are a work of fiction from the authors and are not meant to depict, or represent any particular person.

Names, characters, places, and incidents are either the product of the author's imagination or are used fictitiously, and any resemblances to an actual person living or dead are entirely coincidental.

Inevitable Act II
© 2014 Johnny Jay

ISBN 13 – 978-0996084413

Published by Delphine Publications
Edited by Tee Marshall
Cover Art by Odd Ball Designs
Layout by Write On Promotions
www.DelphinePublications.com

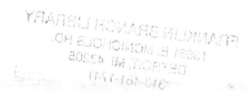

Dedication

LOVE:

The grandest catch 22 ever created. Although the most
scariest thing in the world it is also the most amazing. The
only way to fully experience the latter is to ignore the first.

— *Johnie Jay*

Pushing The Envelope

(The last chapter from Act I)

I stumbled a little walking to my door. Think I'm going to have to cut back a little. One thing drinking is good for though is great sex.

I showered using my mango Bath and Body Works shower gel. Had to make sure I smelled edible. While drying off in front of the mirror I inspected my body from head to toe. "Pretty good," I said to myself as I twisted and turned.

Damn, I was so excited. This was the first time since my ex that a man has come into my place. The only reason that he is getting this privilege is because I know him a little, I'm horny as hell, and because he's fine as fuck. Humph! I guess that's more than one reason.

I slipped on my robe thinking that there was no need for extra clothing. This was an official booty call. There was going to be no watching movies, popping popcorn, or catching up. I'm bringing his ass in my room to take care of business.

I surveyed my room. Candles were lit. Light jazz oozed from the stereo and the Patron still had its grips on me. Seeing the imprints of dicks and grabbing crotches earlier had a sista feeling pretty frisky right about now.

I heard the buzzer from the front door go off and immediately became nervous again. Shit, okay girl breathe, calm down. I'm dedicating this night to you, Darnell. Five feet from the door, I inhaled, exhaled, inhaled...

Knock! Knock! Knock!

I exhaled, then opened the door. "Hey," he said looking just as good fully clothed as he did earlier with shorts and a cut off.

"Hey, yourself," I said welcoming him in.

"Mmmmm, you smell..." he licked his lips, "...edible."

My pussy fluttered with excitement. "That's because I am," I responded calmly, falling back on the door.

"I'll be the judge of that." His sniffs turned into licks and soft kisses on my neck. My kitty turned into a fountain as I moaned and swooned to the music in my head.

"Mmmm, you weren't lying. You are delectable." He lassoed swirls around my neck and ran his fingers through my hair. Damn, I loved that!

"Kiss me!" I had to speed things up, had to taste him back. Liquor still lingered on his palate. His tongue was so thick and fat that it filled my mouth. If it was any indication of his width, this was going to be a good night.

Our slow kissing turned into an intense tongue lashing. I couldn't wait any longer. It was time to take this into the bedroom.

"Come on baby." I grabbed his hand. "Follow me." I led him into my sanctuary that glowed from the flickering candles. "If I'm not mistaken, you owe me something," I said seductively letting my robe fall to the floor. By the look on his face, he appeared to be very pleased at what stood before him.

Pierre licked his lips and walked closer to me placing his hands on my ass. "You have oil?"

"Of course." I have to admit, I was a little disappointed. I was kind of hoping that he would see me naked and say, "Fuck the massage." Then throw me on the bed and bang me to sleep. However, I did really need a good rub down.

By the time I retrieved the oil out of my top drawer he had already taken off his shirt. I reminded myself not to drool as he started to unzip his pants. This guy's body was amazing, reminded me of Terrell Owens. He had muscles on top of muscles, abs of steel. His pants dropped to the floor exposing his black Calvin Klein boxers. The darkness of the room and the dark color of his underwear did me a disservice. It hid the most important muscle on his body.

We both climbed on the bed and he instructed me to lie back and relax. After about five minutes into the massage, I was glad that he stuck to the plan. I didn't realize how tense I was until he kneaded me with his fingertips.

He now had me on my back, one leg flat on the bed, one leg on his shoulder. He massaged my foot, my calves, my hips, and my thighs. "Damn she's pretty," he said. I slightly lifted my head and saw that he was staring at my parted pussy lips.

"Is she?" I snickered. "You know she loves to be kissed."

"Mmm, French kissed I hope."

"Is there any other way?" He gently grabbed my leg and slid his tongue down until it rested in the crease that connected the inside of my leg to the outside of my kitty. His tongue was so warm. He teased me for a few more seconds before diving in.

"Mmm, baby, that's it. Suck this pussy." I tried to hold still but couldn't. I was squirming all over the bed. He darted his thick tongue in and out making me cream even more.

"Ooouuu yeah, that's it right there, just like that." Yeah he was good. Pierre found my spot with his tongue and tried to make it his permanent residence. "Oh, my God!" I would have to pray for forgiveness later for using God's name in vain.

He rose up for a gasp of air. "You like that baby?"

"Mmm yes, I love it."

"Tell me." he said, while flicking again. "Tell me that you love it."

"Ooouuu shit yes...I do, I do. Damn baby, I'm about to cum, yes...yes!" My orgasm was so strong that I couldn't even get the scream out. I just stopped breathing. I thought I was going to faint.

"Baby," I managed to get out in between gasps of air.

"What's up?"

"Ba...by." I had managed to start back breathing.

"Yes," he answered again.

I inhaled and then exhaled. "Fuck me! Fuck me right now!" Pierre started rubbing my clit, throwing kerosene on my already blazing fire. I was ready, ready for anything that he wanted to do. "Condom?" I asked in between pants.

"Yep." He reached over the side of the bed into his pants pocket. I laid my head back on my down pillow enjoying the one finger that he now had inside of me. "Mmmmm, your pussy is so hot." His voice was low and deep. "Can't wait to be inside of you."

"Please...don't...don't wait. Take me now." I was drunk and horny. Don't know exactly what I was saying, but I know if I was sober hearing it I probably would've cracked up. It made me wish that I had a tape recorder so that I could get a good laugh later.

I heard the condom wrapper rip and a couple of seconds later I felt Pierre kneel over me. With my eyes closed, I anticipated his dick. I let out a long sigh, finally real dick. Not rubber, not plastic, but a real dick. He continued to finger fuck me, faster, harder. Instead of his middle finger, which he was using before, now it felt like he switched to his pinky.

"Come on baby, fuck me! Fuck me!" My pussy was longing to be filled but he continued ramming me with his finger. At this point, I'm thinking maybe he's doing this because he couldn't get hard. If that was the case, don't go down on your digits to the pinky, shit, go up! Use your thumb or add more fingers if you have too, but the pinky? My walls needed stretching.

"Baby! Come on, fuck me."

"What?" Pierre sounded a little confused.

I was a little drunk so maybe I was slurring my words or something where he couldn't understand me. "Stop teasing me and put it in." I put more effort into my word pronunciation this time. I made sure that I spoke more clearly. I felt his pinky inside of me moving slower and I decided enough talk, time for some assistance. "You know what, let me help you out," I said, sitting up a little. I thought that if I jacked him off for a little while that he could get hard and break me off.

I reached down for his dick and thought, maybe I grabbed to hard because I pulled the condom right off. I felt my face tense up as I reached back between his legs and felt what had to be his navel.

"What the..." I sat all the way up and looked at what had to be a joke. I saw what had to be the smallest, skinniest dick on planet Earth. "You...you, you were actually fucking me?" I don't think that the situation had really registered in my brain yet.

He looked as if he had an attitude as he made his way off the bed. "What are you trying to say?" His voice wasn't low and sultry any more. It was high and squeaky.

"I mean..." I pointed at the small package between his legs. "What is...oh, my God!" I started chuckling. "You got to be fucking kidding me. God, you are obviously punishing me for something," I said looking toward the heavens. I hurried up and put on my robe.

He put on his boxers and fumbled with his pants. "You know, you fucking black women kill me!"

No he didn't. "Excuse me?" I asked putting both hands on my hips. I didn't see that coming at all.

"You heard me. Acting like every man has to have an 11 or a 12 inch dick."

I cut him off. "First of all I never said that I want an 11 or 12 inch dick, but damn, can you at least give me a four or five? I'm the first one to say that size doesn't really matter but when you are two inches...and it's skinny, what the fuck am I supposed to do with that?" I shook my head and laughed at the mental picture that was in my head of his tiny dick,

He fastened his pants and buttoned up his shirt. "That's why all y'all are lonely to this day. White women never complain."

"That's because they are used to small ass dicks."

He looked stunned. Like this was the first time he realized he had such a small penis. "A few minutes ago I had you catching the Holy Ghost, calling on Jesus, now you are up here tripping."

"I'm saying, that's true, but I'm not a woman who can be ate out all night baby. I like dick, inside of me, deep inside of me." I placed my finger on my temples and tried to prevent what felt to be the beginning of a stress headache. "Your tongue is longer than your dick for heaven's sake. And I really thought that you were fingering me," I said lowering my voice.

Pierre rushed out of my bedroom. I followed behind him. "If your pussy was a little tighter then..."

Oh, don't even go there. Don't you dare try to put you having a tiny dick on me. I haven't had sex in over five months. My kitty is tight." His eyes widened at the shock of my confession. Actually, hearing the months that I've went without dick shocked me a little as well. "The blown out coochie excuse ain't even going to work."

He rolled his eyes as he reached for the doorknob and opened it. "Fuck you!" I guess he ran out of excuses.

"That's what I wanted you to do daddy, but you're obviously," I held up my index and thumb approximately two inches apart, "not a big enough man to get the job done." He walked away and slammed the door.

Walking back to my bedroom, I yelled out loud, "Shit, shit, shiiiiiiiit!" What the fuck a bitch gotta do to get some good quality dick? I dived in the bed and stared at the ceiling trying to think of what to do next. I have to let my girls know about this one.

I reached over for the phone and after a few grabs I managed to finally retrieve my phone from the nightstand. I was too frustrated to even spend the time looking through the phone log for Brianna's name and decided to enter the numbers from memory. Instead of calling, I decided to text a message just in case she was occupied with something or someone.

I texted, **Girrrlll you aint gonna believe this one...I think I'm done with men...can't even get a decent fuck nowadayz. I think muscle man had surgery to remove most of his dick...had 2 inches...no fucking lie, lol.** Then I pressed send.

After about a minute with no response I looked at the time and figured that she was probably sleep. I stood up from the bed, blew out the candles, and turned my stereo down. As soon as my head reconnected with the pillow, my phone alerted me to a new text message.

You can't find a good fuck because you are not looking in the right place!!!

Wow, that's weird. I was looking in the same places that she was. I texted back, **And where do you suggest I look...smart ass...lol.**

My phone chimed again and I read the response. **Well Gabrielle, I suggest that you look in my direction.**

Okay, now I was really confused. I sat up in the bed looking at my phone. Wonder why she's calling me by my text signature? Even though Bri was the one who gave me the name Gabrielle, making a play off the angel Gabriel from the Bible, she has never called me by it before.

I don't think I'm shocked that she would hit on me especially after the night that we had, but it just didn't sound like something that she would say. Maybe someone has her phone, I said to myself as I texted back. **Who is this...better not have my friend's phone.** Then I pressed send and waited.

Hold on baby girl, you texted me...check the number that you sent your message too.

I did just that and on further inspection noticed that for the last number instead of pressing eight I pressed seven. I had sent my message to the wrong person. I felt a wave of embarrassment engulf me. Shit! And I sent it to a guy. Shit, shit! How stupid do I look right now airing out all of my business? Maybe he will just forget the entire thing.

My phone vibrated in my hand. **Gabrielle, I was serious about helping you out with your LITTLE problem...lol.**

I laughed at the caps. I text back, **Ha haha, very funny.**

So...do u want help or not? Mystery man texted back.

Couldn't believe he was still texting, oh well, can't go to sleep anyways and I have nothing else to do, I began pecking on my phones keyboard. **And how do you plan on helping me out, wait, let me guess, you can fuck good and you have a big dick?** I pressed send.

New message! **Damn, you must know me huh?**

I laughed and texted back. **If I had a dollar for every guy who thinks what you think.**

No thinking baby, I know.

His cockiness was beginning to pique my interest. Time to make him choke. A sly smile crept across my face as I texted him back. Okay Dirk Diggler, if you're all that...prove it! That ought to slow him down. I immediately thought differently after reading his response.

Sure what do you have in mind?

Actually, I didn't have anything in mind because I didn't think he would even respond, well at least not that quick. Couldn't let him back me down though. I had an idea. Show me.

What? You want me to come over?

Come over? You're not worthy of that yet baby. Prove what you said is true. You have a camera phone right?

I'm following you now!

Put up or shut up, Big Boy!!! I pressed send. "Your move," I said as I stared at the clock. One minute went by then two then three. "Humph," I knew it. Must admit though I was actually a little disappointed, I was just starting to have fun.

My phone sounded and vibrated in my hand. I saw that I had picture mail and my heart rate sped up. I had three pictures sent to me. "Okay, let's see what you are working with," I said as I opened the first picture. "Whoa!" I slowly maneuvered my phone as I stared at a fat juicy dick and an even juicer head. I hurriedly opened the other two pictures and saw that this gorgeous ass dick from two more angles. It didn't look enormous, it just looked, well, perfect.

So...what do you think, do I qualify?

I texted back, **Mmmmmm definitely, if this is really you.**

Lol, wow! Guess I'm over here taking pictures of another guy's dick huh?

You never know these days.

Well before you even ask, no! I'm not gay or bi. I'm straight like Indian hair. So what do you want me to do to prove it's all me?

I thought for a second before texting him back. **You have shaving cream?**

Yep!

I want you to write a "G" for my name in shaving cream, right on that juicy dick and send me a pic of it. About four minutes later my request was fulfilled.

Anything else my queen? He texted back.

Hold up! I'm still admiring your dick.

Lol...well I'm glad you approve. I apologize for the night you had. If I was your man, I'm sure you would get mad at me for some things, sometime or other, but I promise

you it would never be for not satisfying you sexually.

Mmmmm. More wetness. I contracted Kitty as I continued to look at his pictures. After a couple of minutes of me not responding, he texted me again. **What's the matter...done playing?**

Naw I'm here, still playing...so what do we do now? I typed curious and eager for what was next.

Now it's your turn!!!

My eye's became wide and felt like they were going to pop out of my head. I texted back pretending that I didn't know what he had in mind. **What do you mean, my turn?**

Come on now, I know you're a smart woman...I showed you mine now show me yours.

That wasn't in the plan!

It's in the new and revised one lol.

I thought long and hard, and the more I thought about it the wetter I became. He didn't know me. Didn't know who I was or my real name. It's not like we were sending face pics. Oh what the hell. I said tonight that I was going to be more carefree and as far as I'm concerned, the night was not over yet. I slowly spread my legs.

My phone vibrated as I prepared to take a picture and startled me. I read the text. I'm waiting...

I texted him back. **Okay, okay give me a minute.**

I zoomed in and took the picture. I knew that I was still drunk because I was now getting wet looking at my own kitty. I decided to take another picture, this time I used my fingers to spread my lips and took the money shot. I grouped the pics and sent them together. I immediately became nervous. I liked the way Kitty looked but would he? What am I doing?

He texted back. **Oh my god!!!!!**

Oh my God? Why would he text that? Shit, he doesn't like them. I knew it. **What's wrong?**

.

No...what's right? Are you really that wet or did you pour something on you?

Whewwww. I exhaled deeply and responded to his message. **No additives...that's all me 100%.**

Baby, I would suck on you all fuckin night...you have a beautiful pussy!

Beautiful and pussy in the same sentence, that's a first. I laughed as I pressed send.

You're funny, I like that.

The dick looks delicious, hopefully you know how to use it...but are you good at oral? I pressed send.

A couple seconds later, he responded. **That's my specialty.**

Lol, so what aren't you good at? I texted and waited for him to answer.

Commitment! His answer threw me off for a minute. I definitely wasn't expecting that. My phone vibrated again. **Haven't found anyone who makes me even want to give it a try.**

Wow! And you're honest.

That's the only way to be.

I had fun with you tonight...thanks for making me feel better.

You're leaving me???

I thought about my date tomorrow and even though I didn't want to go, I had to end the fun. As I texted him back I began to yawn. **Yep! Have to get some sleep.**

Do you have to get it right now?

I laughed at his obvious objection to me leaving him. Guess I'll leave him with something good, I thought to myself as I texted him back. **Actually I'm about to masturbate to your pic...then I'm going to sleep.** Send.

Are you ever going to text me again?

Do you think you deserve that? I texted back while smiling.

Definitely!!!!

Cocky huh?

Confident.

I like confident.

Then you'll like me.

Well I'll see how hard you make me cum...that'll decide if you deserve me texting you again lol.

I'll take it.

Lol okay, bye.

Bye!

I'd never sexted before. It was somewhat different but fun nonetheless. I think it was the anticipation of what the next text was going to be. Whatever it was, I liked it a lot. Kitty definitely did too. I slid my middle finger through my warm folds. Mmmm, Kitty definitely did!

Even though I was turned on my mood was quickly soured by other thoughts that were going through my head. I mean don't get me wrong, I was absolutely happy to finally be done with my ex, and I thought I was ready for the single life but thinking about my recent encounters had me thinking that maybe I should be a nun. It's really starting to feel like I'm being Punk'd. I can't even get fucked! The best things that I have going for me right now are a multi-millionaire that I'm not so sure I'm into, a mystery guy that I haven't said one word to, but constantly captures and completely takes over my thoughts; and a wrong-number-texter that's giving me more pleasure than my last two sex attempts, big dick that came too fast and a baby dick that I confused with a finger. God, if you want me to stay single just say so, but, if my one is out there, please let him be known!

Prelude

What is the one thing that you want more than anything in this world? The one thing that makes you feel incomplete without having it? Now imagine if you will, actually having it in your life. Wanting it for so long; and then finally, actually obtaining it. Feels good doesn't it?

I'm sitting here looking at that one thing, the one person that I wanted more than anything. He's lying in my lap, eyes closed, body limp and breathing softly. He is still handsome as the first night that my eyes locked in on him despite the stream of blood now trickling down his forehead. My once brilliant-white dress now resembles a peppermint with the red traces of blood swirled and smeared all over it.

I am now living that scene in the movies where background figures and sounds become blurred and muffled. My heart feels like it is trying to rip its way out of my chest and jump into his. Through the smothered voices, I hear my name called repeatedly but my mouth will not respond, all letting me know that something had definitely gone wrong. Whatever it is has to turn out right, because I'm here, with my one thing—my everything.

Now imagine again the feeling you would have, if you were fortunate enough to get that one thing that you wanted more than anything in the world. Imagine having that feeling only for a split second, because the second that you got it...it was taken away!

INEVITABLE

ACT II

Kandi Is Addictive

The warmer the weather, the less clothes women wore. And that was definitely the case tonight at Elysium. Cleavage and ass cracks were running rampant. Caesar and I were into our second round of drinks and feeling kind of toasty. The club was packed and the dance floor was jumping. This definitely had the makings of a good night.

"What up dawg, you taking it slow tonight?" Caesar asked.

"I'm just surveying my territory that's all. It's too much of the same thing in here. I need different prey, you feel me?"

Caesar looked at me like I was crazy. "Too much of the same thing? And by that you mean young, pretty, and naive? Shit, that's exactly the type that I'm looking for."

"I just need a challenge, that's all."

"Challenge huh?"

I took a nice sized gulp of my Henney and Coke. "Yep, challenge."

"Well tonight might be your night, because I have just what you're looking for."

"Oh yeah, and what's that?"

Caesar nodded in the direction across the bar from us. When I saw her, I damn near dropped my drink. She was gorgeous. "Now what am I looking for again?" I said, trying to play cool.

"Beyoncé and her girls. You remember the girl I told you I

danced with, and then her girl came over and I wished I had met her first?"

I rubbed my temple as if I was in deep thought. "Yeah, okay, that's them huh? So which one were you digging again?"

"Shit, all of them. If I had to choose, it would be redbone hands down. But since I don't have to choose, I'm picking neither."

"Neither? Why is that?"

"Future, you can look at them and tell that they are too much work and effort to try and get. Now why go through all of that, when I can get a young lady just as pretty but easier. Like, for instance... her!" He pointed at a young lady who stood near us by herself looking like she was looking for someone. You could tell by the way she dressed that she didn't have too much game. She wore too much makeup, her jeans were a little too tight, and her bra was at least two sizes too small. She was cute nonetheless.

"I'll holla at you in a few," Caesar said as he walked over to the young kitten. He whispered something to her and she immediately started cheesing. He then looked back at me and gave me a nod then walked away. I couldn't help but to smile; he was indeed becoming a player, maybe not as good as me, but definitely a player.

I looked back over the bar and refocused on her. She and her girls were damn near naked, but she still managed to look sexy instead of trashy.

I tried to remember what they were drinking on the last time that they were here. "Cosmopolitans," I said to myself. To get her attention, I figured that I would send them all drinks; that way she wouldn't think that I'm too pressed with just her, but it should get her to sit up and take notice.

I flagged over my favorite bartender. Have to make a mental note to call her this week.

"What you need baby?" she asked.

2

Johnie Jay

"You mean besides you?" I answered, watching her blush. "I need three Cosmos and I need you to deliver them to the three lovely ladies standing over there."

She looked across the bar then back at me. "Great taste!" she said, winking. I gave her a fifty and told her to keep the change. I like the fact that even though she always sees me hitting on other women and them on me, she always plays her position. Never acted jealous and never said anything out of order. She was passing my test with flying colors. If she kept this up I would definitely have to break her off some.

I watched as she delivered the three fuchsia-colored drinks to possibly the three best looking females in the club tonight. The stunned looks on their faces were priceless; I could tell they were not used to having someone buying them drinks. Tammie pointed over at me and they all looked in my direction. Light-skinned mouthed something that I couldn't quite make out and flashed me a smile. If I wasn't so into her girl, I would be all over her pretty ass. The other friend with the long ponytail was basically drooling. She was cute, but a little too easy for my taste. I bet Caesar wouldn't think so. However; the one who mattered, locked eyes with me and didn't let go.

We both stared like we knew each other from another place, maybe another lifetime. She broke our connection and started speaking to her girls. I looked around the club aimlessly to occupy a minute of my time. It was a real struggle to have my back to her, knowing that she was only a few feet away. Okay, one more little look won't hurt.

I set my attention back to her and at the same time she was turning to look back in my direction. "Thanks," she mouthed, with the corner of her mouth turning upward.

"My pleasure," I whispered back and then her girls stole her attention away from me again. I had to think of a way to get her alone. I had to talk to her, had to get into her world. I wanted to reconnect.

And then out of the blue, I felt a small hand softly touch me on my lower back. I turned around to see Kandi smiling up at me wearing another killer blood-red dress.

"Hey baby! Do you miss me?"

"Should I?" I asked, trying to play hard but it was difficult to do with those luscious light caramel-colored melons popping out at me.

She stood back and pouted, making her look even sexier. "Well, I think you should, because I miss you."

"Puhh!" I started laughing. "Who do you think you're fooling woman? You don't miss anyone."

"Future, why are you dogging me out?" I could tell that she was starting to get a little frustrated from the cold shoulder that I was giving her. "We are both grown adults with very busy lives, who happen to want the same thing—no commitment. Now I know I haven't called you since the last time you did me...and did me so well I might add! But your phone works also and I haven't received any calls from you either."

"Look baby, I'm not tripping, I mean, do you! If it seems like I'm a little testy, then I apologize. I had a long week that's all but it has nothing to do with you." I had to diffuse the situation because I didn't want her to think that she was getting to me in any way. I still couldn't believe the way she played me after I fucked her lights out.

The most important thing right now was how good she was looking. I didn't want to ruin the chance of me tapping that again. I looked at her from her pretty toes, to her curvy hips, up to that cute ass face of hers. Naw, can't fuck up fucking her again.

She crept over to me cautiously. "So we are on then?"

I took a sip from my drink. "Of course we are," I said letting Buddy do the thinking for me.

She ran her hands from my shoulder down to my

4

forearms. "You really didn't miss me?" she asked, pouting again.

I laughed at her trying to butter me up. "How can I not miss you woman?"

She smiled, probably because she felt that she had won the power struggle. "And did he miss me?" she asked, moving her hand from my forearms to my jeans, making a home smack-dab on top of Buddy. I thought about how she squirted all over the place when she came and immediately sprung to life. "Whoa! Never mind, I think he answered for himself."

She moved closer to me, using her body to shield her hand gently massaging my genitals. My boxer briefs were doing an okay job of holding me down. I tried my best to be cool but it was damn hard...literally! Kandi stood on her tiptoes and put her mouth to my ear.

"Baby, my pussy is so wet right now. I need you to eat me out. Mmmmm, I need you to suck on this clit, I need you to kiss this pussy. I want to put my juices all over your face."

By this time, I think we were starting to get some attention from the partiers, and the fact that she was licking my lobe right now wasn't helping out any. Shit, I forgot about ole girl across the bar. Guess all the blood that moved from my brain to my dick had something to do with that. Hopefully the tight packed crowd provided a smoke screen. I had to look to find out.

"Damn girl! You know how to turn a brother on. What are you drinking?" Before she even had a chance to respond, I twisted my body to act like I was trying to find a bartender. I looked across the bar. Yes, she's not there, must've walked away, hope she didn't see the raunchiness that was going on.

Kandi turned me back around. "I'm not drinking anything tonight...unless it's you." She winked, turned her back to me and grinded her butt on me to the fast-paced baseline that was playing over the speakers. She had me so worked up that I wanted to grab her, throw her over my shoulder and carry her out of the club caveman style, but she grabbed me first.

"Come on baby, this is my song!" She didn't even give me a chance to answer. She was no doubt used to getting her way. I surveyed the area and made sure Buddy was situated while being dragged to the dance floor. I didn't see her but I knew she was near. I felt her presence. I did see Caesar and the chick he had just met a minute ago dry humping on the floor.

Kandi went to work immediately, throwing her ass back on me. She moved so sensual and seductive, never bumping or jerking. She stayed smooth like milk and honey. Kandi turned to face me and moved in closer. I had one hand in the air and one on her ass, when I saw her going upstairs to the VIP section, escorted by the big security guard from the front door.

On the way up she slowly looked over the stair railing as if she was looking for something or someone. Then our eyes met again and locked, letting me know that she had found her target. My eyes asked her, Why the fuck are you going up there? Everything you need and more is right here. Hers were asking, why are you wasting your time with that? You need to be coming up these stairs to come get me! I smiled and she did the same until she disappeared. I focused back on Kandi, who was really into the music and had missed my stare-down.

One thing is for sure, Kandi demanded attention. I laughed to myself at guys that were dancing with women and gave more attention to Kandi's ass than to their partners.

She slowed down and motioned with her finger for me to come closer. I leaned in. "You never responded to my question that I asked you at the bar."

"And what question was that?" I asked.

She playfully punched me in the arm. "Stop playing Future! You know what question." She leaned in closer to my ear. "Are you drinking me tonight?"

"Oh, I'm sorry; I thought he—" I looked down at Buddy,

"answered that for me."

She smiled as she followed my gaze down to my dick. "He did, but now I want you to."

I switched my face to the other side of hers. "I can't wait to have my face buried in that sweet ass pussy of yours."

She switched her face back to the other side of mine. "Mmmm hmmmm!" She dragged her M's out so seductively. "Wait, on second thought, I think I want to squat over your face this time." I turned her around, putting her back to me to hide my erection. She giggled as she flipped my dick around with her ass cheeks while dancing. "What's wrong baby?" she asked with a devilish grin, "are you okay?"

I smiled. "Yeah, I'm good, just stay close to me. I don't want to poke anyone's eye out." The DJ slowed the music down and I immediately grabbed her by the waist. "Come on let's get off of this floor," I said, knowing that she could do more damage to me with a slower song than a fast one.

"Not yet, I'm just getting warmed up."

I smiled, "Oh yeah, well I'm getting overheated." And then I felt a slight bump.

"Excuse me." I turned around to see some guy who looked exactly like Juwaun Jones walk pass me.

"Oh my God!" Kandi said holding her face. "Is that Juwaun Jones from the Detroit Lions?"

"Looks like it," I answered, unimpressed.

"You think that's his woman that he's with?"

I looked at the sexy chocolate, short haired, short skirt wearing cutie on his arm and realized that she definitely wasn't his woman, because she was mine whether she knew it or not. "Naw that's probably just a groupie," I said trying to control my breathing. This was the second time that I've seen them together. What if they were dating? Naw, couldn't be. She wouldn't be looking at me like she wanted me if she was really with him.

7

By now, most of the partygoers had stopped dancing to look at Juwaun and her get their dance on.

"Future, do you know how to ballroom?"

I felt my temperature immediately start to rise as Kandi compared me to Mr. Famous. "Naw...never learned."

"You should, I'm telling you; women love a man who can dance, I mean really dance."

What was she trying to say? That I couldn't really dance. Ain't this a bitch! She still has the nerve to have her ass all up on my crotch. Those fluid movements and freaky grinds from earlier were now gone. Juwaun had managed to steal my personal attention from my personal groupie—and from the looks of it, he's trying to steal the only woman who has personally managed to grab my interest.

"I can't believe that he can dance that good." She was now holding on to my arm. "You would think that with him being as tall as he is and an athlete that he would be, I don't know... stiff." She had to be kidding. Bring me out to the floor to give her attention to another man. I'm Future! I reminded myself. I don't care how pretty you are, I'm out. Fuck her, fuck the receiver, and fuck the bitch on the receiver's arm. I turned around and parted the crowd. When I stepped off the dance floor, I glanced back to see how fast Kandi would be running to catch up with me. She must have had other plans, because she was in the same spot and the same position as when I left.

"Ain't this bout a bitch!" I said, as I walked towards the restroom to relieve myself. I ran into my boy on the way.

"Whatup doe? Damn it's off the hook in here tonight!"

I looked around. "Yeah, live as hell. Where is ole girl?"

Caesar laughed. "With her girls trying to make up an excuse to leave with me."

"Whaaaa, she dissing her girls for you? You must have been spitting mad game boy."

8

He stroked his goatee. "Something like that."

"You almost ready to leave?" I said, looking at my watch.

"Yeah I'm good...you?"

"Yeah, got to go piss first, but you know that valet line is going to be crazy."

"Damn, forgot about that," Caesar said.

Nearing the bathroom, I was greeted by a long line of girls lined up on the outside of the women's room.

"Hey ladies," I warmly greeted as I passed.

"Hey!"

All the urinals were occupied, so I went to the stalls. The first two were occupied by women. I mean they had no shame. The doors were wide open and they were squatted over the stool pissing away. Fuck it! You don't care, I don't either, I'm not moving and I'm looking. Shouldn't have come in here.

The woman I stared at blew me a kiss while freshening up. I blew one back. She stood up, wiped, and pulled her dress back down.

"Your turn," she said, holding her hand out and letting me walk past her into the stall.

"Thank you," I said, smiling at her.

"And my turn to watch you." She came up from behind me just when I was whipping Buddy out and wrapped her hands around me stroking my chest. "Mmmm, work out huh?"

"Little bit." She then leaned to the side to see what I was working with. Buddy was in good shape, semi-erect from all of the piss I was holding.

"Nice, very nice." She pulled back and pulled her phone from her purse. "Give me your number."

I thought against it for a couple of seconds but went against my first mind. Even though she was raunchy, she was cute and definitely fuckable. I figured that if nothing else popped off later, maybe I would hit her up. My phone vibrated and she told me to lock her number in.

I washed my hands and tipped the bathroom attendant. I was hoping I didn't run into Kandi as I was walking back up the stairs, because I probably would curse her ass out.

"That's him right there," my new bathroom friend notified her girl. "Yeah, I'm calling him for sure." I smiled and gave her a nod as I walked past. The valet line was getting thick and I jumped in it.

"Damn Future, did you have to take a shit?" Caesar asked.

I laughed. "Naw, it was a little packed, that's all."

"Did you ever holla at redbone or her girls?"

A little bit of my attitude returned. "We spoke...I said hi to them, but that's all."

"I think the one with the short hair might be kicking it with Juwaun Jones. This is the second time that I've seen him on her in this club."

I pretended not to give it too much thought. "So where is your girl?"

"Oh, I'm about to pick her up in front of her girl's crib. You want to follow me? Her girls asked if I had a friend."

"Naw I'm good. Good looking out though. I got a little something lined up already." I thought about who I should call to come over tonight. I had to take my aggression out on someone.

One of the attendants brought Caesar his truck first. "Alright Future, hit me up tomorrow."

"I will. Peace out and be safe!"

The scene outside was almost as packed as the club. I pulled my phone from my pocket and saw that I had two missed messages. One was from a chick that I had fucked three weeks prior, asking for seconds. The other was from Ricka, my ghetto Superhead, telling me how bad she wanted and needed my dick back in her mouth.

The attendant pulled Sally around with the top down. I

always threw in a couple of extra dollars for that. Guys were talking about how good my car sounded, and the women talked about how good it looked. Sally was an attention magnet for real.

After pulling out, I hit Jefferson Avenue and headed towards home. Just as I flipped my phone open to call Ricka, it vibrated in my hand.

"Hello."

"Hey baby."

I looked at my phone to make sure I was hearing correctly. "Kandi?"

"Yes Kandi. What happened to you in there? Why did you leave me, I was looking all over for you," she said, raising her voice.

"Had to use the restroom. I mean, I told you, but it was at the same time that you were admiring Juwaun." I had to put a little jab in there to make the story look good.

"Oh my God, I'm sorry. I really am. I don't want you to think that I was ignoring you at all. He's just my favorite player." She laughed. "Look at me sounding like a groupie. Baby I apologize, I guess you don't want me to come over huh?"

In my mind, I was saying, Hell naw, not after playing the kid like that. But my dick was saying, Come on over bitch and get this pussy whipping. "I am a little tired, long day." There you go Future, stay strong, I said to myself.

"Mmm, okay, I—mmmmm, I understand. Ouuuushi—mmmm, you sure you don't want to recon...mmmmm...sider?"

What the fuck were all the noises? "What's wrong with you, are you okay?"

"Yeah, yeah, I'm okay just driving and mmmm, playing with my pussy...ooouuu shit. I'm so horny...and so fucking wet!"

Stay strong Future, stick with it. "Playing with yourself huh?" I asked nonchalantly, clearing my throat. Buddy, had started to awaken.

11

"Yeah," she answered while panting, and then she started making smacking noises. I pressed my ear closer to the phone. "Mmmm, and she tastes so good, you should see how glazed my fingers are."

Shit, Buddy stay down. "Girl, you're crazy." I heard my voice crack.

"I'm not crazy baby. I'm horny, really...really horny. Need this pussy sucked on so bad!"

I tried to catch my words and prevent them from escaping my mouth but failed terribly. "I'll see you when you get here," I said, shaking my head on how weak I was. Shit! I thought to myself while shaking my head.

"Byyyyyee baaaaaby," she answered victorious. "See you in a few." She had won again. I couldn't seem to say no to this woman when it came to sex. No matter how hard I tried.

I took a quick shower and threw on a pair of gym shorts. About 10 minutes later, I received a call from downstairs alerting me of my guest. A light knock at my door shortly followed.

"Hey," I said uninterestedly, while letting Kandi in.

She looked down at my erection and smiled. "Damn baby, you sound so...not happy to see me." That's one thing about being a male. You can act one way, but females can always look at your dick and tell what you were really thinking. I closed the door behind her and looked down at Buddy, shaking my head.

"You are so easy," I whispered to him.

"You say something baby?" Kandi asked, turning around looking at me.

"Huh? Oh naw."

She stood in the middle of the living room looking sexy as hell. I have to take the power back, I reminded myself. She had a look as if she knew that I was silly putty in her hands.

I dimmed the lights. "Take your clothes off," I demanded, while looking at her already nearly non-existent wardrobe.

12

She smiled at me, obviously liking my tone. "Yes daddy." She unzipped that short red dress and let it fall to the floor, unveiling a matching red bra and panties. I walked over and sat on the edge of my bed. She walked over to me and unhooked her bra. She then turned around showing me that thin piece of material in-between her ass.

"Pull it out baby." I went to grab her G-string and she moved away from me. "Uh unn, with your tongue." Buddy was at full attention. She backed up to me again and arched her back. I grabbed her hips and turned my head to the side. Before pulling her G-string out with my teeth, I swirled my tongue over her asshole. With Kandi, I never would have to worry about smelling her. I could tell that from the first time I saw her. I don't know what she does before she comes over here, but just like the last time her ass really smelled like strawberries.

After pulling off her panties, she stood up straight and stared at Buddy. She squatted down, and slowly inch by inch without stopping, took all of me down to my balls. She then slowly pulled back, making gagging noises, and left my dick covered with thick gooey spit. Buddy was now jumping up and down with excitement.

"Touch it baby, feel how wet this pussy is." She grabbed my hand and directed it to her clean-shaven camel toe. She spread her legs and revealed a trail of wetness that had made its way down the inside of her thigh.

I arched my middle finger while entering her juicy lips and scooped out some of her honey. "Mmmm, damn you taste good," I said, slurping on my now glazed finger.

"I told you," she said smiling. "Eat me baby, lie back." Kandi gently pushed my head back, didn't even wait before my head connected with the bed before she mounted me and squatted over my face. "Yeah suck it, suck it!" I loved how vocal she was. I lightly kissed her clit while she grinded on me. "Mmmmm, kiss my fucking pussy baby." Her juices were now dripping down my chin and creeping down my neck. She started to take matters into her own hands and fucked my tongue, speeding up her pumps with each stroke. "Yeahh...that's it. Keep your fucking tongue right fucking there...right...there!"

My neck started to cramp a little but I wasn't going to let that prevent me from giving her the first nut of the night. "Oh shit, I'm gonna cum! Ouuu baby I'm about to cum on your face."

Wetness hit my face with a forceful stream in short spurts. Her liquids were dripping from my chin and down both sides of my neck. I really couldn't get enough of this squirting shit.

"Damn you taste good," I said, licking her from my mouth.

"Future," she called out, panting, trying to catch her breath. "You...you are the fucking best. Believe it or not, sometimes it takes years for guys to learn how to do their sexual partners right. But you, whewwwww! You get it right each and every time."

"I don't think every guy loves doing it as much as I do," I said, getting up from the bed. I walked to the bathroom with my chest poked out. "Now who's the man?" I whispered, while going to get a cloth to wash my face.

She raised her voice so that I could hear her while I ran some warm water in the face bowl. "That's why I like you. You're a freak, just like me. My only regret is that I wish I had met you sooner. I've been missing out."

I walked back to the main room wiping my face, and looked over towards my bed for Kandi. Buddy and I both were ready to get down to business. "What the fuck? Where did she go?" I said, barely above a whisper.

"Baby over here." Kandi was now standing by my kitchen's island fully dressed, except for her heels and she was in the process of putting them on.

14

"What are you—where are you going?" I could hear the displeasure in my voice, so I know that she was able to.

She giggled then looked at me with what seemed to be pity in her eyes. "I have a couple of errands to run."

I looked over at the clock on the wall. "At three in the fucking morning?" My voice raised one octave higher than someone who didn't care.

"Damn baby, you starting to sound like we're married."

"Wait a minute," I said, waving my hands and shaking my head. "Look, don't get it twisted. I don't give a fuck about what you're about to get into, that's not my concern. I'm just tripping that you are about to leave me with my dick pointed north like a fucking compass."

She walked over closer to me. "Future, baby!" The same voice that turned me on earlier was pissing me off now. I was beginning not to like that whiny ass voice now. "I told you that I needed you to eat me out, and you did. If I wanted to fuck you, I would've said that. The truth is I knew I wasn't going to have enough time for all of that, not with you." She wrapped both of her arms around my neck. "You know how long you last." She tried to sound seductive again.

I gently removed her arms. "Look Kandi, I'm not a lame. Don't build me up and shit thinking that'll make me forget about how you're playing me. Usually with normal humans, eating out and sucking dick is followed by fucking."

"Trust me, it's not because I don't want to. I just..."

I cut her off mid-sentence. "Look, save it! I ain't tripping. You better get going. I wouldn't want you to be late."

"So you're going to be mad at me now?" she asked. She wore a smirk that suggested that she wouldn't care one way or another. This chick was really trying to play me.

She walked towards the door and turned around with her hand on the knob. "I'll call you." She waited for a response.

15

I jealously looked at the door and thought, At least your knob is being handled, "Sure, I'll be waiting for that," I said sarcastically. She opened the door and exited. I was now standing in the middle of the floor, with a massive boner and an even larger attitude. I even had my arms folded like a little bitch that had just been dumped. She was starting to make me feel like Marcus in Boomerang.

While washing up in the bathroom, I thought about Ricka and all of the times I'd picked her up, just to have her suck me off and drop her back off at home. Karma is a motherfucker. I've come a long way from where I was a few years ago—I have a good job, money, nice ass car, and a bachelor pad. The one thing that hasn't changed, is the feeling that I get when I feel that I've been rejected. I hated that shit and I'm not trying to feel that again. I have to let this crazy bitch go before she drives me crazy, or even worse, keeps me living in the past.

I walked back over to the bed and looked at my phone. "This is your lucky day Ricka." I was going to actually let her see the bachelor pad. I'm going to upgrade her from those cheap motels I would usually take her to, invite her to my spot, and at least for one night, treat her like she's special.

I looked at my phone and noticed a missed text message. I didn't recognize the number and after reading the message, I thought someone was playing a trick on me. Then looked at the text signature from the sender. Gabrielle, who the hell is Gabrielle? I searched my brain for any woman that I may have fucked with or talked to with that name and drew a blank.

I read the message over a couple of times and concluded that someone had sent their message to the wrong person. From the looks of it, she'd had a worse night than me. As I reread the message I shook my head, feeling sorry for little dick dudes. I wonder if she'll play with me? Let's see!

I texted her and waited for a response. Two minutes later

16

she did. I laughed at the message. She must be drunk. She didn't even realize that she was texting a stranger.

After a couple of texts, I decided that if this wasn't going to get dirty, I was wasting my time. She responded exactly how I wanted her to, Wait let me guess, you can fuck and you have a big dick. It looks like she may know me after all.

The more we texted, the more it seemed that she was opening up—especially when she asked to see a picture of my dick. I played dumb like it was all new to me. Buddy sprang up at the thought of a mystery woman seeing him. He wasn't camera shy at all. I took about five pictures, selected the best, and pressed send.

Gabrielle took a little while responding, so I made sure that I had replied to the right number. I started getting a little nervous, thinking that she might not have liked the pictures. I looked down at Buddy, Hell naw! That couldn't have been it.

I texted her again to see if she had received my package and this time she responded swiftly letting me know that she was over there admiring the pictures. "Yeah, I got her ass now," I said to myself while grinning.

I laughed at her trying to act like she didn't believe that the pictures that I sent were not really mine. It was no doubt a sorry excuse for her to see more of me. I could tell that this isn't something that she partakes in regularly. Probably doesn't do phone sex either, but it's nothing wrong with that. I take pride in turning inexperienced women out.

I had to give her credit though; she was trying to step her game up. Other women would've wanted to see a guy jack off or cum pictures but she wanted me to put the letter "G" for her name in shaving cream on my dick. So cute, original and innocent. I took the picture and sent it. I wondered what she looked like. Was she white? Black? How did she smell? What did her voice sound like? Was she cute or ugly?

It was time to use my power of persuasion and see how

shy she was. I asked her to send me a picture. I wanted to see her pussy. After a few excuses and stalling, I received three pictures of a kitty that was so wet that I had to study it for a few to make sure that it wasn't Kandi's. The neatly manicured landing strip indicated that it wasn't. Kandi kept hers completely waxed. Damn, I was all in now.

I started stroking Buddy while looking at her pictures. Because of the bragging that I did earlier, she asked if there was anything that I was not good at. This was the perfect time for me to let her know up front, that I didn't want to be in a relationship at all. Just in case, I don't know, we ended up actually hooking up later on down the road, she would know exactly what I wanted from her. I texted her, telling her the one thing that I am a work in progress at is Commitment. Then I texted a little something to give her a little hope and a challenge. I texted, haven't even found anyone who makes me even want to give it a try. I knew how all women loved to feel like they can change a situation.

She let me know that she was about to go to bed, but I was just getting warmed up and still wanted to play. I didn't want to seem desperate or like I would be a stalker, so I asked her if we could do this again. She didn't give me a definite yes, but she didn't give me a no either. I'll take that, but I'm figuring that she is just as interested as I was.

I had forgotten all about Ricka. Oh well, it was too late now and I didn't feel like going out this late anyways. But I did have to release this nut. Haven't jacked off in a while, so Gabrielle consider yourself privileged.

I woke up the next morning at 11:00A.M. I had a 1:00P.M. appointment with Carolina at what hopefully will be the family's newest piece of property. I was looking forward to seeing her as always.

After getting dressed, I looked out of my large panoramic picture window and viewed the city. What a difference a day makes. Michigan weather was totally unpredictable. Yesterday it was 79 degrees and sunny. According to The Weather Channel today it's going to be 68 degrees and rainy out. I watched as rain bounced off the buildings and cars below. If you let it, the weather could really affect your entire mood. I was determined that I was not going to let it decide how my day was going to go.

When I was about five minutes away from the ranch-styled house, I dialed Carolina.

"Hello," she answered, cheery as always.

"Hello, may I speak to the best looking realtor in all of the land?"

She tried to hide her snickering. "Um, she's on vacation right now, but can I be of any assistance?"

"Yeah, I guess you'll do. Girl stop playing; you know that I'm talking about you."

She couldn't contain her laugh any longer. "Boy, you are so silly. Where are you?" she asked.

"Right down the street."

"Good because I'm pulling up now."

"Cool, I'll see you in a few."

I pulled up to the house and it was now pouring down raining. Carolina was standing in the door waiting for me to come in. I hopped out of the car and sprinted to the door.

"Hey Future," she said, displaying a huge smile.

"Hey." We hugged and held it a couple seconds longer than maybe we should have. I figured that I would break the uncomfortable silence that followed.

"What's up, how have you been?"

"Can't complain," she said, closing the door behind me.

"And how's the hubby?"

I caught her eyes rolling as she walked towards the kitchen. "Working of course." I took that as my cue to leave it alone. "The inspector is supposed to be here in about 30 minutes. I just wanted to bring you here to let you look things over."

While she leaned back on the counter, I turned the sink on letting the water run. I bent over and opened the cabinet to feel the pipes to make sure there weren't any leaks. "I'll give it a once-over; but for the steal that I'm getting this house for, I'm sure there is not much I'll complain about."

"I hear you. I looked it over pretty good too. The inspector is a good friend, so he'll do a good job also. It's actually good that it's raining cats and dogs out now; he can make sure there are no leaks in the roof."

We took the next 10 minutes walking around the house, checking things out, and joking around. I leaned back on the countertop, while she propped herself on the wall.

"I want to thank you again Carolina, for hooking this up. Like you really didn't have to do this, for real—and I really do appreciate it."

"Aw, it's no problem. I can't think of anyone else that deserves it more. You're setting yourself up to be in a nice position in a couple of years."

I smiled thinking about my future net worth. "That's the plan."

"How long are you going to stay at Ford Motor Company?"

"Now that's a tough question, because eventually I'm going to need more free time to do what I want to do, but it's going to be hard to give up such a beneficial job. I just don't know right now." She was staring intensely at me. "What, you didn't like that answer?"

She now looked confused. "What? Oh naw, that's not it. I...I thought about you that night."

"Okay, now I'm confused," I said. I knew exactly what she was talking about but I wanted to her to go more in depth.

"When we..." she put her head down and sighed before

20

she continued, "when we met up at the martini bar." Carolina was now blushing. It seemed like she was struggling with telling me or not telling me what was on her mind. "Later on that night, I thought about you in... in a way..." she started to shake her head from side to side, "a way that I shouldn't have."

"And what way was that?" I asked, slowly stepping closer to her.

She kept her face to the floor, but now tried to shield it with her hand. "When I was in bed."

I was now standing in front of her and raised her chin up towards my face with my index finger. "And what's wrong with that?"

She continued to shake her head. "I can't do this."

I moved my mouth closer to hers. "Do what?"

She tilted her head back welcoming anything that I might impose. Her words still saying that she can't, her lips softening saying that she wanted to. My lips were now close enough to feel her warm soothing breath, then there was a knock at the door.

We both jumped and regrouped from the sudden surprise. "Get a grip Carolina," I heard her say quietly to herself, as she walked into the living room to answer the door. I waited for about 10 seconds before I joined her and the inspector. After Carolina introduced us, he went right to work.

"If you have somewhere else to go I can take it from here," Carolina said.

"Are you trying to get rid of me?" I said, looking at her body from a side view. Absolutely delicious!

"Not at all, I'm just saying, it's really nothing left for you to do. When he gets done he'll let me know what he finds, and I can send the results to you or you can come and pick them up."

"You sure?"

"Of course I'm sure."

I stepped closer and lowered my voice. "You sure you

want me to leave?"

She looked down the hallway and then matched my volume. "I don't know if I'm sure I want you to, but just for your sake and mine, I think that maybe you should."

I sighed in defeat and hunched my shoulders. "Okay well, I guess I'll talk to you later." I extended my hand for a handshake.

She smiled, knowing I wanted to do more than that, but under the circumstances it was the safest thing to do. "I'll call you as soon as he's done."

I released her hand and walked to the door. Pulling my hood over my head, we said our goodbyes and I hopped in Sally and drove off.

I called my parents on my way to the gym just to keep them in the loop about the house. Shortly after hanging up with them, Carolina called to tell me that the inspection went well and to meet her at the office Monday. Dealing with her saved me so much time. I could always find the best deals on property, and even though she was into commercial real estate now, she always took care of me.

Powerhouse parking lot was packed. I didn't really like it when the gym was too crowded but it was getting closer to summer. Most of that crowd was going to be women, trying to make that last push to lose any and every inch that they could before it became too hot.

I walked in the gym and just as I suspected, women were everywhere. Most of them were overweight, but there were a couple of them that were in good shape and looked as if they frequented this gym regularly. I started off on the treadmill to get my heart rate pumped and checked out the new prospects. When I first started working out, I made it a rule never to fuck around with women at the gym because when it goes sour, you'll have this tension at a place where you visit a lot. But upon further inspection, I realized that the average amount of months that a black woman worked out at this gym was about two, if that.

After warming up and watching a couple of juicy rumps move up and down on the elliptical machine, I decided it was time to get down to business. It was back day, my favorite next to arms. A lot of guys overlook the back, not knowing that it is what gives you that V-shape. It makes your shoulders look broader and waist smaller. And if you like thick girls like I do, in bed, that strong back really comes into play.

I sat down and just as I began to reach upward for the bar on the pull down machine, I felt a tap on my shoulder. "Excuse me can I bother you for a second?" I turned around to a fat imprint of a camel toe, staring me right in my face. Mmmm, thick thighs and hips. I continued my trip upwards to find out all of this was attached to a woman with a schoolgirl face.

"It would be my absolute pleasure for you to bother me," I said with a smile.

She blushed and pointed to a leg machine that was right behind me. "That's the machine that works the inside of the thighs right?" She rubbed both of her hands over her shapely legs.

"Yep, that's the adductor and the one beside it is the abductor, it works the outside of the leg.

"Oh okay, one more thing, could you watch me do it for a little while and make sure that I'm doing it right?"

"Of course I will." I watched her as she sat in the seat and opened her legs wide to fit the pads in between her knees. She then squeezed both of her legs together and returned them back to the starting position. I tried to make it look like I was really focusing in on where the machine was supposed to be working, but instead I was locked in on that fat mound between her legs.

"Is that good?" she asked.

That's what I want to find out. I snapped out of my daze and answered, "Yes, real good. I would lower the weight a little though, wouldn't want you to go too heavy and hurt yourself."

While adjusting the weight, she said something that sounded like she was asking how much I charged.

"What was that?"

"Oh, I'm sorry," she said turning her face back towards me, "I asked how much do you charge?"

Damn, kind of bold. "Charge...for what?" I asked, with my eyebrows now raised.

"For a session? You are a personal trainer aren't you?"

"Oh no, I'm a normal member."

"I can't tell. I'm sorry; it's just with all of those muscles popping out all over the place, I figured you worked here or you were a personal trainer."

I tried not to smile too much. "Thanks for the compliment; and by the way, there is one of the trainers over there." I pointed to the squat machine on the other side of her. She looked at the trainer then back at me.

"You mean him?"

"Yeah."

"That guy?" she asked, as she nodded in the direction of the squat machine, "the chubby guy with more gut than me?"

I laughed. "That's the one." I understood her sarcasm. I didn't understand how personal trainers gained clients, when they didn't look any better than the people that they were training.

"Well you definitely should be one if he is. I mean, you could train me anytime, or any way. I could be your first customer."

"If I decide to do that I'll let you know," I said, smiling and sneaking another peek at that fat kitty cat of hers.

"And how are you going to do that? You don't have my number and you haven't asked for it." She looked at me seriously. I admired her bluntness. She was handing the ass over to me.

I looked at her baby face. "How old are you?"

"Twenty-four."

"Sure about that?

"Yes I'm sure. I know I look young; I get it all the time. Do you want to see my license?"

"That won't be necessary love." I took out my cell phone and flipped it open. "What's your number?" She ran down her digits along with her name, and I stored it in. "Alright Chante, I got it." I placed my phone back in my pocket.

"You can call that number whenever you want. And I'm ready for you to start training me," she ran her hands inside of those juicy thick thighs of hers again, slow and meticulously, "effective tonight!"

Wow! Here we go again.

Consumes My Thoughts

I double and triple-checked myself again in the mirror before Juwaun pulled up. It took me forever to figure out what to wear. I didn't want to be too conservative or sexy, so I called my girls for their opinion. They both told me to be myself.

I decided on a pair of Rock Revival fitted jeans and a crisp, white, tapered-waist, button up blouse. I unbuttoned the top two buttons, one more than I normally would and then...I buttoned one back up, "Damn it!" I shook my head as I went back to two buttons undone.

Ding!

I damn near pissed on myself when I heard my doorbell ring. "Who...who is it?"

Juwaun laughed on the other end of the door. "It's me, Juwaun."

Okay here we go. I opened the door. "Hey!"

"Hey beautiful," he said, looking as scrumptious as ever.

"Come in, please." I closed the door behind him while discreetly checking him out. He walked slowly into the living room, and into my personal space. Every step he took, his calves flexed at the bottom of his linen shorts. He wore a soft yellow sweater vest on top of a white tee and a pair of crispy white Nike Air Force Ones.

"Very nice!"

"Why thank you."

"Yeah, you have good taste." He was staring at a painting on the far sidewall. "Is that a Jonz painting?"

"Wow, I'm impressed. Yes it is," I answered. "What do you know about Jonz?"

"I used to paint a little bit. And I dibble and dabble in the arts from time to time. The first time I saw one of his paintings, it gave me goose bumps. You look at his paintings and see yourself in them somehow."

I walked over and stood beside him. "That's exactly what I felt when I saw this piece."

He smiled. "This is crazy because I just bought one of his paintings a week ago, should be here any day now."

"My mother bought this one before he was famous. Two more will complete the set." I pointed to the adjacent wall. "That one, and there's one that's still at my parents. When I move—"

"You're moving soon?" He asked, cutting me off.

"Yep, in about a month to a condo in Dearborn. But when I do, I'm asking for that third one for a housewarming gift."

He turned towards me and placed his hand on my shoulder. "You ready?"

"Yeah I'm ready." Please let's hurry, because your touch is driving me crazy.

We walked outside to a brilliant white on white Range Rover, with huge shiny chrome rims. He walked me to the passenger side, opened the door, and let me in. I can't even remember the last time I had someone other than my daddy open the door for me. His truck still had the new car smell. I took a deep breath, inhaled, and leaned over to pull the door handle to open his door.

He sat in the truck, looking confused, "Never had that happen before."

"What's that?"

"A woman actually returning the favor by opening my

27

door."

I laughed. "Yeah, my mom taught me that."

"Sounds like a good woman," he said, putting the Range in reverse.

"Very!"

Juwaun made me laugh all the way to the Renaissance Center where we were having lunch. I had never been, but I had heard that the food was excellent.

From the time we stepped out of the truck, there were people pointing, yelling, and asking for autographs. Being with him in a setting other than the club, really let me know that I was with a real superstar. He was very humble and handled fans graciously without making me feel left out. Before we stepped in the elevator, he signed a little kid's jersey. The joy in his face and Juwaun's was priceless. It was the little boy's lucky day; he just happened to be wearing the right jersey at the right time.

I thought hypothetically; if we were ever to take this to another level, that this would be my life every single day. Could I really deal with that? I looked at how handsome he was and then thought about how much shopping I would be able to do... Hell yeah! I could handle that.

"You ready Angel?"

"Yes." He grabbed my hand and escorted me into the elevator. I had a mental fight with myself trying to stay focused, but another part of me was thinking of all the nasty things that we could do inside of this elevator.

He smiled at me and shook his head. "What?" I asked, leaning back on the wall.

"Nothing," he said, laughing.

"What? Tell me."

"You have that same look on your face that you had last night." I blushed and dared not to ask him what that look meant because I already knew.

Ding!

Yes, saved by the bell! We had reached our floor. I smelled the aroma of the food as we walked into 42 Degrees North, and my stomach started rumbling. We were seated and handed menus.

"So what do you usually order when you come here?" I asked Juwaun, still looking at the long list of choices.

"The buffet, no doubt. Look up there, they have everything you need."

I placed the menu back on the table. "So why didn't you tell me that, instead of having me look through this menu?"

"Well, I didn't know. Maybe you felt that you were too good for a buffet. Or you could've been one of those women who is scared to eat, and wanted to order breadsticks and a glass of water."

"If there is one thing I'm not scared of—its food, baby. I love to eat. Maybe a little too much."

"My kind of woman. Let's go up there and handle business."

"Puh, you ain't said nothing!" I said, following his lead.

The lunch buffet was wonderful, very elegant. There was everything from Louisiana gumbo to Mississippi fried catfish. Their lunch buffet looked better than a lot of restaurant's dinner entrées.

We ate until we were totally stuffed. I didn't even have room for dessert, which looked tantalizing as well.

"Whoa!" Juwaun said, sitting back and rubbing his belly. "You weren't playing girl, you do love food."

"Shut up Juwaun, I am not greedy." I felt my cheeks tightening from blushing.

"I can't tell." We both cracked up. We sat for a few minutes more, and then Juwaun paid for the bill and left a fifty-dollar tip.

As we walked out of the restaurant, I was getting the same looks from women that I received at the club. Juwaun put his arm around me, probably noticing the tension on my face. "Baby, what's wrong?"

"Huh, nothing," I answered, trying to play it off.

"You sure?"

"Yes, I'm good." I tried to smooth the wrinkles from my forehead. We stepped into the elevator and he pressed L for lobby.

"You know you can't let them get to you."

"I told you that I'm fine." I was trying to forget the situation, but he obviously wasn't having it.

"Yes you did, but your face is saying something entirely different. I see how they look at you, but I'm going to tell you it's not just because you are with me. It's because you are beautiful and you are with me. If they saw you with anybody they would still hate."

My attitude immediately disappeared. Juwaun knew how to make a woman feel good and on the way to valet, he made sure he kept me close to him as he spoke to fans and signed a few more autographs.

"So did you enjoy the food?"

I stopped looking outside of the passenger side window and focused on him. "Of course I did, you saw how much I ate."

He chuckled. "So you're not going to mind when I ask you again, very soon, to go back?"

I turned my face back towards outside, and peered at the freeway traffic. "I don't know; we'll see when you ask."

"Do you have room for dessert yet?"

"Dessert?" I did have a little sweet tooth. "What do you have in mind?"

"I was thinking Coldstone Creamery, ever been?"

"Juwaun, what are you trying to do, fatten me up? If you have a big girl fetish, then I suggest you let me know now," I said jokingly.

"What? Naw girl, I just thought that you would want to

30

top off a good meal, that's all."

I thought about how good the ice cream looked on the Coldstone commercials. "Maybe I could get an extra small or something."

"Mmmm hmmm, I knew you wanted to go. Sitting over there fronting."

"Shut up!" I said, nudging him in the arm. "I have a question for you. Why don't you travel with bodyguards? Aren't you supposed to be protected or something?"

Juwaun turned the radio all the way off. "I guess when you're in my position, you are supposed to have bodyguards, but I'm just not that type of guy. I like reaching out and touching the fans, and don't want to seem untouchable—so for right now, I choose not to have any."

Juwaun was a lot different than I originally thought. We had good conversation all the way to Coldstone, where I ordered the Like It serving of Cheesecake Fantasy. He had me cracking up all the way back to my apartment. I struggled with the thought of whether I should give him a kiss or not at the end of the evening. A couple of traffic lights before arriving to my place, I made my decision.

"Juwaun?" I called his name out nervously.

He took his eyes off the red light. "What's up?"

"Come here," I said, beckoning him with my finger. I knew he didn't expect what was coming by the surprised look on his face. He leaned in closer and I met him halfway.

We kissed. Soft, slow, no tongue, all passion...mmmmm felt so...

Beep beep! The driver behind us honked his horn and broke our connection. I laughed at how hard he jumped.

"I just wanted to get that out of the way, so we wouldn't have an awkward moment."

He smiled. "Whenever you want to get that out of the way

again, feel free to do so."

He parked in front of my apartment door, and this time the kiss flowed much easier and lasted a little longer. Still there was no tongue, and I tried my best to mask the fact that I wanted to jump his bones right then and there.

I called my girls and gave them the details of my date. Of course Tierra asked, "Did y'all go back to his place and fuck?" She was a trip. I opened a bottle of Moscato and poured me a glass full. As soon as I raised the glass to my lips, I heard my phone ringing. I looked at the display as it lay on the coffee table. It was Juwaun.

"Hey."

"Hey Angel, don't be scared, I'm not a stalker."

"I know that silly."

"Anyways, I forgot to tell you about the get-together that my older brother Antonio is having at his loft. It's a couple of weeks from now, Fourth of July weekend. It's sorta like a housewarming 'slash' holiday party."

"So that means if I come that I have to bring a gift?" I asked half-jokingly.

"No, not at all. I have the gift part covered. Believe me; his place is laid, there's not too much he's lacking. It's really an excuse for him to have a get-together and to meet all the other tenants in the building. So...does it sound like something that you want to attend? Good food, good drinks, good music, and good people."

"Wow, you're really selling it huh?" I said, smiling.

He laughed. "Yeah, a little too hard I take it?"

"Naw, you're doing good. But I might have to go over my parent's house that day."

"Oh, that's cool," he responded quickly, almost sounding as if he was expecting that answer. "The party doesn't start until seven."

"Seven...that sounds cool. I think I can swing that."

"Good. Okay, I'll talk to you later then."

Johnie Jay

"Okay."

As I flicked through the endless number of meaningless cable channels, I started my second glass of wine and started feeling a little frisky.

Juwaun was a gentleman indeed and happened to be very handsome, but he still didn't turn me on as much as the mystery guy from the club. That guy just does it for me and I wished he was here with me. There is definitely a difference between handsome and being sexy.

If I had to grade both of them on a looks scale I think that Juwaun would score a little higher, but not by much. He just has the traditional looks that women would call handsome and good-looking. This mystery guy is handsome in a different and strange kind of way, but there's something about the way that he moves, the way he walks, and the way that he looks at you that make you think...sex! He makes you horny if you think about him for more than a few seconds. Like now, I'm thinking about that bulge that I saw in his pants. Damn, what I wouldn't give to wrap my hands around that.

I laughed at myself. I used to be so good and conservative. I would suppress thoughts like that, but they were always there. Now look at me, a freak, and it didn't really come all the way out full force until after my breakup. To pinpoint it even further, the real freak in me didn't really come out until the night I laid eyes on Mr. Sexy.

Okay, I have to calm myself down. I stared at the phone on the coffee table. I grabbed it and went directly to the three saved dick pics from last night. So fat and thick, think I'm going to show my girls, hell, it isn't my man. I sent all three pictures to Tierra and Brianna.

Five minutes later, I received my first text from who else but Tierra. **Who does that belong too and how can I get a piece?**

I texted her back my response. **Don't know who he is, made a mistake and texted the wrong number last night, the next thing I know...we were damn near fucking through texting lol.**

My phone vibrated a couple of seconds after sending the message to Tierra. **I knew you were a freak! lol it looks so...suckable.**

Then I received my first text from Brianna. **Damn Angel is that Juwaun's?**

Nawwww, haven't seen his yet. This is some guy that I mistakenly texted while I was trying to tell you what happened last night.

Brianna texted me back. **What...you don't know who the guy is? And by the way, how did it go last night?**

My phone vibrated again. I read Tierra's text. **Damn Angel...can't stop looking at it. I've had bigger or I should say longer but never a better looking one!**

Yeah, does look juicy doesn't it? I texted back.

Scrumptious, Tierra responded.

My fingers started to get a little cramped texting both of my friends so I came up with a better solution. I texted, **Hey Bri, I'm going to call you in a few so we can talk about last night...on second thought I'm going to call you and Tee both on the three-way."**

Cool, she responded.

Tierra obviously still had her mind on one thing. I read her incoming text. **You don't mind if I save this pic do you?**

Girl I don't care...I'm 'bout to call you on the three-way with Bri. Then I pressed send.

Okay, she responded.

I called Brianna, then conferenced Tierra in to connect the three of us.

"Hey y'all!"

34

"Hey Angel," they both screamed.

"Okay y'all forgive me if I'm slurring, but I've had two glasses of wine. But um, oh yeah, so do y'all want the short version or the long version about last night?"

Tierra quickly spoke up. "Well as much as I love a good sex story, I have to get ready for a date."

"It don't matter to me," Brianna said, "but you might as well cut to the meat and potatoes."

I smiled. "Meat and potatoes huh? Okay, well how's this for meat and potatoes? Pierre has a two and a half inch dick, and I'm giving him the half because of his dick head. Is that enough meat and potatoes for you, because it surely wasn't enough for me."

"Hellll naw, that ain't enough. I think I'm going to need another helping. What about you Brianna?" Tierra asked, laughing.

Brianna could barely stop laughing. "I'm definitely going back for seconds."

"Both of y'all go to hell!" I couldn't hold it in any longer, and started laughing and crying at the same time. I think I'm going crazy. I mean it was somewhat sad. I think the tears were coming down because I really wanted dick that bad.

"Maybe you saw it wrong; I mean Angel, I have never seen or heard of a man with such a small dick."

"I have to agree with Tee on that one Angel. I've had some small dicks in my day, Lord knows, but two and a half, that's like a newborn. Was he hard?"

I took another sip of Moscato. "That's the worst part. He was hard. Just think; it could be even smaller than that. I'm telling y'all and this is no joke, when I saw it I thought it was his navel." The girls continued on their laughing spree. "Go ahead, laugh it up. Ugggghhhhhh! And to think that he had his little thingy inside of me, felt like he was fucking me with his pinky."

"Damn I wish you would've taken a picture of that, I want

to see it for myself," Tierra said, laughing.

"So what happened? Did he finish, did he cum?" Brianna asked, wanting to know more.

"No, I didn't give him the chance to. I made him get up, and get this; he really copped an attitude, tried to blame him having little dick syndrome on black women. Talking about white women appreciate him, and not just his dick size. He said size doesn't matter."

"Shit, the hell it don't, especially when you are that small," Tierra blurted out.

"That's exactly what I said."

"And white women aren't really concerned about little dicks because they are used to them!" Brianna chimed in.

"I told him that too!" I quickly agreed. "So that's when I went to my phone to text y'all about what had happened, but I guess I was too intoxicated and punched in the wrong number because instead of Bri responding, Thick Dick did."

"I have to try that wrong number game if you can get that out of it," Brianna joked.

I shook my head. "Yeah, but that's just one part of him, he might be ugly with bad breath or something."

"Oh well, turn the light off, pop a Tic Tac in his mouth, and have him bang you from the back. See, all taken care of."

"Angel, I don't know what to say. Maybe…" Bri paused as if she was trying to pick the right words, "…maybe you are supposed to wait."

"Wait? Wait for what?" I questioned.

"I don't know, maybe you're supposed to be waiting on the right guy I mean, maybe this stuff is happening for a reason."

"Oh please!" Tierra interjected, "This ain't rocket science or psychology, and you shouldn't have to wait for anything or anyone. If you're horny, then damn it, you should be able to call someone to take care of that. Angel is just having a strip of bad luck with running into a bunch of lames. What's up with Juwaun?"

"Girl, I'm almost getting scared to even take it to a sexual level. What if we get all into it and he has two dicks or something?"

"What?" Bri screamed.

"Mmm wait...two dicks on one body?" Tierra asked. "One for each hole...damn that doesn't sound half bad. If he don't work out, you send him to momma."

"Tee, you need to see a doctor," Brianna said, sounding serious.

"I agree."

"What I say wrong?" Tierra asked.

Brianna went back to trying to make me feel a little better. "It'll happen Angel, just don't force it, that's all I'm saying."

I took another sip of my Moscato. "This is just all new to me. I haven't been single for a long time and a bitch is mad horny. I just want a good lay, not a boyfriend, not a man, just hot sex on a platter."

"There's always your ex." Tierra said barely loud enough for anyone to hear.

"Tierra, don't make me hang up on you—you can't be serious. Why would I ever give him the privilege to get some of this again? Please tell me."

"Because according to you, he had that fire and some say the ex makes the sex spectacular," Tierra said, repeating one of Biggie's lines.

I thought about the numerous times Damien had made me cum. "Mmm, yes he did. But after all the shit he's put me through, if he even said one word, I would probably dry up like the Sahara."

Brianna jumped in, "I agree, it's not even worth it."

I thought briefly about my ex fucking me. Hated him, loved his sex. Catch-22.

"Okay girls; I gotta get out of here, what are y'all doing

later tonight? If y'all want, I can ask my date if he has any friends."

"No thanks Tee, I'm going to chill here with some more wine and cable."

"Okay then, Bri what about you?" Tierra asked.

"Thanks Tee, but I'm in for the night."

"Okay party poopers, talk to y'all tomorrow."

"Bye Tee," Brianna and I responded.

After clicking Tierra off, Brianna and I continued talking.

"Wonder who she's going out with tonight?"

"Ain't no telling Bri, I think she goes out at least four nights a week."

"Are you going to be okay?" she asked apprehensively.

"Yeah, I guess I'm cool. It's just sex. I know one thing though; I've been spending too much money on batteries lately." We both laughed. "And sipping on this wine isn't making it any better. Almost seem like wine makes you think about sex even more."

"I know," Brianna said, giggling.

"Wine, no matter where you are makes you feel sexy," I let out a sly grin, "and feel like sexing, not fucking but sexing. Slow, slippery sexing, you know what I mean?"

"Definitely, I'm drinking some right now. You know, if you are not getting into anything tonight, you could come over here and watch a movie or something."

"Girl if I came over there tonight, how I'm feeling right now, you and I would probably end up sleeping together." I chuckled, not paying attention to what I was saying. I became a little nervous when I didn't hear anything coming from the other end of the phone—no laughing, no agreeing, no objections. Then Brianna's phone clicked.

"Hold on Angel." Whewww! That was an uneasy situation. Then Brianna clicked back on. "Um Angel, this is Joey. You know white boy from the other night? I'll call you back."

"Oh that's okay, I might be asleep in a few anyways," I said, trying to avoid an uncomfortable situation.

"Okay, well I'll call you tomorrow."

I stripped down to my undies after getting off the phone. Much more comfortable. I went to refill my glass. My chest was now feeling warm and cozy and I noticed my nipples protruding out of my satin bra. I picked up my cell and went back to the dick pictures again. Guess I couldn't resist.

While sitting on the couch I spread my legs a little more and touched myself through the thin satin. I was so hot, so moist. While looking over at the clock I wondered what my mystery texter was doing at this moment. Was he touching himself? Was he fucking? I wish that he was fucking me.

I grabbed my phone, went into my text message inbox and selected the unknown number that had excited me the night before. After a couple of seconds of contemplating, I made my decision. "What the hell," I blurted out as I began texting. **Mmmmm, can't stop looking at u...getting really turned on.** Then I pressed send.

He probably won't even respond. I hopped up from the couch and went to empty my bladder. When I came back to the couch, I saw that my phone was displaying a new message.

What took you so long? Was about to start without you lol.

I smiled wide and hard as I texted him back. **Now why would you do a thing like that?**

I read his response. **Lol cause I thought that you were over there probably starting without me.**

Lol truthfully...I was about 2.

Now that's not very nice of you...I am glad you waited though...so, what are you wearing right now?

My heart started thumping. I was so excited with anticipation. **Satin low cut bra, matching boy cut panties.**

39

Boycuts mmmmm, my favorite, love the way it leaves half of the ass cheek out. You do have a nice ass right?

While texting him back I stood up and looked at my backside in the mirrored wall. **Nice? No baby, I have a terrific ass!** Send. As I waited for him to respond, I looked at my booty again this time from the other side.

My phone vibrated in my hand and I instantly felt more juices building up to make their escape. Terrific huh? And what makes it that?

I looked at my ass from all angles holding the phone in my left hand as I gripped my ass cheek with my right. Then I texted him my answer. **It's firm, plump, juicy and round.**

Damn baby...sounds good...is it a teardrop booty or a half moon?

I read his message and laughed. He sounded like someone who was really into booties. I didn't know the difference between the two choices, so I sent   ? and about a minute later, he cleared the air.

Lol, sorry about that...that's guy talk, teardrop is when you have more ass at the bottom than at the top...half-moon is when it's a perfect half circle. Round, starting at the lower back to the bottom of the cheek.

I laughed at his definition and texted him back, **In that case I definitely have a half moon lol. Are you home alone?**

Nope, wifey is downstairs vacuuming...is that okay?

"Shit!" Don't think that I was expecting that answer. Should I leave him alone? Hell, it's not my man, maybe I should...

His new message interrupted my thought. **Just kidding...yes I'm at home alone, and I'm single with no roommates and no kids...absolutely free!**

"Whew!" Reading that lightened my mood right back up. It's not as if he couldn't be lying, but for right now, him actually saying it was all that I needed. I continued looking at myself in the mirror, and wondered what a picture of my ass would do for him. I took a picture of my booty from the back and the sides through the reflection of the mirror and sent them to him, along with a heading that read, **Something to think about while you're alone.**

My phone vibrated. **Dayuuummmm, your ass looks good, yummie!!! By the way nice abs. Love a woman who takes care of herself.**

He had me smiling now, as I rubbed my hands over my flat stomach. I really liked when someone complimented the results of my hard work. By the time I sent my thank you, I received a front picture of him showing off his chest, torso, and abs. "Damn," I said, bringing my phone closer to my face. He definitely had it going on.

Where are you? he texted.

Sitting on my couch. I responded.

Undies still on?

Yes.

Wrong answer...take it off!!!

I don't know what it was, but the way he demanded it turned me on even more. I sat the phone down, used my left hand to slide my panties down, and with my right hand, I unhooked and removed my bra. **Now what?**

Now show me that pretty pussy again.

I did. He was my director and I was open for direction. I couldn't believe how quickly and easy he had me touching, rubbing, even tasting myself. I had lost all reserve and had turned into a chick from a porno flick. Reading his words was making me high.

I want you so fucking bad right now, he texted.

I feel the same way, wish you were here. I really meant it too. Then the game changed when I read his next text.

Call me...I wanna make you cum, wanna hear you cum.

I instantly froze up, didn't know what to say. Texting was one thing—it kept things impersonal. Hearing words, listening to voices was an entirely different world. While rambling all these thoughts through my head, I received another text from him, **I'll do all the talking, just wanna hear you breathe, feel your breath. Call me!!!!** He must've felt my hesitation and tried to make me feel more at ease.

I now had my fingers on the green dial button, debating, wondering, thinking. My heart was beating like a bass drum trying to pound a hole through my chest and my pussy was beating in Morse code. "Okay, I'm not saying shit. I'm not giving any information. I'll just listen to him do all the talking." I whispered, trying to convince myself. Hormones had now taken over me. I pressed dial. The phone rang once. He answered.

"Are you still horny baby?" His voice was a low raspy whisper, deep and vibrating. Only five words and he already had me under his spell.

"Mmm hmmm." I answered, not opening my mouth. I tried not to let my nervous breathing come through over the phone.

"Mmmm, lay back and spread your legs." I obeyed and couldn't help the sigh that escaped my mouth. "Ouuu your pussy looks so good, so delicious." I had my eyes closed and imagined him there, in front of me looking and staring.

He directed me to spread my lips with one hand and squeeze my pussy muscles to make my hole open and close. I was so moist that every time I opened and closed my hole, it made a squishy noise.

"Scoot down a little more. I'm about to get comfortable, gonna be here for a minute." His low seductive voice was driving me crazy. He continued to talk to me as if he were a narrator or an author of a book—a book that I was the main character of.

"I'm bending down in front of you. I can tell that your

42

pussy wants to suck my tongue. Mmm, your scent is so intoxicating, so sweet. I'm bringing my face closer to your pink rose. I inhale you, invite you into my lungs, my soul. Damn mami, you are so wet. Do you feel the warmth of my breath?" I let out a low moan. I was there with him and he was here with me. I felt everything that was going down. "Do you feel me, baby?" he asked.

"Mmmmmm hmmmmmm." My mouth had opened wide. I was breathing heavy as I fondled my clit.

He went on describing how he was softly kissing on my clit and doing figure eights on my inner lips. I had stopped touching myself, didn't even need too at this point. He was fucking my mind and making it a reality. I felt every flick and every suck. All the way, up to my explosion. That was the first time that I had an orgasm from a guy telling me what he was doing, instead of actually doing it.

I tried so hard to catch my breath, but it made me gasp even harder. "Ooouuu yeah mami, cum on my tongue, you taste so good." The more he talked, the more intense my orgasm grew, until another even stronger one followed closely behind.

"Oh my...God!" escaped my mouth, as I lowered the phone from my face. I'm sure he heard it though. I brought the phone back to my ear and basked in the afterglow.

"Mmm you sounded exactly how I thought you would cumming...absolutely beautiful. Talk to you later sexy." And then I heard the dial tone. I dropped my phone to the floor. I was totally satisfied and drained. Now I'm really glad that I made the decision to buy a leather sofa. I had leaked my juices all over the place. After cleaning up, I prepared myself for a good night's sleep ahead.

The next couple of nights, I pleasured myself to his pictures on my phone and the thoughts of that phone call. It had become my sleep therapy. During the day I would be excited, hoping that I would get a text or a picture. I had gotten neither since Saturday night. It was almost like he did it to me to get me addicted, and then left me feigning. If that was his intention, he definitely had succeeded.

Always On My Mind

One thing I loved about working in an auto plant is that there was a lot of downtime. You were often sent home and sometimes laid off for weeks at a time. A lot of different factors determined that: like no stock, damaged stock, or another plant running bad parts that your auto plant needed. Any combination of those factors could shut the plant down.

Today we were sent home early because one of the machines from the pump department went down. Usually when someone from a department gets the word that they might be leaving early, they make sure that the word gets around. This time was no different.

A chick that worked in the pump department that I fucked around with at least once a month, texted me to let me know that they were leaving early at lunch, and that everyone was meeting up at the usual early out spot, Malarky's Pub. She also notified me that we could skip the bar altogether if I wanted to, and that she would be more than happy to be my lunch.

Shortly after, texts from other people started pouring in, every one notifying me about Malarky's. I placed my phone on the table and turned to the sports section in the Detroit News. I felt my body stiffen when I saw an enlarged picture of Juwaun Jones of the Detroit Lions, aka the fucking guy that I'm starting to see a little too often with the lady that I'm trying to get.

The picture showed him leaning up against a brand new

electric-blue Lamborghini Diablo. "I bet it's not his," I said out loud. I glanced at the caption under the picture and discovered not only was the Lamb his, it was a gift from a newly inked advertisement deal with the car company. My eyes traveled back up to the headline, "The Sky is the Limit for the Young Prince of Detroit." Who the fuck told him he's the Prince of Detroit?

"You alright dog?"

I looked up and met Caesar's questionable stare. "Yeah, why do you ask?"

"Cause ya face is all frowned up like you're about to set the newspaper on fire!" He busted out in laughter.

I noticed that my forehead was wrinkled and my eyebrows were squinted up and quickly tried to relax my face. "Naw man, I'm good. It's just crazy that the richer you become, the less you have to pay for. It's like people just hand you shit."

Caesar came around the table to get a closer look. "Sounds like hating to me, because you know if you get to that stage, you won't be complaining about anyone handing you anything for free."

I couldn't help but to laugh at that one. "Whatever, nobody asked you anyway."

"Is that Juwaun Jones? Damn that Lambo is tight, look!" Caesar pointed to the article below his picture. "Says he has a better chance than anyone to be the next Jerry Rice. It must be nice to be him right now."

"So everybody is going to the bar huh?" I asked, changing the subject.

"Yeah, that's the word." Then he went right back to the subject that I tried to change. "Look, says that he is in the Detroiter magazine as number ten on the fifty most eligible bachelors' list and he is younger than twenty-five years old."

"For real, wow that's good." I tried my best to seem interested, but every time I thought of Juwaun, I got a mental picture of him with her. "I heard they're not letting us out of here till 11:00." I tried again to change the subject, but Caesar obviously wasn't getting the hint.

"And he's just—"

"Aye, Caesar, for real man, I get it. He's the man."

Caesar put the paper down and looked at me confused. "Okay anyways, on my way over here I stopped at department 454 to see if they were really getting sent home and I saw ole girl that you used to fuck around with." He paused, and looked up to the ceiling. "Daayummm she have a fat ass."

I zoned out remembering the last time I had that juicy booty up in the air, in the men's restroom right at this very plant. "Yes she does. She just texted me, trying to make a detour from the bar."

Caesar looked at me. "I know that's one detour that you are not going to mind taking."

I ran my hand across my beard making me glad that tomorrow was Friday, the day that I visited my barber. "I don't know. Think I'm going to pass on that."

My boy grabbed at his heart as if it had stopped beating. "Am, am I hearing right? Future is turning down a big butt and a smile? Wow, you're really changing on me man."

I sat back in my chair and interlocked my fingers behind my head. I pondered for a few seconds before responding. "I don't know Caesar. I think I'm just getting bored with the same old same old. I just need...I don't know, I need more than ass, titties, and sex. The women I meet, body-wise are great, but mentally they bore me. I mean, I can't even think of one that really challenges or stimulates me mentally." I paused for a second and did a quick mental check to make sure that I wasn't overlooking anyone. "Nope, not one!"

Caesar hunched his shoulders. "And the problem with that is...?"

I looked at my boy and laughed. "The problem with that is, my immature little friend, that when you become older—"

"Older? Nigga you're only 27," he interrupted.

I continued my speech. "Like I was saying when you become older, a little more mature and wiser you start talking about going out with a woman, to places like plays, concerts, dinner, or dancing. You know, somewhere other than the bedroom. Don't get me wrong, it's cool hanging with the fellas, even going out on dates with women. But I think it would be cool if I had that one that I can chill with, no matter what the occasion or situation is."

Caesar sat on the edge of the table and stared at me as if I was a stranger. "Look, I don't know what the hell you've done with my boy, but you better bring him back now; because if I'm hearing correctly, it sounds like to me you're talking about settling down."

"Not really settling down, just slowing down a bit." I must admit, hearing my words even shocked me a little. No matter how hard I tried to deny it, I knew that I didn't really even start to entertain thoughts like these until I saw her at the club.

During The Michael Baisden Show yesterday, I became confused because thoughts about her started to invade my head. I wondered if our paths were really on a collision course to meet. The feelings that come over me whenever I see her, is like no other feeling that I've ever had for any other woman. I guess I can't say for sure if she's my soul mate, or an angel sent to me from Heaven. I mean why would God care enough about me to send me anyone? Especially after how I've been acting towards him. One thing's for sure; I wasn't going to let a star football player or anyone else stand in the way of me finding out what part, if any, she'll play in my life.

"You know what?" Caesar asked, standing up from the table. "You need a drink, that's what's wrong with you. The first round is on me."

"Yeah, maybe that's it." I tried to cut down the concern my boy seemed to have, and to minimize me sounding like a lame.

48

"Maybe you should get the first two rounds."

"See now you're pushing it. I'll see you up there in a few."

"A'ight." Caesar walked back towards his department. I remember when we first met about three years ago. He was recruiting people for his basketball tournament. We played a 10 game 10-week schedule, then a playoff series. Our team swept through the other teams like a broom and we've been tight ever since.

As soon as I stepped in the bar, I had two beers forced into my hands from co-workers. That was one thing that I loved about white people, when they drink they become really generous.

"Instead of real estate Future, you should be thinking about owning a bar." Caesar leaned back on the edge of the bar and looked over the thickening crowd.

"Yeah, I know, they are making a killing up in here." It was 11:35, the same time that I sent my text to Gabrielle yesterday. I flipped my phone open to see if I had any missed messages; I didn't.

"So what are you going to do with the rest of your day?" he asked, after taking large gulps of his beer.

"I don't know. It's so nice out, I might go jogging down by the riverfront or something."

"Aw, that sounds so romantic," Caesar teased.

"Shut up!" I laughed at him trying to flutter his eyelashes like a woman. "You need to come and start working out with ya boy."

"Naw, I need to start going with you for real. I'm getting a little tired of hearing all these chicks talking about how good you look, and making all of these 'mm mmm mmmm' sounds every time you walk by."

"Maybe you're mistaken. Maybe they're making all of them noises for you." I laughed, before downing the rest of my beer.

"So now you're gonna play dirty? Oh now, you got jokes?"

"What do you mean?" I said smiling, "I'm not joking, I mean some women like a little gut," I said, giving him a slight pat on his belly, "as opposed to a chiseled up six-pack."

"I don't have a gut. This is nowhere near a gut. Now that...is a gut." He pointed to one of our hi-lo drivers, whose stomach overflowed out of his pants and over his belt.

"You guys go 'head and fight over whose gut is bigger while I do these sit-ups, crunches, and jog all of these miles. Who knows; maybe one day y'all women might need a washboard to clean their lingerie on, and might need to borrow my abs." We busted out laughing and I felt my phone vibrate on my hips. Upon opening my phone, I saw that I had a new text message and instantly became excited to read it. When I saw that it came from my big booty freak who I boned every now and then, I became less enthused but read it anyway.

I hope that bulge in your jeans is for me. I looked down at Buddy who appeared to be bulged because of the pants I was wearing, and then looked straight in front of me and saw the sender of the message sitting three tables from the aisle. She locked eyes on me and placed her phone back in her purse, but not before giving me a swipe across her lips with that tongue that she knew how to use oh so well.

One thing I give her credit for; she was crafty and slick. Even though we've been messing around for over two years, I never got the feeling that she's gone back and spilled the beans to her girls, which was a good thing—because out of the eight women sitting at the table with her, I've screwed three of them. I knew that even if all of them found out, they would still fuck around with me in a heartbeat. In today's times, it seemed as if women had no loyalty for each other anymore, which was in turn a good thing for me and for men in general.

I received another text and laughed when I realized it was from her co-worker sitting two chairs from her. She texted, **Damn**

50

you're looking good over there Future, still can't get over how good you fucked me the last time. Got me over here anticipating the next!

I figured I would play around with her for a moment, since Caesar was trying his best to kick it with one of the bartenders. I texted her back, **Sorry baby...I just wanted to make sure you really really wanted me before we fucked again.** I sent the message. About a minute later, I watched her open her phone back up and smile wide and bright.

She typed for a few, closed her phone and continued her conversation with her girls without skipping a beat. **Well it really really worked because I find myself really really wanting your ass more than I know I should.**

I texted her back. **I miss that juicy ass pussy of yours too!! Whenever you get a chance send me another picture of it so I can lick my screen lol.**

Monique wasn't shy at all about showing her goods, because a couple seconds after I sent my text I received another from her informing me, **There is no time like the present**, and then I saw her excusing herself from the ladies at the table and making her way towards the ladies room. She might have been going in there to use the restroom, but I knew I was going to get my requested picture of that juicy peach of hers.

Caesar and I continued our conversation and he noticed me opening my phone checking my messages. "Who are you waiting on to hit you up dawg? You've been flipping that phone open since you've got here."

A few seconds later, I smiled as I opened the pretty pussy picture that I just had received under the heading "Licky Licky". I watched as Monique sat back down in her chair to rejoin her girls. "Your girl just sent me a nice little picture of her pussy."

His mouth dropped. "Are you serious? What she do, take it at the table?"

"No fool, she just came from the ladies room. But I'm going to keep it real with you. I've been kind of waiting on this other chick to text me."

"Waiting...you? On who? What time did she say that she was going to get in touch with you?"

I closed my phone and put it back on my hip. "Damn, one question at a time man. It's kind of a long story, but um there isn't a specific time that she said she would call or text. I just texted her yesterday around this time, so I was thinking maybe she'll text me around the same time today."

Caesar looked at me and erupted in laughter. "Okay! Um maybe I missed something but again, why are you waiting on her again?"

I waved my hand in front of me. "Man, you wouldn't believe me if I told you."

"Try me." Caesar hunched his shoulders and took another swig.

I looked at my boy and tried to decide if I wanted to spill the beans on my recent text escapades. "Okay, short version. One night I get this text from a wrong number. We went back and forth, traded a couple of nasty pics and we've been doing the same thing ever since."

I looked at Caesar who was staring at me. "Yep, you're right, I don't believe that shit. Sounds like something that happens in fiction novels. How does she look?"

He kept staring at me waiting for an answer. "Body is banging," I informed him while looking around.

"Okay...and the face?" I could only look at the floor. "You're kidding right? You haven't seen her face? I mean what is her name?" I continued to look towards the floor, because I knew Gabrielle was more than likely not her real name; it may be a tag just like I use Futre Lux Bryt for mine. "Are you fucking kidding me? You haven't seen her face, don't know her name, and you've

52

talked to her how many times?"

"Talked?" I asked, playing dumb.

He laughed. "Yeah, talked, spoken to, kicked it with."

"Once," I answered quietly.

"Once?"

"Once," I repeated.

"Once, I've actually spoken to the chick once, and you are sitting up here sweating her waiting for her to text you?" The way he came at me did make the situation seem worse than it really was.

"I can't explain it man. Some weird shit has been happening to me this last month."

"Yeah I see. This some shit you would've schooled me on a couple of years ago. Role reversal like a motherfucker!" Caesar was now shaking his head from side to side.

I smiled as I started on another beer. "Do you believe in soul mates?"

Caesar turned his head coughing from swallowing and choking on his drink. He was now laughing uncontrollably. "Are you serious? You have to be kidding me. I have to be on camera right now. This has to be some kind of new reality show!"

I had to laugh myself. I mean what else could I do? It was funny. Me, the womanizer, tripping over a woman I haven't even met. "Forget you! I'm getting out of here. Stop by later if you're not getting into anything."

"Yeah, I might," he said, continuing to smile. "I might be hooking up with old girl from last week."

"Alright, well, hit me up." I started heading towards the exit.

"Aye Future." Caesar yelled out my name and I turned around. "Go get checked out!" he said, pointing to his head.

I waved my hand at him and walked out to Sally. After dropping the top, I headed to the bat cave.

INEVITABLE ACT II

Soul Mate

A couple of days ago, Juwaun prearranged another lunch date for today. I tried to tell him that it wasn't necessary, but he insisted. I loved the fact that he was persistent. My phone rang just as I finished balancing my last account before lunchtime.

"Hello."

"Hey you!" Juwaun responded, sounding cheery.

"Hey what's up, you sound like you're in a good mood."

"Why wouldn't I be? I get to see you again. I'm out front when you're ready."

"Okay." I grabbed my purse and walked down the long corridor to the front door. The closer I came to the door, the louder the commotion from outside became. Someone must be fighting, I thought to myself, which caused my steps to quicken. I walked out of the door and passed my good friend Darnell. When he saw me, his happy face instantly changed into a shocked one, and he quickly walked in the opposite direction. What a waste.

When I finally walked out, I saw what the commotion was about. Juwaun was parked in front of the building in a sparkling electric-blue Lamborghini. It was breathtaking. I have never seen a blue so...blue. The car was absolutely stunning.

I felt the stares as I neared the car. Then Juwaun hopped out of the driver's seat, walked over to the passenger side and opened the door for me, which opened up towards the heavens. I looked out at my new fan club before being closed up in the cockpit. Juwaun joined me in the car, bringing his sweet good-smelling aroma with him.

He smiled wide. "Hey you!"

"Hey," I responded, unable to help the large smile spreading across my face. "Oh, and I would've opened your door for you again, but I didn't know how."

He laughed. "It's cool, just knowing that you would have is good enough for me. But in the future if you want to," he said smiling, "it's right here." He pointed to a button above the handle. I tried hard to smooth out my smile. "What's wrong?" he asked.

"Nothing, just kind of happy to see you again, that's all."

"Kind of? We have to work on that. So where are we going?"

"That depends on if you don't mind going somewhere normal. I mean you might be only used to eating at fancy places," I teased.

"What? Oh you're gonna play me out like that? I'm not uppity. Besides, even if I wanted too, there isn't anything fancy around here anyways." He looked at me and smiled.

I punched him in the arm. "Don't you go dogging out places that I spend time in."

"I'm just saying."

"Whatever, I want to go to Arby's. Is that too regular for you?"

"Oh that's my spot," he said, overexcited. "I love the Market Fresh sandwiches."

"Me too, and their cheese sticks."

"Mmmm, and the strawberry banana milkshakes." There was a brief silence as we both seemed to picture Arby's entire menu. "Damn I'm hungry," Juwaun said, rubbing his abs. I was hoping that my stomach wouldn't growl too loud and embarrass me.

I looked at drivers pointing and staring as we sped by. He

had limo tint to keep him an incognegro. I imagined myself in another car looking at this one. Probably would make my pussy wet.

We pulled into Arby's parking lot and walked inside. The look on the cashier's face when she realized that her next customer was Juwaun Jones was priceless.

We ordered and received our meals then sat down and began grubbing. "Somewhere you have to be?" he asked, seeing me eye my watch.

"Uh yeah, work," I teased. "Some of us have real jobs."

He smiled, "You have an hour right?"

"Well actually, I'm my own boss, so I don't actually have a specific time to be back; but to stay professional, I usually only take an hour."

"Okay, well I'm driving a pretty fast car, so don't worry. I'll get you there in time."

"Play if you want to, police out this way are no joke. When did you get that gorgeous toy anyway?" I asked, prying a little into his life.

"About three months ago. It was a gift from Lamborghini. I'm their new face for the urban sector, as they say."

I tried to take it all in. "A gift, are you serious? Wish I could get gifts like that." He looked at me and smiled. "What?"

"Nothing, just looking at you that's all. Is that okay?" he asked with a mock attitude.

"I guess so," I responded sarcastically. In reality, I loved the way he looked at me, like he really thought that I was beautiful. He glanced at his magnificently covered diamond encrusted watch. "That's a gift too?" I asked, wiping crumbs from my mouth with a napkin. He took the last couple sips from his shake and looked at me, raising his eyebrows. "You're kidding right? Please tell me that you're joking."

He smiled. "It was from the Fords for breaking the

league's records for receptions, yards, and touchdowns last year."

"Must be nice," I said. The volume of my voice was on low.

"It is," he responded, taking our trays to the trash. I felt my phone buzzing in my purse. I remove it and saw that I had two text messages. One was telling me I had an urgent voicemail. I dialed it immediately, not knowing who it could be. I looked around to see where Juwaun was and he was occupied with a fan. The message was from The Michael Baisden Show, telling me to call them as soon as possible with a direct number to the show.

The other text message was from the mystery texter, the guy that invaded my life a few nights back. I had saved the unknown number with three question marks. My heart raced when I read the mystery texter's message. **How about dessert tonight**...I'll bring the caramel, the honey, and the nuts. Mmmm, he was trying to set up a session for later and I was long overdue.

I texted him back, **How about I bring the caramel and honey...and you bring that thick chocolate Snickers bar of yours, with the nuts of course lol. I've been having a sweet tooth lately.** As soon as I pressed send, Juwaun tapped me on the shoulder. I damn near pissed on myself and almost jumped out of my seat.

"You ready?"

"Sure!" I responded, almost before he finished the question.

"Are you okay?"

"Yeah, I'm okay." I stood up and grabbed my purse. "Why do you ask?"

"I don't know, maybe the way that your face is all flushed and rosy right now, might have something to do with it. I have that effect on you huh?" he asked, smiling.

I grabbed my face as if I would be able to feel myself blushing. "I guess you do."

58

About 10 minutes later, we pulled back up in front of my workplace to more pointers and gawkers.

"Thanks for the lunch."

"Anytime, and I do mean that. But since I kind of know you a little, I know I'll be asking you before you ask me."

"You never know, I might just surprise you." There were a few seconds of silence before I decided that I would give Juwaun another kiss. This one flowed much smoother than the first. I think that he may have been expecting this one. "You better not say anything about my breath either."

"Not a word," he said, laughing.

I pressed the button on the door handle and the door went up automatically. "That's so neat!"

"We still on for next weekend right?" he asked, as I stepped out of the car.

"Yeah, thanks for reminding me. I have to find something to wear."

"What size are you by the way?"

I looked at him with curious eyes and a frowned forehead. "Why, are you trying to say that I'm too big for you or something?"

He laughed. "Big? Woman, the only thing big on you is your booty."

"My booty is not big," I said, unable to mask my smile.

"Yeah, okay, call me later on."

I slid the door back to its original position and he sped off. The rest of my day at work went pretty well. I decided on my last break that I would call The Michael Baisden Show to see what was so urgent. When I called, I was reconnected with my young chipper friend, Jada.

"Michael Baisden Show, this is Jada speaking."

"Hey Jada, this is Halo."

"Hey girl, how have you been?"

"I've been okay. How about you?"

She sighed. "I've been okay if you erase the problems I've been having with my boyfriend. Oh and you were great on the last show by the way."

I smiled. "Thanks, and you are too young to be having man problems. I had a voicemail from earlier telling me to call in."

"Yep, that was me. Michael told me to see if you could do the show today. I think he was originally going to ask if you guys could do it Friday for "Men Versus Women," but he was able to score an interview with Johnie Jay, the renowned author."

"Yeah, I'm familiar with him, have a couple of his novels."

"Well, Mike thinks that you guys' comments on the subject would make good conflict."

"So what's his new book about?" I asked, curious.

"Soul mates!"

If I were in a movie, this would be the part where the 'dun dun duuuuunnnnnnnnn!' would play. Instantly I thought about Him, and knew in my heart that I felt he was supposed to be in my life. Maybe not exactly how I wanted him, but definitely in my life some kind of way. "Soul mates huh?"

"Yeah. I don't have all the details, but it's something about a woman and a guy who always seem to run into each other, but don't meet because of some kind of obstacle that always ends up in their way."

I laughed. "Wow, some storyline huh?" I said, still in semi-shock.

"Yep, he's good, but I'm not going to lie, I read his books because of the juicy sex scenes. Mmmm mmm! They are the best, so detailed. But anyways, yeah, Michael wants you to give your views on soul mates, and then have Baby Boy give his take—which I'm sure will be different from yours," she said, laughing.

"I'm sure."

"So, do you believe in that kind of stuff?" Jada asked cautiously.

"Actually, I think I do."

"That's good, because I'll bet any amount of money that Baby Boy doesn't. You ready for him?"

"Come on now girl. He's lightweight. He does not want it with me." I was ready for him though. I actually looked forward to his brash cockiness and his off the wall beliefs. I really loved when he tried to convince me to see things his way.

"Cool. If you can, call between 3:30 and 3:50. I think you guys go on at 4 P.M."

"That should be good. I get off at three."

"Okay Halo, talk to you then."

I was a little excited about doing the show again. It was a good thing everyone in my department had their own cubicles, because right now I needed a dick fix. I looked around to make sure nobody was coming and flipped open my phone. When I scrolled to his pictures, I pressed zoom and got a closer view. "Yummie!" I whispered as I turned my phone horizontally and imagined myself kissing and sucking all along his shaft. The only thing that was missing from this picture was a stamp of USDA along the length of his dick.

I felt like a junkie, I needed more. I needed to tell him to send me more pictures without seeming desperate. Hell, I need a subscription, a new dick picture every day. It seems like all that I think about is sex. And that's not even the bad part. The bad part is that I can't seem to get any.

Last night my ex called saying that he wanted me back. I cracked up laughing. He's obviously with who he wants to be with. Speaking to him did bring up memories though, not all of them bad.

But right now I'm enjoying being single. Actually, by being alone I'm learning a lot about myself, and for the first time ever I think I'm starting to like this Angel woman. I do need a little maintenance from time to time. If I did start to think about a man,

I think Juwaun was a pretty good candidate.

I closed my phone and tried to calm back down to normal. I looked at my watch. Yes, almost time to go.

"Hey Angel, what's up?" I was greeted by Tina, a woman who works three cubicles down from me. Tina thinks that she's the best thing that God has created. In fact, this was only the second time in the three years of me working here that she has actually spoken to me. I tried to be cordial a couple of times, but was totally turned off by her snobbishness.

I looked around to make sure that she was talking to me. "You're...talking to me?" I asked pointing to my chest. I was shocked that she even knew my name.

"Of course I'm talking to you," she responded, lightly tapping me on the shoulder. "How are you doing today? Time's going by slow isn't it?"

"Yeah, it's been a long day."

"What are you doing after work? We should go to Fridays and have a few cocktails; I mean we work in the same department, and don't even know each other."

I tried hard to conceal the shock that I was feeling. Maybe she was alright after all. "Um I'm a little busy after work today, sorry. But thanks for the offer."

"No problem, maybe some other time." She turned away, and not even taking one step, turned back towards me. "Hey, I forgot to ask you, was that Juwaun Jones that you hopped in the car with at lunch?"

"Yes," I answered short and direct. I really didn't like telling people my personal business. If you saw it then that's another story but me actually telling someone was another.

"Okay, I thought so. Is that your man?"

Okay now she was being a little too nosey. I leaned back in my chair. "We're friends."

"Oh okay. So you've probably met some of the other

62

players on the team too! I heard they party hard and ball out of control."

I saw where this was going now. Sneaky ass was planning this all along. I might as well have fun with it. "Yeah, they're very generous. Always buying the bar out, Dom P and Ace of Spades everywhere. Making it rain with twenties and hundreds." The look on Tina's face was priceless. It looked like she was about to start salivating. The sign of a true groupie. "They really go overboard," I threw in for good measure.

"Damn! Those are my type of niggas." Tina said, staring off into space. "Yeah girl...we definitely have to go out, soon."

"I'll get back with you and let you know," I said, signing off my computer.

"Okay girl, and by the way I love your haircut. Did you just get it?"

"Yep," I answered, lying through my teeth.

"Alright Angel, see you tomorrow."

"Okay," I said, shaking my head.

On the drive home, I tried to prepare my head for the show. I couldn't be weak with Mike and Baby Boy, especially after Brianna told me that women were starting to take a liking to Halo. Now I had to come correct.

I called and spoke briefly to Jada. She informed me that Baby Boy was on the other line.

"Angel, I'm not kidding, this guy sounds sexier and sexier every time I hear him. Be having me squirming in my seat."

Even though I was laughing, I could definitely understand where she was coming from. Baby Boy did have a sexy voice. I thought about the other night, hearing the mystery texter's voice on the phone. Even though it was one octave above a whisper, he made me cream all over the place.

While on hold, I listened to the interview on the radio with Michael and Johnie Jay. He was one of my favorite authors. And even though I didn't have his newest book yet, I was certainly going out to get it real soon.

He explained how the characters in his book overcame obstacles in their life and started on two different paths but through the magic of love found each other's hearts. But more importantly, before they found each other, they found themselves.

I sighed, it sounded so nice. I wish it could really be that easy. After the interview with Johnie Jay, Michael connected and reintroduced me to Baby Boy.

"How are you sweetheart?"

"Hey Michael."

"You remember your arch nemesis, Baby Boy?" he said.

"Yeah, how could I forget the one and only?"

"Hey beautiful!" Baby Boy answered.

Mmmm that voice. Jada was right it was almost hypnotic. "And how do you know that I am beautiful?" I asked.

"Believe me I know. I hear it in your voice."

"Whoa hold up, save it for the show. We go on in thirty seconds," Mike said, playing referee. I could tell that this was going to be a good show.

"Hey people, we are back and I want to talk more about this soul mate thing. But first I was talking to my good friends on the break, and one of them said something amazing. Ladies and gentlemen, Baby Boy and Halo, what's up y'all?" Michael's program manager cued the imitation applause to welcome us both to the show.

"Hey Mike," we both responded.

"Now Baby Boy, tell the listeners what you said on the break."

"Oh boy," I said, starting the beef.

"Sure, I was just telling Halo that I can tell that she is beautiful from her voice."

Michael laughed. "Wow, now that is deep. And how can

you do that, because I have heard some pretty pleasant voices on women, but when we finally met I was like, who are you and what have you done with the lady that I was talking to over the phone?"

"You see Mike; every man is not equipped with this mechanism. Fortunately, I am. It's not just about how she sounds, but how her voice feels. Like when I'm talking to a beautiful woman; whether I can see her or not, the hairs on the back of my neck and on my arms stand to attention. You know what I'm saying, I can't really explain it."

"So you're saying when you first heard my voice your hairs stood up?" I was curious to find out.

"I'm saying beautiful, that when I heard your voice over the phone, more than just my hairs stood up."

"Whoa whoa!" Michael interjected. "This is supposed to be a nice wholesome show, what's going on here?" Baby Boy and I both laughed. "I don't know if we should go on with the show, or if y'all should just go take a cold shower." Michael did a good job pretending like he wasn't with us boosting his ratings.

"Okay, if you're just tuning in we had Johnie Jay, the world-famous romance fiction writer in the studio, and unfortunately he had other engagements to attend. He just released We Are Meant, his new book that's already on the bestsellers list. I'm telling you, I read the book and it's very intense. I guess because it shows the behind the scene stuff that goes on, all the way up to you finding your soul mate. How their paths perfectly align with yours. It is as if every move you make, is setting you up to find your soul mate. That is some deep stuff right there. Take for instance my two callers; who knows, maybe they are meant to be together."

"Puh!" I blurted out.

"What Halo? You can't see that or something?" Michael asked.

"Mike, I don't know why she's fronting, she knows she

wants me," Baby Boy bragged.

"Baby Boy is too much of a ladies' man to be my soul mate." I wanted him to come back with an excuse or deny my accusations, but he never did, temporarily banning himself from my short and almost nonexistent list of possible soul mates.

Michael cut in, "Well according to this novel, your soul mate can very well be someone that you don't think is ideal for you. So the question I pose to you two today is—do you believe in soul mates?"

"Hell naw!" Baby Boy shouted before Mike got the question out good.

"Nooooo, Baby Boy, not you. I am totally surprised," Michael said, while laughing.

"Look Mike, this isn't happily ever after or fairy tale world. There isn't this magical person out there waiting for everyone. Soul mates, or the person for you or whatever you want to call them is straight bull, because no one is going to get with a person that's the perfect match for them."

"And Halo, do you agree with him?" Michael redirected his question towards me.

"I know I might sound like the typical female but I do believe in romance and I do believe in soul mates. Now I don't know how it all works in the scheme of things, but I do think that God makes somebody for everybody. Every time I see my parents' together, it makes me believe that even more."

"So how are you supposed to know that this...person is your actual soul mate? Because I'm sure a bunch of people have been with someone who they thought was their soul mate, only to come and find out that they are the devil reincarnated."

Michael and I laughed. "Not the devil reincarnated, Baby Boy! No you didn't."

"You know I'm telling the truth Mike. The reason for that is there is always someone in the relationship that is not going to hold up their end of the bargain. If you give a hundred, they're going to give eighty. Then if I feel you are only giving eighty, I'm going to bump my giving down to fifty to preserve. There's no sense of me putting in my all when you're not."

I quickly responded. "I think if you meet or shall I say when you meet your soul mate, you will know it, the both of you. You won't have any doubt that this person is supposed to be the one in your life."

"Wow," Michael said with a calming voice. "Halo, I thought you said that you were single. It almost sounds like you are speaking from experience."

"I am single Mike, and I wasn't saying that when you meet your soul mate you're going to stay together forever, because Baby Boy is right; it's up to both individuals to work at staying together. I think that God will only ensure that you two will meet, the rest will be up to you."

"That's a great point Halo," Michael said.

"I think my parents would agree with Halo too. They have been married for twenty-five years and I think that they would say that they are soul mates. I just think they just simply dedicated themselves to make it work. I don't think that they got together and everything clicked like a fairy tale."

"But like he said, soul mates, according to the book can be two unlikely individuals. Actually, someone who doesn't have the same views as you can actually be a good thing. Both people in the relationship should be able to learn something from each other so that they can both grow. It seems more likely that God would send someone that you can learn from by being different, rather than to send you someone just like you to keep you in the same state that you are in."

Both guys were silent and I have to say I think that may have been a first. Baby Boy was the first to break the quiet. "I know you said that you were single, but do you think that you have already met your soul mate?"

I thought about the question and if I should answer it. Nobody knew who I really was except Brianna, so I decided to tell the truth. "Yes!" When I answered, I felt like a huge weight had been lifted off of my shoulders.

"Yes huh?" Michael's voice started to pick up steam. "So does he know that he's your soul mate?"

"I don't know, but I think he knows that something about us is...inevitable."

"You two haven't talked about it at all?" Baby Boy asked.

"Nope as a matter of fact, we haven't spoken at all...period."

"What?" Michael's voice rang out. "Baby Boy, are you getting this?" Baby Boy didn't respond. "You mean to tell me Halo, that there is a man out there, that you have only seen, never spoken to, and don't know, and you're thinking that this guy may be the guy that you are supposed to be with? You sure you're not crazy?" Michael started laughing. Baby Boy was still silent.

"I know how this sounds Michael, and I haven't even told my friends about it. But the first time I saw this guy, I knew it was something special about him. And the funny part about it is he keeps popping up." Still there was no interjection from Baby Boy. "I see him when I'm out, and even when I decide to stay in, he invades my dreams."

"Baby Boy, you're a little quiet over there. I understand man. She's scaring you with all this crazy talk huh?" Michael asked.

Baby Boy let out what sounded like a halfhearted laugh. "Yeah, that's probably it. So Halo, you're telling me that you and this guy haven't said a word to each other, at all?"

"No, but when I do see him looking at me—"

"Oh so he has seen you?" he said, cutting me off.

"Yes."

"And when he does see you, what does he do? Like, how

68

does he look at you?" Baby Boy could've been a prosecuting attorney the way he was interrogating me.

"When I do see him and our eyes meet, it's like we kind of look like we've known each other forever. Like I said earlier, it just feels like he's supposed to be in my life. Now I'm not saying that he's going to end up being my man or my husband, because he may already have a woman or a wife, who knows. One thing I can say is that I think I got a glimpse at my future.

"Wow! This is too deep. We are running out of time family and have to go, but I'm going to leave you with a song that fits this topic perfectly, "Supposed to Be" by Toni Braxton. Until next time family...I'm out!"

I heard the click and Michael came back on the line. "Halo?"

"Yes, I'm here."

"Good show, very good. I mean you really tied into that theme perfectly," Mike said, congratulating me. "Baby Boy?"

"What up Mike?"

"Your girl had you speechless, man."

"Yeah, she was going off on the deep end today." Both of the men started laughing, as I took in the soothing sound of Baby Boy's voice. It sounded so familiar. I tried to pick my brain to figure out if and where I've heard it before. It definitely wasn't in the bedroom, because there was no way I could forget that voice whispering raunchiness in my ear.

"Go ahead, laugh it up boys, but when you find that one, y'all are going to think back to this day and think about me," I said, smiling.

"Uh huh! Right, yeah, so anyways—" I laughed at Michael blowing me off. "As you guys know our annual Eyes Wide Shut masquerade ball is about to pop off. Baby Boy, you've been there before, but Halo it'll be good if you came. It's going to be at the MGM Grand Casino. The dress code is Show Off of course and you must have on a full or half mask. Not the Halloween ones either but the sexy kind, feathers, paint, bling, you know Phantom of the Opera Mardi Gras type. How does that sound?"

"Sounds great, when is it?"

"First weekend in August. I'll have Jada email you all of the details."

"That'll work. Baby Boy, are you going?" I tried to ask, not sounding too concerned.

"Depends," he answered, just as nonchalant.

"On?"

"On if you'll be my date." I didn't know what to say, I was stuck. I mean I would definitely want to see him, but what about Juwaun? That's a little while away and who knows how we'll be by then. What about my girls? I knew they would love to go to something like this. Men dressed in tuxedos and suits surrounded by an air of mystery—yeah, they'll love it. And finally, what about Him...what if we actually... Arrgghhhh! I silently screamed inside about the fact that he's always on my mind.

"Halo?"

"Um, yes, I'm here. I think it would be better if we just met up there," I said, really wishing I could have given a different answer.

"Okay, I can dig that, but when we meet up, you're mine for the night." Damn, he was cocky and I loved every bit of it.

"I think that's a good idea," Michael said. "I would love to see you two together and I know the listeners would. That's if Halo's soul mate doesn't mind." The guys broke out in laughter again. I figured this was a good time to shoot them down.

"Why would he? It's not like this is a date or something, nothing more than a meet up."

"Ooouuu!" Michael was always in instigating mode.

"Whatever, Halo. You might actually like this meet up."

In my mind, there was no might about it. "Yeah, I'm

sure," I said, with a fake attitude.

"You never know, I might just be him."

"What, did you say?" I pulled into my parking space at the apartment building and pressed my ear to the phone, to make sure I heard what I thought I just heard.

"How do you know that I'm not your soul mate?"

"What do you mean, how do I know? I just told you about him."

"Yeah, but you've never seen me before and I've never seen you, so there is a slight chance that this...this guy you have been seeing, popping up all the time, is in fact, me."

I looked down at my hand that was now on my heart. I shook my head, trying to deny the possibility of Baby Boy's statement. Naw couldn't be. I paused, trying to think of something else to say. "Well for one, he doesn't think that he's God's gift to women." He got a kick out of that one. I heard someone in the background telling Michael that he had an important call on another line.

"Okay boys and girls, better wrap this up fast."

"Can we exchange numbers?" Baby Boy asked.

"I don't think that's a good idea."

He laughed. "You know I'm not going to stop trying."

I smiled. "I'm counting on you not to."

"Okay y'all, I'll be in touch with the both of you next week. Talk to you then."

"Aye Halo!" Baby Boy tried to hurry up before we were cut off. "See you around." Then I heard the dial tone.

But You Say She's Just A Friend

I got home in no time. Traffic was light due to the fact that it was still early. After parking in my underground parking lot, I walked to the elevator to begin the ascent to my floor.

"Hold up!" I pushed the open door button just in time. "Thanks man," the out of breath stranger said.

"No problem." I tried to remember where I'd seen him before.

"You're...on the 15th floor right?"

"Yeah," I said, extending my hand and wondering how he knew my floor. "Future."

"I'm Antonio, you can call me Tone. We met at the beginning of spring at the Loft Bar out on the yard. Remember we were both eyeing the big booty Asian woman at the same time?"

I laughed at the recollection. Funny how men could become cool all through the love of a female's fat fanny. "Yeah, yeah, I remember her. I didn't even know that they could support all of that back there."

"I hear you. I was thinking the same thing. She had an ass like a sista. Fortunately, she and my fiancé have become quite good friends, so I get to see that thang pretty frequently. Unfortunately, she and my fiancé have become quite good friends, so the only thing I can do is see that thang!"

"Lucky you," I said, smiling.

"Yeah, she's good peoples too, a flight attendant, lives on the eleventh floor. She'll be at the party though. I'll introduce you to her. You have the invitation right, for this weekend?"

"Oh that's you? Yeah I got it."

"Cool," he said, wiping sweat from his forehead with the towel around his neck. "I slid it under your door, wanted to make sure you got it."

"So...what do you need me to bring?"

He shook his head. "Naw man, just bring yourself and a lady if you want. If you don't, there will be plenty there. It's just a way that I can meet all of my neighbors and y'all can meet each other. A little holiday mingle. So the food, drinks, music, everything is taken care of."

"Food, women, and drinks. How can a brother say no to that? That's awfully nice of you man."

"Well even though it's my idea, I can't take all of the credit. My baby bro is helping foot the bill." The bell sounded as we reached the twelfth floor. "Alright Future, this is my stop. If I don't see you tomorrow, I'll see you Saturday?"

"Definitely. See you later Tone." The door shut behind Tone and the elevator continued its climb until it reached the fifteenth floor. I wonder what he does for a living? Whatever it is, it must be nice because I've seen him a couple of times driving in or out of the parking structure. If I recall right, one time he was in a Lexus, the other in a Benz. If his brother is helping him front the bill for the party, he must have just as much cake. Now that's the kind of people I like to associate myself with.

While changing to get myself ready for my afternoon jog, my phone rang. Before answering, I saw that it was

Carolina and smiled. "Hello, Future speaking!"

"Wow, so formal! Hey, how are you?"

"Great now. I was just about to go to Belle Isle to get my jog on before it gets too crowded down there."

"Jog? Aren't you supposed to be at work? I wasn't even expecting you to pick up the phone. I was going to leave you a message on your voicemail."

"They sent us home early, and don't sound so disappointed to talk to me," I teased.

"Whatever, you know it's not like that. By the way...that jog sounds just like what I need. Mind some company? I'm right down the way from you at the Coleman A. Young Building. I mean...that's if you're not already meeting someone."

"Of course I don't mind company, especially not yours. You have your running gear?"

"Keep it in the trunk. A real woman is prepared for anything." She snickered at her own comment.

"Anything?" I asked suggestively.

"Anything! So what's the address?" she asked, quickly changing the subject.

I gave her my address and directions to my place. She said she should be here in about ten minutes, so I tidied up a little bit. Out of all the years of knowing her, this is the first time she's falling through my place. I wondered if she wanted to see me or if she really did need that jog. One thing is for sure, I was definitely going to find out.

About fifteen minutes later, I got a buzz and told Carolina to ride the elevator to the fifteenth floor. Shortly after, there was a faint knock at the door.

"You're late," I sternly said, opening the door.

"Wow, a whole five minutes." Carolina looked at her watch as she stepped through the door.

"Time is money darling. You of all people should know that."

"Boy please—where can I change?" Her silver hair was flat ironed and pulled behind her ears with a small tendril gracing the side of her face.

"Guest room is to the left." As she walked down the hallway looking professional as always, my eyes felt as if they were the Libra scale, balancing between her radiant silver hair and her picture-perfect rear end. I haven't seen her dressed down in a long time and looked forward to seeing her that way.

She stopped just before reaching the hallway. "Are those Takashi Murakami pillows?"

"Yep!" I answered impressed. She's the first woman that saw the artistic pillows and didn't say, "Ooouuu, I like your multicolored pillows." Not knowing that each of those pillows could pay their rent.

"God, I love those. And you have an original painting?" She took a detour, and stared at the art on my wall with her hands on her hips. "Wow! Jean-Michel Basquiat and Ernie Barnes. I must say, I am way impressed." Then she caught a glimpse of my favorite one, hanging over the fireplace. "Jonz? Look at your grown ass. Who put you up on game?"

"Come on baby," I said, stepping to her in cocky mode. "I put myself up on game."

"And how did you score the Jonz?"

"I know people who know people." Truth is, I know a guy who put me up on a guy who was in a jam, and was selling all of his art for a super discounted price.

"Mmmmm hmm, like I said, I'm impressed." It felt good to have someone appreciate things that you went out of your way to do. Carolina was that woman who knew the difference between fine art and pictures you would buy at Art Van. I started jogging in place to give her the clue to hurry it along. "Okay, okay, I get it."

She went into the guest room to change. I followed her perfume trail for a bit and inhaled. "Mmmm, down boy, down!" I whispered to Buddy. A couple of minutes later Carolina came out with a clip in one hand and twisting her hair into a ponytail with the other. She was now standing one-person length away from me. Didn't even look like the same person. She wore a pair of track shorts that came to her upper thigh, revealing a pair of shapely legs that I didn't even know she owned. Her matching sports top showed off a stomach that was flat and defined. Her arms were nice and toned. There was no way this lady had me by almost ten years.

"Okay," she said, dropping her hands to her side. "You ready?"

I looked her over again. "Um, yeah."

"You sure?" she asked, smiling.

"Um, yeah," I repeated.

"Okay...let's go then." She walked toward the door and I purposely let her walk ahead of me while I grabbed the keys from the countertop. She had the body of a twenty year old. Ass sat up and stood to attention. I tried to hold my composure as I held the door open for her. "After you," I said, before closing the door behind us.

Carolina was quiet the entire drive. Seeming to enjoy the fresh air from the top being down, she stared outside with her oversized Donna Karan shades on, bobbing her head to Faith Evans' first album that I was playing. It seemed like she didn't want to talk and I didn't want to press her. Something was obviously bothering her. Then out of the blue she grabbed my hand, lightly at first and then a little tighter and firmer.

I flipped her hand over and interlocked our fingers. While looking over to the right to switch lanes, I saw a tear making its way down her left cheek. Guess it's more serious than I originally thought.

I crossed the bridge and entered onto the island. After passing the first corner, I pulled over and parked across from the giant water fountain. Carolina exited the car and began to do her stretches.

"Are you going to be able to keep up?" I jokingly asked, trying to break her overcast mood.

"With you? Please, no problem."

"Confident are we?"

"Enough talk," she said, and then sprinted off. It took me a full ten seconds to catch up to her. We jogged about a half mile before she broke her silence.

"The fucking secretary!" she said, panting. "Out of all...fucking people, the fucking...secretary. How cliché is that? I mean...I knew! Why am I trying to act as if I didn't know? The overly nice way she treated me when I came to his office." More panting. "The way she looked at him when we stepped out of his office. The numerous times she would call his phone for shit that could've waited until he came to the office."

The more Carolina spoke, the faster she jogged. "Even when we talked about having a threesome... I asked him does he have anyone in mind that would be discreet about it and she was the first name out of his fucking mouth! 'She seems to be sexually open-minded and very mature.' The bitch didn't seem to be; she was and he knew it! And I knew it all along but still played the naive wife!"

I quickened the pace of my jog to keep up with Carolina. I guess the pent up energy was fueling her run.

"I remember when she first got there, the day he hired her. He introduced me to her as, 'My lovely wife who I love more than anything', can you believe that?" I almost answered but realized that it was a rhetorical question.

"I knew she was trouble. I mean who wears a red dress to their first day at work? I guess I thought as long as he didn't put it in my face...I probably could've lived with it, but the other night we attended a banquet at his CEO's mansion."

We were in full sprint mode now, and she hadn't even broken a sweat, but she continued. "I was mingling with the other wives after dinner and was looking for him, not for any particular reason—just because I hadn't seen him in a half hour. So I figured I would use the restroom before he showed up; I asked one of the butlers where one was, and she pointed me down one of the corridors. I must have made a wrong turn somewhere because I ended up in another hallway where I heard faint noises. I kept walking and the closer I came, the clearer it became that those noises were indeed moans and groans."

By this time Carolina and I were flat out running. I tried my best to keep up with her but it was becoming incredibly difficult. She was running like a woman possessed. "So being the woman that I am, I figured I would steal an earful. Hell, if it sounded real good, maybe I would hide out in the other room next door and play with myself, while the mystery couple got their groove on. Well it was good, too good. Whoever the woman was, was getting dicked down and by the rising pitch of her voice was sounding like she was nearing orgasm.

By this time, my pussy was throbbing and my nipples were hard, until I heard the woman say my husband's name, again, and again and again. She told him how good he made

78

her feel and how much she loved his dick. I thought, naw...couldn't be, he has a very common name. Could be anybody, then I heard him call out her name and tell her that she had the best pussy in the world. Now I knew this couldn't be my husband, because that's the same motherfucking line that he used on me!"

Gone now was the proper, womanly voice. It was now replaced with that young girl who grew up in the heart of Inkster. The one who had to be hard to protect herself from getting walked over.

"I stuck my head in the doorway, but I couldn't see. So I opened the door completely and saw my husband with his tuxedo pants down around his ankles, and a set of legs wrapped around his waist and a pair of arms around his neck, pumping away. It was her, the devil in a red dress, and her red dress was hiked up over her waist, as she sat part of her ass on the table while my husband held the rest in his hands. When she first saw me she gasped from the initial shock, then she cracked a devilish grin and continued fucking him, while he stood clueless with his head buried in her breast. 'Mmmm, whose dick is this?' she asked, while staring at me. 'Yours baby.' 'Who does it belong to?' 'You baby, you.' While asking him her next question, she smiled wide. 'And who do you love baby?' 'Mmmm you baby, I love you.' 'Then make me cum, make me fucking cum.' I backed up from the door. We held eye contact for a few, and I went back to the celebration like nothing ever happened.

He later joined me and kissed me on the cheek, his goatee smelling like the remnants of her orgasm. I didn't even say anything, just sat there like a quiet little good wife and said nothing."

She stopped running. Stopped dead in her tracks and looked at me. Even though I couldn't see her eyes through the limousine tent of her shades, I saw the tears that fell from beneath them. "I don't know what to do Future. I'm so scared, and I don't know what to do." I held her in my arms as we walked the last quarter mile back to Sally.

There was more silence on the way back to the bat cave. This was such a change from the always upbeat Carolina, but I would be the friend that she needed. Don't think she wanted advice or an explanation. She just needed to get it out.

"Do you think I can use your shower?"

"Of course you can," I answered, and directed her to the bathroom.

"Nice...very nice," she said, admiring my spacious bathroom.

"Thanks," I said, still not wanting to say much. I walked her to the linen closet, grabbed one of my Ralph Lauren plush terry cloth robes, and handed it to her.

"Thanks baby," she said, standing on her tiptoes while giving me some sugar on the cheek.

"Make yourself at home. Under the cabinet is some Oil of Olay soap and there might also be a bar of Caress under there. If you don't like those, there is a new bar of Zest in the shower."

"Wow, so many choices. What is a girl to do?" she asked, smiling.

I smiled back, wishing that I could take credit, but in actuality a woman I used to date schooled me to the fact that most women more than likely wouldn't choose to wash up with a man's soap. I sat on the couch and watched TV for about fifteen minutes, when Carolina rejoined me in the living room.

"Oh my God...I didn't even want to get out of there. The water coming down from all directions is the bomb. You didn't tell me you had heated floors. And I thought I loved my bathroom."

"You should feel grateful to experience the shower. Only a few females can attest to being in there," I said, smiling.

"Oh thank you almighty king, thank you!" she mocked me by starting to bow.

"Aw shut up." I hopped up off the couch. "Mi casa is su casa. Time for big daddy to shower now."

"I saw the sound system in there. Why didn't you put on some music for me?"

"Oh, I didn't know if you..." I caught myself not wanting to bring up the recent gloomy mood. "Tell you what, when I hop in the shower you can put something on." I pointed to my stereo on the nearby wall. "Just push the big green button to sync it to the bathroom so I can hear it. And don't be trying to come in and get a glimpse of me while I'm naked either." I looked at her and laughed, but she didn't even break a smile, she just stood there and watched me walk.

The oversized hooded robe drooped over her head and covered that silver hair that I loved so much. We didn't break eye contact until the hallway wall forced us to do so.

I closed my eyes as the steamy water trickled down my face and onto my body. I felt for my soap tray and retrieved the White Water Zest bar. The steamier the shower became, the more I smelled the remnants of the Oil of Olay soap that Carolina chose to use. As I began to lather up, I heard music cascading from my surround sound speakers. It was Janet Jackson's "Any Time, Any Place." Damn I love this song!

Janet began to serenade me, 'In the thundering rain...' At that moment, I felt a small hand come from behind me and grab the soap from my hand. I felt her soft mounds pressed against my lower back.

"I hope you put that song on repeat," I asked, without turning around.

"Of course I did," Carolina replied. "I love that song!" She began to rub the soap in a circular motion around my chest, the front of my shoulders, then on my abs. All this while still standing behind me. She put the soap back in the tray and turned me around to face her. Through the steam, I looked in her eyes and saw pain. They told me not to ask because she wasn't sure, but right now, it felt right, it felt good.

She placed both of her hands on my chest and began to make the soapy substance turn into thick rich lather. Her hand definitely felt better than any washcloth that I have ever used on my body. Her touch was so light and feathery that it almost tickled. Buddy was getting a kick out of this, that's for sure.

I think Carolina knew that if this were a normal situation, I would be all over her like bees on honey. But this wasn't a normal situation. I was going to let her tell me how far she wanted to go.

She used her fingertips and traced every nook and cranny of my abs. Her face was pointed towards Buddy and her hands began to circle lower. My hands caressed her shoulder. Her fingers massaged soap into my trimmed pubic hairs. Buddy nodded up and down his approval. She brought her hands back up to my chest and traced my pecs. Janet kept on singing to us, 'I don't wanna stop just because...people standin' 'round are watching us'.

Carolina grabbed the soap again and lathered her hands until it began running down her forearm. She placed her small hands over her full C's, squeezed them, and cupped them under letting them slide out causing them to slightly bounce. I was enjoying the show. She continued lathering her breasts until they were nice and soapy, then she looked at me, head slightly turned to the side as if to say, "Okay, your turn."

The titty sign was the sign that I had been waiting for, so I took over the massage. She placed her arms on the inside of mine and went back to my crotch. This time she used both of her hands to caress my balls. I spread my legs a little to make sure that she didn't miss a spot. She played with my testicles like they were Ben Wa balls.

Her eyes were closed and her head was back. She had positioned herself so that the water was now running on her face. Her silver hair looked even better wet. What was once straight was now wavy and clinging to the sides of her face and neck. The soap on her breasts was now rinsed away. Gone was the lather on my chest, abs, and crotch. There was nothing to hide us from each other.

Carolina's lips slightly parted and I joined her under the waterfall and tasted her mouth. We pressed lips for what seemed an eternity. No tongue at first, just lip to lip and then she introduced her taster to mine. They mingled for a while, hit it off quite nicely and then mingled some more.

Her hand had gripped Buddy like a golf club. My hand was cupping her pussy and from the heat escaping her, I could tell that Carolina was ready to tee off. I fiddled with her clit and strummed along to Janet on her second go around of "Any Time, Any Place". Her wetness made itself known and distinguished itself from the wetness that flowed from the showerheads.

She was a lady. There was no aggressiveness, no animalistic behavior, she was all feminine. She moaned, hummed, and swayed as my hands moved from her stringed instrument to grip her tight snare drum. Her ass fit perfectly in my palms. I didn't want to stop kissing her, but she pulled away, grabbed me by the hand and led me out of the shower.

She placed the oversized robe back on. I did the same with mine. We faced each other and kissed again while momentarily enjoying the heated marble floor.

She grabbed my hand, led me out of the bathroom and into my bedroom, where two glasses of white wine were poured and ready for consumption. We stood holding hands. I looked at the glasses, then back at her and couldn't help but smile.

She hunched her shoulders. "What? You said mi casa is su casa." She released her hand from mine and handed me a glass of wine while smiling. "For you," she said, knowing that I should be the one handing her a glass.

"Thanks," I said, joining in with the role reversal. We drank with our robes untied partially exposing our bodies. Carolina downed the last of her wine while walking over to the stereo to select a Janet Jackson slow songs playlist. Next up was "Funny How Time Flies". She sat her glass down, placed both of her hands inside of my robe, and lightly traced my six-pack as I finished what was left in my glass.

"Love your abs."

"You want a refill?"

"Yes, please."

I picked up her empty glass and went into the kitchen to replenish our drinks. After taking Carolina her refreshed Riesling I walked to the bathroom, reached under the cabinet, and grabbed a bottle of warming massage oil. She's gonna like this. A massage would do her good.

When I stepped back into the bedroom, Carolina had her head back and glass tilted. Glass number two was gone now, along with her robe. I walked closer and held the massage oil up towards her.

"Mmmm." She nodded her acceptance to my

unspoken proposal. I stood admiring her body, which was now highlighted by the tangerine and crimson sunset creeping through my drapes. She was beautiful. Her skin was so smooth, complexion so rich and even. My eyes trailed from those cute heart-shaped lips to the lips that were just as plump that rested in between her thighs.

"Lay down baby," I said, directing her. She followed my directions and stretched out on her stomach. I continued to survey her body. My eyes stopping on her ass. It wasn't a donk by far, nor what some would call an apple bottom but it was really nice.

With her legs closed, I could see her juicy peach poking out at the bottom of her ass cheeks. Sometimes a nice medium ass was cool. She was the type that I could fuck from the back standing straight up with no problem. No lifting, no spreading, no separating. I removed my robe and straddled her. Buddy was pointing in the direction where it wanted to be. I had to be strong.

I grabbed the massage oil and poured small trails on her back then I poured a dab into my palms and rubbed them together vigorously like Mr. Miyagi did in The Karate Kid. When I placed both of my palms on the back of her shoulders, she jumped. "Damn Future, your hands feel like heating pads."

"Sorry!" I said, momentarily removing them.

"No, no, feels good." She returned to her relaxed state and I began massaging her shoulders, up by her neck, the back of her triceps, and went down to the middle of her back. I scooted until I was down by her calves and started kneading her ass. "Mmmmm!" Moans escaped her and that pretty peach that was visible from the back was now creating its own juices.

"You like that?" I asked, licking my lips.

"Mmmmm hmmm, I like it." I used both hands on the right cheek, then on the left. Then I used one hand on each. Carolina continued to groan. She propped her chin up on the pillow and stared out of the window towards the orange sky. "Future," she called out my name faintly, with hints of uncertainty and fear of what she was going to say next.

"Yes baby?"

"Make love to me!" she finally said, after seconds of silence.

I stopped squeezing her ass and looked at her face from the side. "You sure?"

She moved her head up and down. "Yes, I'm sure." She looked back at me. I stood up and before I could take those couple of steps to my nightstand to grab a foiled gold square, she pulled my arm. "Kiss me, please, kiss me some more." She pulled me over to her. I kissed her with all of the passion she needed and wanted. The passion that I've been longing to give her all this time. She nudged me to the bed and I sat. She then straddled me with her knees on the mattress, and kissed my nose as I looked into her eyes.

There was so much pain in them, there was no way I could take advantage of her and eventually add to that. I wrapped one of my arms around her back and the other hand I placed behind her head. I fell back on the bed, still holding on to her.

"Why? I don't understand...why? I've been nothing but good to him." Another question that really wasn't a question. I squeezed her tight as she lay on my chest. She sobbed uncontrollably for about five minutes. Snot and tears mixed and ran down the left side of my chest. No woman; nobody period, deserved to feel this miserable. I thought about the numerous women that I've slept with and the many

86

husbands who probably felt like her. Funny how something like this brings shit into perspective. I decided right at that moment that I was not going to do anybody's wife...ever! I wasn't going to add home wrecker to the long list of bad titles that I already owned. I owed that to Carolina. Of course, girlfriends were still game. I'm not fully rehabilitated yet.

After about ten minutes, the sobbing slowed and Carolina's breathing became calmer but heavier. "You're staying?" I asked, before she dozed all the way off.

"If it's okay with you?" she answered softly.

"Of course it's okay. What about...him?" I asked, referring to her hubby.

"Out of town," she flatly stated.

"Okay, well if you have to leave out after I go to work in the morning, a spare key is on top of the fridge under the coupon box. You can stay as long as you want, no rush." I meant every word.

"You are too good to me, you know that?"

I smiled and decided to answer that question. "Yeah, I know." She playfully nudged me on my arm. "Let me get up and make sure everything is locked up."

Before she rolled off me, I kissed her on the cheek. She folded the sheets back and climbed under. "You holding me tonight?" she asked, turning her body towards me as I walked away.

"Of course!"

"Kay."

After securing the locks, I went into the guestroom to check my missed calls and messages on my cell. There was one and it was from Kandi. She had left a voicemail.

I unhooked my phone from the charger and dialed one to access the message. "You have one new voicemail, 8:03 P.M." I looked at the clock hanging on the rear wall and noticed it was 8:15. Damn, just missed her call.

I listened to Kandi's message. "Hey Future, this is Kandi. I'm in dire need of a tune up ASAP. I think it's around eight. Call me before nine. I have to make a stop first, but after that I should be on my way, so hit me back. Bye sweetie!"

"What the fuck!" I whispered low enough not to alert Carolina. Be on your way? Call me back before nine? This chick really had some fucking issues. I think she's really used to always getting her way. My mind was made up...Kandi had to be cut off! This is the woman who made me eat her out and left me with a hard dick and a sticky beard. But even after all of that, my dick still wanted another piece of her. I didn't want Carolina to hear a potential spat with a woman right now so instead of calling Kandi, I texted her.

Not going to be able to swing it tonight...let you know when. Send. That'll show her ass for trying to play me like a sucker on our last meeting.

I walked back in the bedroom and saw no movement from Carolina. My phone chimed out loud from the guest room. Shit! I walked briskly to retrieve my phone and turned the volume down.

When I opened up my text message box I saw that the new message was from who else but Kandi. **What do you mean...can't swing it? I was on my way over.**

I immediately text back, **nobody told you to be on your way so that sounds like your problem, not mine.** Send.

About a minute later my phone vibrated again. **Okay baby, stop playing...do you know how much I thought about you and that juicy dick of yours today? I'm going to show you just how much I've been missing you.**

I sat down on the bed and laughed because she just

wasn't getting it. When you're first physically and sexually attracted to someone instead of mentally, a lot of times you miss or ignore warning signs, because you're entire mental is focused on what's below the neck. While I texted her back, I tried to think back to see if I missed any signs. **Maybe you didn't understand my text so let me try to put it a little plainer...AIN'T SHIT HAPPENING!**

She sent a response immediately. **Well fuck you mother fucker! How dare you turn this down. You'll never have anybody who will fuck you better than me! When you play with Fyre...you will get burned! Fuckin asshole!**

Wow! Okay! I stared at this fire statement with concern and shook my head at the fact that she could have at least spelled the word right. I think somebody is a little psycho for real. I turned my phone to silent, and figured I would turn in and hold Carolina for the rest of the night. That's when my phone lit up again. I opened and read the message. Awww shit! **I was very busy today and had to work through my lunch but looking at that yummy dick of yours more than satisfied my appetite. Think I'm starting to get a-dick-ted 2 u!**

My heart rate sped up a little and a smile came across my face. The text that I've been waiting for all day finally came through. The man who usually gets excited over a fat ass and a nice pair of titties is now giddy over a text message with a damn smiley face.

My phone illuminated again and I noticed that I had an incoming picture mail from Gabrielle. I was really excited now. The picture was under a heading that read: **I made you dessert...Melted Caramel Sundae.** There were four pictures, each one of her fingers. She used at least two of her fingers in each picture, and they were covered in thick, gooey pussy juice that resembled melted vanilla ice cream mixed with hot caramel. I contemplated licking my phone's screen right there and then but decided against it.

I peeped back in my bedroom. Carolina was still motionless. I started texting. **Thanks for making dessert and for satisfying my sweet tooth...looks scrumptious.**

She texted back, **if you think that's something...u should've seen them right after I came! I could've glazed a ham 4real, lol. Okay baby, I've got a long day tomorrow. I'm moving!!! Yay...and have to meet with my realtor.**

Hopefully not far enough where you can't text. I became a little concerned about the moving part, hope that wouldn't put a detour in my plans to meet her one day.

Naw, not that far lol.

I actually look forward to reading your words on my screen.

That was so lame, I thought as I pressed send.

Same here ☐ Talk to you later!

Okay Honey Suckle, talk to you later.

Lol, mwaaahhhh!

Gabrielle texted me a kiss and had me floating on cloud nine. I had to figure out a way to meet this woman. I don't know how exactly, but I had to think of something.

It was now time for me to attend to the woman who happened to be in my life at the moment. She was sleeping like a baby, calm and peaceful. Definitely a big contrast from a little while ago. I crawled into the bed still naked, and slid under the sheets. Buddy found him a nice spot and cuddled up in the crevice between Carolina's butt cheeks. I wrapped my arm around her. She instantly grabbed my hand and kissed the inside of my palm. I inhaled her soft hair and closed my eyes. Even though I had a beautiful woman in front of me that I've wanted to cut into for God knows how long, tonight I was going to have dreams of me eating a Honey Baked ham, and topping it off with a caramel sundae from Dairy Queen.

Red bone

I couldn't even get out of my car. What-if's kept running through my mind. What if Baby Boy really was the guy that has been popping up in my life? I tried to shake it off. "Get a grip Angel." He is obviously trying to fuck with your mind and you are letting him. It's Baby Boy for God's sake. He is a professional. Don't be weak. I had promised myself after my ex that I wouldn't let a guy take advantage of me emotionally or in any other way again and damn it, I'm going to make good on that promise!!

I stepped out of my car and slammed the door behind me. I did the same to my apartment door after I walked in. I kicked my heels off and watched as one flew under the couch and the other under the coffee table.

"Huhhhhhh!" I tried to calm myself by messaging my temples. "Woooosaahhh, wooosaahhh." I let out a long sigh, sat on the couch, and immediately reached for the remote control. "Okay Oprah, help a sista out." I turned up the volume as I watched Oprah in her usual chair, doing what she does best.

"If you are just tuning in, today's show is very special. Today we have on the show, couples that swear they were destined to be together." I was now sitting up straight on the couch. "They say that they are not like normal couples who might meet by accident, get to know each other, and then fall in love. They say that the stars aligned and that the events in each of their lives led them to each other. In other words, today's show is about soul mates."

I clicked the television off and hung my head. I need a bubble bath, bad! I started my steaming hot water and poured a capful of Freshwater Cucumber bath salts with two capfuls of matching bubble bath. I inhaled the sweet aroma. Funny how something I dreaded to eat as a child, would be something that I absolutely loved to bathe in later in life.

I walked to my bedroom and stripped naked, stopping briefly in front of the mirror to strike a quick pose. I grabbed my booty and made it do a quick bounce. If the apple in the Garden of Eden looked anywhere near as good as mine, it's no wonder why Adam couldn't resist taking a bite. Scrumptious!

I went back to the bathroom and turned the hot water off while turning on the cold. I sat over the edge and counted to ten before turning the blue knob clockwise as far as it would go. Just looking at all of the suds made me momentarily relax.

I walked to the kitchen to poor myself a glass of Sangria and decided that today, I needed all of the trimmings. I sliced up a couple pieces of pineapple and while placing the unused portion of fruit back in the fridge, a jar of cherries caught my eye. "Why not?" I spooned four cherries from the jar and included them in my fruit medley. I took a sip. Mmmmm, delicious. I licked the excess wine that began to trickle down the rim. Sangria is the shit, you can drink it like Kool-Aid and it's inexpensive. I took another sip. Yep, the shit!

Now I can take my bath. I grabbed my phone and realized that I had two missed calls. One was from Brianna. The second missed call was from my ex-boyfriend and ex-headache, ex-lover, ex-ecstasy giver, ex-multiple orgasm maker, and ex-superb pussy licker. I couldn't even pretend like I never thought of calling him for a late night romp. But I knew once he arrived here, either looking at him or hearing him speak would make me regret it.

I pressed the up arrow until Brianna's name appeared and

pressed call.

"What up A?" Brianna answered in a gangstered out voice.

"Ain't shit big B," I imitated.

"Nothing's up over here either nigga." We both laughed.

"You must be drinking on something over there," I stated, knowing the silly mood she entered when alcohol was involved.

"You know it, on my second glass of Red Ziffy."

I looked at my half-empty glass of Sangria and took a few more sips. "Damn it, you've got a head start on me, give me a couple of minutes to catch up."

"Whatever girl. By the time you catch up, I'll be on another glass. Are you okay over there? You breathing all hard and shit."

I laughed when I reached the refrigerator. "Girl," I said catching my breath, "I just trotted to the kitchen to refill my glass before I hopped in the tub." I carefully walked back to my awaiting bubble bath. "Give me one second girl." I cautiously sat the phone on the edge of the tub along with my glass of wine. Standing in the water, I graciously made my decent. "Ahhhh yes! Whewwwww!" I picked the phone back up. "Okay I'm back."

"Damn, what are you doing over there, having an orgasm?"

My pussy twitched at the thought. "Mmmm how I wish. That sounds so good, but I was just sitting down in this hot bath water."

"That's what I'm doing too. Wine goes so perfect with a nice bubble bath."

"Doesn't it though? And candles," I added, as I looked around and noticed that I hadn't lit any.

"Yeah, candles." Brianna let out a long relaxing sigh. "It's been five weeks." Her comments had gone over my head. "Angel, did you hear what I said, it's been five weeks since I had any. No tongue, no lips, no dick!"

"You're doing good girl," I answered back nonchalantly. "I've lost count it's been so long for me." I sank down until the bubbles covered my chocolate covered breasts. "Brianna I have a question for you since you've opened up the sex talk."

I think Brianna felt my hesitation. "Angel it's okay. I told you before that you are my girl and you could ask me anything. Honestly, it's alright."

"Okay, umm." I still hesitated a little even though I knew Brianna was bisexual, asking her any questions that involved her and the same sex made me feel uncomfortable. "Umm, which do you miss more?"

"I'm assuming that you're talking about dick or pussy?" she asked, with no reservation.

"Yeah, like, which one do you think about more."

"I know that this sounds cliché, but I really can't choose one over the other. Like take for instance dick."

"Mmmmm hmmm," unexpectedly escaped my mouth.

Brianna laughed. "It's nothing that takes the place of it. How it feels, how it penetrates you and takes control of your entire being. Then attach that to a manly body, a hard muscular body."

I cut her off. "Hopefully not too muscular where it takes away from the size. I've had one of those." We both laughed as I dipped my washcloth and wrung it out to dab the beads of sweat that were forming on my forehead from my rising body temperature.

"Then the smell of a man is even a turn on, not his cologne or his soap, but his natural scent. Their voice, their touch. Men are absolutely irreplaceable. So is a woman."

"When you have sex, well when I have sex with a woman, it's not to replace a man. It's an entirely separate and different experience. Being with a woman is like," she paused, perhaps thinking about how she could explain it in layman's terms, "It's like making love to yourself. A woman's touch is so different from a man's. Everything is delicate, soft, and sensual. She's going to finger you the way you would yourself. Suck your titties the way that you would and suck on your clit the way that you wished a man could. It's less about penetration than it is about feeling good. She is female, therefore she is you, feel what I'm saying?"

"I don't think I've ever heard it described that way, but yeah, I feel you."

"But in the end when it comes down to it, pussy is like Chinese food, sometimes you have a craving for it and it tastes good as hell but not long after you eat it you're hungry again."

I laughed at my friend as I dipped my towel again and ran it across my face. I sat up a little, leaning my back on the rear of the tub and noticed my erect nipples and the fullness of my breasts. I enjoyed the fact that Brianna has always been open and willing to explain her sexual orientation.

I remember when Tierra introduced us a little over two years ago and I found out she was bi. I automatically set a barrier for our friendship based on that fact alone. In reality, I wasn't being a friend at all. Now our friendship has reached new heights and depths, surpassing that of Tierra's and mine. I mean Tee is my dog for life, but on certain subjects and issues, I think her maturity level is subpar. I now can say that I'm truly comfortable in every way with Brianna's bisexuality.

We sat for a couple of seconds in silence. I was so relaxed, my body was buzzing now. "What are you doing over there Brianna? Are you sleep?"

"Mmmm, all this freaky talk got me over here squeezing my nipples," she said seductively.

"You are so nasty," I said, rolling my nipples in between each finger.

"I am aren't I?" She let out a low laugh. "And what are you doing over there Ms. Goodie Two Shoes?" She asked in a way that suggested that she knew I was being mischievous.

I gave my left breast a squeeze, which sent a tingle on a direct route to my pussy. "Same as you...playing with my nipples." We both laughed.

"Quick question, I know that you would never, but if you would...hypothetically...who would you do?"

"What?" I asked, caught off guard by her question. "Who would I do as in... a woman?"

"Yeah!" she excitedly said, and then repeated her question.

It was a no brainer for me. I thought of a woman that I have imagined what it would be like to experience a sexual escapade with, but I had to make it seem as if the answer didn't come to me right away. "If I had to pick someone, I would saayyyy, ummmm I don't know...Angelina Jolie."

"No! Angelina, get out!" Her excitement made me feel a little insecure.

"What? What's wrong with Angelina?"

"Oh, nothing's wrong with her. It's just that for your first bi experience, I think that you should go with someone a little tamer. Girl, did you see her in Mr. and Mrs. Smith? She would have you turned out, first time."

I laughed at my best friend but totally agreed. "You are silly. I don't know though, she just seems, so...so sensual and those pillow top lips." I stopped myself, realizing I may have been getting a little too much into the physical attributes of Angelina.

Brianna and I went on for another ten minutes about what females in the industry we would do, and who we thought were closet bi's.

"Okay before we get off of the phone, I forgot to tell you what this guy asked me today."

"And what was that?" I asked, noticing my fingertips taking on the characteristics of a California Raisin.

"He asked me was my booty fake."

"Are you serious?"

"Dead serious. He was like, 'Yo ma, is that all you or do you get booty shots?' Like if I had shots I would go around announcing it."

"So what did you tell him?" I asked, curious.

"I told him that injections don't look this good, then I walked away popping my ass side to side to give him something to think about."

"Oh my God, are you serious?"

"Yep, had that fool drooling like a toddler."

We laughed. "Bri you are sick."

"Yeah, I know. I mean what is it about asses Angel? I really don't get it, do you? What is it about a big butt that drives men crazy?"

"I really couldn't tell you. I always ask the same question. Don't get me wrong, I do like mine but guys love it much more than me. I think they all equate it to sex and how it'll look while humping doggy style."

"Mmm love that position," Brianna responded. "Have you ever fucked in front of the mirror doggy style?"

"Mmm hmmm," I answered reminiscing. That thought brought a huge smile to my face.

"Ass making all those ripples like a tsunami. Does your ass make waves like that?" Brianna asked, sounding serious as a heart attack.

"Yes silly, I think every woman's booty does that."

"I wouldn't think yours would, seems like it's too firm to ripple."

"My ass does make waves," I said, defending my derriere. "And how do you know my ass is firm by the way?" My eyebrows went up in anticipation of Brianna's answer.

"I know because when we are out and you drink, I always cop a feel," she said giggling.

"You are so nasty."

98

Johnie Jay

"So!"

"Alright girl, I'll talk to you later. Messing with you got my entire body wrinkled." I squeezed my hands together and stretched them back out looking at my senior citizen looking fingers.

"Mine too. I'll talk to you later baby. Sweet dreams about me!"

I felt my cheeks warm as I thought about my pussy jumping during our conversation. There was something about her. She possessed a type of sexual energy that was undeniable. No wonder she attracted both male and female. When I finally got around to doing a quick wash-up, my phone vibrated. I expected to see a raunchy message from Brianna, but on further inspection realized that it wasn't from her, but from the person that I've become kind of addicted to. Just seeing those three question marks flash across my screen made me so excited that I dropped my phone. "Shit!" I picked up my phone and examined it. It's a good thing that it fell on the bathroom rug in front of the sink.

Yes! I had picture mail. "Mmmm yummie." I had received a picture of a gorgeous Godiva chocolate package of hard abs, muscular arms, chiseled chest and legs and a thick, juicy dick. The only thing that was missing was his face. The icing on the cake was that he must have just stepped out of the shower because he was dripping wet. Damn he looked good as hell.

I reached for my robe and decided against it. "Yeah, I'll repay him for this," I said to myself as I admired his body. I quickly walked my bedroom mirror and took two pictures, full body from the front and from the side. I pressed send after examining them to make sure my face wasn't in any of the pictures. "Now take that!"

I went back to grab my robe and to pour me another glass of Sangria. By this time, I had lost track of how many glasses I drank. When I first hooked up with my ex, I was drinking maybe every other weekend. Stress from being in a relationship with Damien caused me to drink wine more and more to relax.

Now it was time for provocative texting. While rubbing cocoa butter on my legs, my phone vibrated. I read my new text message. **Damn mami...I want my mouth on every inch, every part of that delicious body of yours.**

I was feeling devious tonight. No more Ms. Nice Girl. Tonight I was being nasty. I texted back, **every body part huh? Sure you have the stamina for that?**

My stamina will be the least of your worries baby, instead you should be more concerned about drowning in ecstasy and cumming uncontrollably.

I liked the sound of that I thought as I read his message, and immediately began to text him to let him know. **Mmmm, I like your style. Looked at your dick umpteen times today.**

Lol, umpteen huh? Well ever since you sent me those delectable pictures of your ass, I've been using them as NoDoz when I get sleepy at work. You have that caffeine booty.

I busted out laughing at that one. This guy seemed to have it all, smarts, naughtiness, a brilliant body, gorgeous dick and funny as hell. I text him back, **Lmao...you are silly!!!**

Damn, our bodies would look so good on top of each other. His text made me look at my full body picture, then flip back to his. **You know, I think that you are right,** I texted back.

Light on or off?

Lamp on, candles lit...I love to see...watch.

Mmmm good answer...What about mirrors?

What a coincidence, he made me think about the recent conversation Brianna and I shared. Of course! Send. I liked his line of questioning. Mystery Dick was trying to find out if I was a true freak or just faking the funk.

I see that you are nasty huh? He asked in his next text.

Just call me Ms. Jackson...lol.

Okay Ms. Jackson, let's see how freaky you really are...finish the line to this song...I, must be honest with you babe...

Oh yeah, he was definitely the man now. He was quoting a line from one of my favorite songs by Ne-Yo, "Mirror". I did as he requested. **I love to watch the faces that you make...when we, make love, ouuuuweeee!!!**

He responded quickly, **Okay okay dang! Lol you even put in the extras and all...ouuuuweeee, I like that.**

Okay Mr. 21 Questions my turn to interrogate you. Have you ever recorded yourself having sex...I'm talking audio only.

He texted back, **Can't say that I have, but it sounds very intriguing.**

After sex, you replay what you and your lover just said to each other along with all the noises that you were making, groans and moans and then replay what your partner was doing to you at the time that made you say or make the sounds that you did. Send.

Damn, that sounds great, would be a lot of talking on there on my behalf, lol, I'm a very vocal lover.

Ditto, so what do you think about toys? I figured since I was on a roll, I might as well find out all that I could.

Toys, well, from what I've heard most kids like them, I used to have a lot when I was younger and most are made in China.

He had me cracking up as I texted him back. **Lol, no silly you know what I mean...do sex toys intimidate you?** This was a question all women wanted to ask before becoming sexually involved. A lot of men believe that if a woman has a toy that it means that she isn't satisfied with them or that she wants to replace him. Nothing could be farther from the truth.

New message! **Lol, okay why didn't you just say sex**

101

toys. **Intimidated you ask...are you serious, the more the merrier. Anything that enhances the sexual intensity is cool with me.**

I had a helluva mental picture going on and it was making my coochie leak. I inserted my index finger to the first knuckle and twisted it around. I removed my honey and placed it in my mouth. "Mmmm." I loved the taste of my pussy. I wonder if every woman tasted as good as me? **Guess what I'm doing right now?**

Please do share

Tasting myself. I tasted my finger again and inhaled my scent.

Mmmm, wish I could be there to indulge with you. Tell me how she tastes baby.

I had started to imagine his voice and how it would sound if he were here with me. **It tastes like a Cinnabon, with extra icing...your text makes me cream all over myself.**

He quickly sent his response. **Damn! I love me some Cinnabon and how I would love tasting yours...lol; this is some coincidental shit.**

What is?

I was just talking about this with some friends earlier.

About what...Cinnabons? I didn't know where he was going.

You and I just started texting and all of the things that I feel like I've been missing out on with other women...seems like you got it. You are probably undercover crazy though.

He had me blushing through the text. **Are you trying to run game on me now?** I sent the message and tried to massage my cheeks.

Lol, now why would I run game on my soul mate?

What the hell, I thought as I read his text and then reread it. My eyes fixated on the last two words on my screen. I was momentarily paralyzed. I think this had to go down as one of the

102

weirdest days in my life. Those words, the subject, the thoughts, the coincidences were just...weird.

Well, my sexual soul mate anyways...lol.

Okay, I texted back. That helped a little. He meant sexual soul mate. Not soul mate, soul mate. I had to text something. I felt like he was waiting for more of a response. **I'm digging you too daddy! You better not be gaming me or else that crazy bitch you spoke of will come out...lol. Seriously, I want to thank you for getting me revved up for my finale.**

Whenever I can be of assistance...

I'll make sure I think of you while I'm using one of my toys tonight. I sent the message and opened up my toy drawer to decide which accessory would aid in my orgasm tonight. Yep, Mr. Dependable will do just fine.

You do that, and don't be a stranger...you have me actually looking forward to these...sessions, lol, they are very therapeutic.

Ditto was my last reply. He and I shared the same sentiment. I have to admit it was a little weird to witness a man showing a warm side. Most men could be thinking about you all fucking day but won't admit it. There was something about this guy. He could be putting on a major front but why would he? There was no need to. We haven't promised to meet or date so there was no pressure for him to say what he didn't mean. I mean our arrangement was only physical and semi-sexual. There was no need to bring feelings into it. It's just a friendly text affair. Nothing more, nothing less.

I finished what was left of my Sangria, laid my head on the pillow, and reflected on all of the past events over the last month. My emotions have been in overdrive. Mostly for someone who I haven't even met, actually three people that I haven't met. Baby Boy, the mystery texter, and the Mystery Club Man.

And on top of that, I'm up here actually telling people that

I've seen my soul mate. "Ha!" What I feel is nothing more than infatuation mixed with lust over a guy that I've seen a couple of times and wanted to fuck, that's all. I inhaled deeply and exhaled just the same. If that's all it was, then why does it feel like I'm trying to convince myself?

I closed my eyes. "Okay, just need a couple of minutes before I..." My eyelids felt like weights were attached to them. Darkness became even darker followed by soft frizzy light.

When the light focused in and my eyes adjusted to it, I was looking down on myself lying in the middle of the bed butt naked. I looked really relaxed with one hand behind my head and the other caressing my left breast, but by the steady pace of my breathing, I could tell that I wasn't sleep…I was in deep thought about something or someone.

My nipples pointed north and my robe was hanging halfway off of the bed, a sign that I recently was in the shower. I could hear soft music coming from my stereo. As my vision became clearer and the music, more audible my perspective changed from third to first. I was no longer having an out of body experience, hovering over myself being a voyeur. I was now... myself.

I continued to squeeze my breasts softly while humming along with Sade on the stereo. "Smooth operator, smooooooth operator." My nipples tingled as they slipped through my oily fingertips.

"Oh my God!" a recognizable voice yelled out from the hallway. "That cucumber bath gel is the bomb baby!" Brianna then walked through my bedroom door, butt naked, semi damp while drying her hair off with one of my seafoam green bath towels.

"I told you," I said calmly, as I watched her titties bounce. I was fully aware of my surroundings but I was not in control of my movements or words. I was on auto-pilot. I watched her dry off the rest of her body and admired her perfectly S-shaped body from the side. Her booty automatically formed a deep arch in her back. I don't know if you could be thick and lean at the same time, but that's how Brianna looked. She was all of a size ten, but her ass was more like a fourteen or sixteen. Her legs and thighs looked like those of a thoroughbred horse, shapely and strong. Her arms were sculpted and she had a slim stomach, small waist and looked like she had no body fat. All of that ass with no dimples or dents... amazing!

Her dark brown hair hung over her head and face. The product of her Puerto Rican father and African American mother, she had the hair that most of us black women purchased from the Asians.

I placed both hands behind my head and admired my best friend's body. She must have noticed the look in my eyes because she gave me a wink. I blew her a kiss back. I felt the wetness between my legs. I was so amused and confused at the same time. First of all, why was my best friend stark naked in my bedroom? And why were we behaving like this was not the first time that we've seen each other in the buff? This was too weird but it felt so normal.

"I take it you like?" Brianna asked, referring to the intense stare that I kept locked on her bum. She turned her back all the way towards me so I could get a better look.

"Damn Bri, I think you have the most perfect ass that I have ever seen."

"Other than yours of course," she replied, turning back towards me. She came closer to the foot of the bed and placed both of her hands on the edge. "I've been wet all day at work thinking about being with you." I parted my legs into a V and felt my moist outer lips slightly separate. "Mmmmm." She licked her slippery tongue across her glazed lips letting the excess spit almost drip off them. "Kinda like this," she said, looking at my pussy.

I lightly patted my pussy. "She missed you," I said, looking down towards my crotch.

"Is that so? Well I miss her too and plan on showing her just how much." Brianna seductively crawled on my king sized bed towards me like a feline. Not a kitty cat but something from the wild jungle. A lioness, or better yet, a panther. She kept her eyes fixated on me, her prey—and my pussy, her dessert.

She had both of her hands wrapped around my left ankle and calf, raising my leg and placing my heel on her left shoulder. The contrast of my dark leg and immaculate French pedicured toes against her Palmer's Cocoa Butter colored skin was a turn on in itself.

Brianna started with my pinky toe, licking her long wet warm tongue under and all around it making my thigh muscles tense up. "Mmmm." The sudden warmness of her mouth took my toes off guard but quickly adjusted. She sucked on my toe like it was a nipple, not too hard, not too soft. Usually when I am turned on, I feel my wetness coming down in spurts, almost as if my pussy builds up a certain amount of juices until it can't contain any more and lets it flow. Right now, there were no spurts, just a continuous, constant stream.

I think every pussy has its own scent. No two alike. Mine was intoxicating even more so now that it was mixing with Brianna's. It was like catching a contact from marijuana. I was high and horny. Brianna gave my toes equal attention until she got to the big toe. She held it close to her bottom lip, teasing it with her warm breath. I moaned out loud, "Put it in your mouth baby, suck it." I couldn't lie there mute any longer. She massaged the arch in my foot and continued blowing and breathing making me arch my back off the bed.

Brianna shared her focus between me and Kitty. "Mmmm, your pussy is sooo wet! Looks so delicious."

Before I could respond, she devoured my big toe like it was a plump dick head, sucking it hard, then pulling it from in between those perky lips of hers, causing it to make popping noises. "Ooouuu shit baby, yeah...just like that!" Brianna continued sucking, bobbing her head as if she was giving fellatio. Slob had begun to run from the corners of her mouth and onto my toes and down my foot.

I felt her strokes in my shaft, each flick of her tongue directing more blood flow to my clit. This must be what it feels like to have a dick. It's no wonder why guys can't get enough of this shit. My back kept rising off the mattress and my hips wouldn't stop gyrating. The golden gates to my orgasm had been unlocked and cracked open.

Brianna must have sensed it too. "No baby! Not yet, save it for my mouth. I want that thick, sweet nectar down my throat." She removed my toe from her mouth and returned my leg back to the bed. She crawled over me, putting one of her legs in between mine. She was now directly over me on all fours. I inhaled her, took in the scent that clung to both of our skins. Her long curly hair cascaded over her face and hung down around mine. We locked eyes and she smiled. "Guess what flavor?" she asked me, as she puckered her lips.

Her asking clued me in to the answer. "Better be my favorite, Vicky Secrets Cocoalicious."

"Hmmm could be," she said, widening her smile.

"No, I said better be." I reached my fingers through her spiral waterfall until I reached the back of her head. I wanted her so bad. My body needed her, longed to taste her again. This obviously wasn't our first time. I wonder how many times it has been. Were we a couple? Am I dreaming? I had to be because the passion I had for Brianna right at this moment was too strong.

I pulled her closer to me and devoured her lips. The soft taste of chocolate invaded my tongue. We moaned in between each suck, each kiss. I sucked on her bottom lip until there weren't any remnants of cocoa left.

107

"Give me your tongue Angel. Stick it out for me." I did and she softly slurped it, stealing back the traces of cocoa that had not dissolved on my tongue.

The wetness that had trailed to my ass had now begun to run towards my lower back. I felt droplets falling on my lower abs right above my pussy from Brianna. At first, I thought maybe it was water that was left on her from the shower. "Mmmm baby, do you feel my juices? I'm so wet, you have me dripping." As she spoke to me in between kisses, I smelled the faint sweet smell of Sangria on her breath.

Brianna held herself up and kissed my neck and shoulders until she made it to her new target, my protruding nipples. She hungrily took the right one before doing the same with the left. I felt her breathing getting heavy as her lips softly touched my stomach. I jumped every time she connected with a different spot on my body. Kitty waited in anticipation of feeling her mouth on it. I methodically turned my head to the left and fastened my gaze on the chair by the wall.

Now I was really thrown for a loop, not so much physically as mentally. Things were happening as if they were normal. "You want to see her taste me daddy?" I asked breathily, looking at the man who has of late invaded my life, my heart, and my dreams. He sat attentive and naked, stroking that thick dick of his. He licked his lips and nodded his head up and down.

Brianna swung her head to the side causing her hair to escape her face and retreat to the back of her neck. "Only if you let us help you with that situation you're handling," she told him with a devilish grin.

"I wouldn't have it any other way," he responded. His voice sounded so familiar. I knew it, heard it somewhere before, but where? He fondled his balls as he continued staring at the two women making out before him.

Brianna turned her focus back to me. "Don't you just love

108

watching him play with his dick?" We both laughed as she pushed both of my knees up to my chest.

"Almost as much as I love having it in my mouth," I replied. As my legs went up, I felt my lips parting and my thick juices trying to hold them together.

"I love looking at your pussy baby, it is so beautiful." Those were the last words I heard before she dived head first into my slit.

"Ohh ba...baby, mmmmmm yeah, just like that." My mouth could barely form words. Brianna knew what she was doing. The way she circled my clit and trailed her tongue to my opening was driving me crazy. She licked then kissed then sucked. The noises were getting me hornier. I looked at Him as he stroked himself slow, rubbing his thumb over that fat head and his fingers under that plumped underside vein.

His eyes locked in on mine, we were connected. Brianna pushed back the hood of my clit and fluttered her tongue like she was warming up for vocal lessons, la lalalalalaaaaahhh! She knew I loved that shit. She placed her middle finger in me, and curved it upwards towards my G-spot. I was now getting double pleasure, felt my O trying to escape. He scooted to the edge of the chair.

"Yeah baby, that's it, cum for daddy," he said to me, still stroking.

"Cum for mama," Brianna chimed in at the same time. Not wanting to disappoint either, my pussy obeyed and let out strong spasms making my entire body tremble. I listened to the sounds of Brianna as she sipped on my excess juices.

I motioned for him to come to me and he did. As he stood, his dick stood to attention and throbbed up and down to the beat of his pulse. His body was magnificent, abs of steel and a beautiful chocolate hue. He and the mystery texter could pass for twins from the neck down.

I licked my lips as he came closer. I couldn't wait to taste him. I stuck out my tongue and closed my eyes. Mmmmm, put that dick right here baby. As soon as I felt the tip of his head touch my tongue——

Ring! Ring!

What the fuck!

Ring! Ring!

It was my phone ringing and vibrating. "No no no!" I screamed as I closed my eyes tightly, thinking that if I just ignored it I could fall quietly back to sleep. Shit, not working. I kicked and flapped my arms like a baby bird. I was very upset. To make matters worse, I looked at my caller ID and it displayed XXX, which is the code that I put in for my ex-boyfriend, Damien.

"What!" I spat wondering why I even picked up the phone.

"Hey baby, what you doing?" he asked in a soft calming voice.

"What most normal Americans with jobs do this time of night...sleep!" I took the phone from my face and looked at the time; it was 11:45 P.M. I went to switch the phone to my other hand when I realized it was already preoccupied with something else, Mr. Dependable. I laughed at myself realizing that I had fallen asleep with a dick in my hand, and woke up with one in my mouth—well almost.

Damien continued to talk, taking me out of a good thought once again. "I've been thinking about you so much, baby." He paused, waiting for a response. After not getting one, he continued. "Angel, I miss you."

Okay, I couldn't sit quiet any longer. "Were you missing me when you were with me and fucking your baby momma?"

He took a few seconds to regroup. "Angie, baby, don't be like that. You know I never wanted to hurt you." Guys always killed me with that line. If you don't mean to hurt someone the simple thing to do is, let me see, just don't hurt them.

110

Johnie Jay

"Look Damien, first of all you can't call me Angie anymore," I said sternly about my used-to-be pet name.

"But Angie, I mean Angel—"

I cut him off. "Secondly, I don't have time to waste with you. What do you want?"

There was a couple seconds of silence. "I...I want to see you," he said, barely above a whisper.

I laughed out loud. "Did I just hear you right? There is no reason for us to see each other. I mean, I can't think of one."

"You sure about that?" Damien asked confidently. "Cause I can think of at least one good reason that you should let me come and see you."

Wow, this motherfucker had balls. After cheating and me kicking him out, he still had the audacity to call me to try to get some. I hated when he acted cocky about his sex game, even though in reality, he had the right to do so. He could fuck his ass off, but still I played mad. "I'm listening because I still can't think of any."

"Come on Angie...Angel, you going to sit here and front like Kitty don't think about me anymore. I know you and that pretty pussy of yours like the back of my hand. And my tongue knows it even better." I tried not to think about how good he ate me out. "You remember how good I sucked that juicy pussy, don't you?"

My hands instantly went to Kitty and she was moist, no doubt from my dreams but also from the words of my former lover. I thought of the numerous times he had me bent over the kitchen counter, the kitchen table, the chairs, hell even the garbage can. When you're in the moment, cleanliness goes out of the window. "Nope, can't say that I remember." I shook my head from side to side as if he could see me.

"Well if you can't remember, that just means that it's been too long," he shot back.

111

"Or it could mean that I have someone else taking care of that for me."

He laughed. "Nobody will ever take care of it the way I did." His voice became serious. "I would tell you to think about me tonight, but I'm sure you was already gonna do that. Talk to you later, baby." Then he hung up before I could curse his ass out.

I flipped my phone closed and laid back down. I felt the little devil and the little angel on both sides of my head.

"Don't even think about it," my guardian angel told me.

"It would be easy access. Get what you want and move on," the little devil rebutted.

"You finally got him out of your life, don't let him back in physically, emotionally, or sexually."

The last voice I heard was from the little devil. "So...how long has it been now since you've had dick? Good dick?"

"Shit," I screamed aloud, as I reached for Mr. Dependable who was now lying on the bed. "Shit," I cursed again, as I turned the black knob on the back of the eight-inch chocolate colored dildo clockwise. I thought of my ex, licking me, tasting me, and bending me over the kitchen counter. I turned the knob until it couldn't be turned anymore. Placing it on my love button, I moaned out loud, "Shit, shit...oouushiiittttt!"

Could It Be

The next day at work was a piece of cake. Since it was the last day before our contractual two-week vacation, our production number for the day was cut in half to make way for an extended potluck lunch.

I walked around for a while, gave pounds to a couple of dudes that I knew and said goodbye to a couple of ex-squeezes. On the way back to my department, I stopped and talked to my quarterly stock option. She tried to set up a little booty call during our off time. I told her that I would definitely call, but I had no real intentions on doing so.

While walking back to my department I felt my phone vibrate. "Hello?" I answered.

"Hey, how is your day going?"

A smile came to my face. "Fine and yours?"

Carolina hesitated for a second and then chuckled. "I'm better now, thanks to you. Anyways enough about me, do you think that you can come to the office today?"

"Um, I should be able to. Why, what's up?"

"Well unless you want me to take them, you have to come and pick up these keys to your new property."

"Oh shit! How could I forget about that? Are you there now?" I asked, trying to find out if she accepted my offer to stay longer at the bat cave.

"Yes, I'm here...at the office that is. I woke up this

morning and didn't want any of your hoochies to knock on the door. I wouldn't know how to explain me being there naked!"

"Whatever, I'm not going to take too many more of your hoochie jokes. I would have you to know that I only mess with nice, respectable young women." I smiled and sat down at my gauge table.

"Mmm hmm, anyways, are you coming after work?"

"Sure! I get off a little early today. Want me to come through at about 1:30?"

"Actually that wouldn't work. I'll probably still be finishing up with a client, first time homeowner. She's buying one of the Condos at Wind Crest."

"The market must be good," I said, as I thought about Gabrielle texting me on her moving today. "Must be excited. I remember the feeling I had when I acquired my first spot."

"She's ecstatic," Carolina replied.

"Wait a minute, did you say she?" I asked, joking.

"Yes, she! She's a very nice girl too. She said this is a new beginning for her, out with the old memories, in with the new."

I laughed. "Sounds like she's referring to an ex."

"I thought the same thing," Carolina agreed and we both laughed. "You would like her though."

"Word? And how do you figure that?" I asked, and leaned forward in my chair.

"She has an ass to die for!" she responded with a low but excited voice.

"And...why are we whispering now?"

"Because...she's still here. She just stepped out to use the restroom."

"Oh, okay," I said still matching her low tone. "Nice

114

ass huh?" No sooner than I asked Carolina my question, I received a text message. I looked at my phone's screen and saw that it was from Gabrielle. "Carolina, hold on one sec."

"Uh, no!" she said raising her voice now. "She'll be back in a few."

"Oh okay so...an ass to die for huh?" I repeated.

She laughed. "Future, you are a mess you know that? See you around three."

I tried to get a few words in to tell Carolina to put in a good word for me but I don't know if she heard me before she hung up.

I opened up my text inbox and read my new message. **Was thinking about you, just wanted to say hi!** Texting was cool, but I would much rather be actually speaking to her. I knew that this was more comfortable for her though, a little more impersonal.

I texted her back. **Hey what's up? Took a break from moving huh?**

Moving? I'm not actually moving today sweetie, just closing and getting my keys to my new spot. Yay!!!

I stared at the phone, my mind now rambling. Na, couldn't be **what a coincidence, I'm closing on an investment property today and getting my keys also.**

Investment property huh? Go head you big baller you.

Not balling. Okay it was time to step out on a limb. **We should celebrate, nothing formal, just meet for drinks.** I pressed send.

Two minutes went by and my phone alerted me of the new incoming message. **Would have to think about that.**

Well, no rush, if not today maybe in the future. I texted back and pressed send.

115

Okay baby, have to go now...my realtor's waiting. C U later, I mean text you later, lol.

Lol holla! Couldn't be...Gabrielle could not be the same woman that's in Carolina's office right now, could she? I went into my saved picture files and selected a picture of her ass that she had sent from the side view. I shook my head as thoughts of sending the picture to Carolina's phone, and asking her if the ass in the picture matched the "to die for" ass that was currently in her office crowded my mind. I put the thought to the back of my mind. Maybe I'll dig a little deeper when I go in for my appointment.

I called my parents on the way to Carolina's office.

"Hello?" My dad always has answered the phone in the same way since I could remember, with a long, dragged out country twang.

"What's up old man?" I teased.

"I ain't too old to beat you in anything."

"Yeah right. You don't want none of this."

"Yeah, yeah, I hear you. So what's up, you finished that last day of work?"

"Yep!" I answered, feeling a smile on my face. "I'm heading to Carolina's now."

"She's doing alright for herself I hear. She calls to check up on your mom every now and then."

I thought about last night and me holding her in my arms. My mom would kill me if she knew I was having any kind of relationship with a married woman—let alone Carolina. "Yeah she's good, as far as I can tell. When I finish signing and get the keys, I will swing by so you and Ma can look at the house."

"I wanted to tell you that I was proud of you. This is the first time that you've handled getting property from the beginning to the end by yourself."

116

It felt so good to hear such words coming from a guy who was my living role model. "Well don't speak so highly yet; y'all haven't even seen the place yet."

"We fully trust your judgment Future. If that property didn't make sense, I know you wouldn't have invested in it."

"Thanks old man, means a lot coming from you." I switched the subject, feeling that we were getting to mushy. "Where's your wife?"

"In somebody's store," he responded. "She called a little while ago and said she'll be here in a few, but you know your mom."

"Yeah, that could easily turn into three hours." I pulled into Carolina's office in Southfield and parked Sally. "Alright old man, I'll call you when I get out of here to see if your wife is there."

"Alright Future."

I hung up with my dad and walked into the marble-faced office building.

"Hi, may I help you?" the overly tan receptionist asked.

"Yes, I have an appointment with Carolina Montgomery."

"Okay and your name?" Enthusiasm oozed from the receptionist with every word and movement.

"Future, Future Crowne." I looked at the appointment book as she looked for my name and time, and right before I saw the full name of the person that was scheduled before me, she turned the page. I only saw that the name started with A.

"Future, ah here it is. Okay, I'll let Mrs. Montgomery know that you are here. You can have a seat."

I took a seat in the wine-colored plush leather couch with gold rivets. The waiting area was very chic. Looking toward the two-toned pinstriped cream and burgundy walls, I saw a multicolored Jonz painting gracing the huge, otherwise bare space. I walked closer to see that it was number twelve of twenty-five paintings entitled Self Portrait, where the artist painted his name in a collage of vibrant colors shapes and swirls. In the last ten years, he was one of few artists who made African American art trendy, fun, and exciting again.

"Future, Mrs. Montgomery will see you now!" I walked to the receptionist's desk and she pointed me to the door directly behind her. It was slightly cracked open, so I knocked and walked right in.

Carolina had her back to me, staring out of her window at a fabulous view of downtown Southfield. One hand was on her hip while the other was on her cell phone. She was giving someone an earful about inspection codes. If she were a clock, one of her legs stood straight up and down at 6:00 while the other seemed to be right around 6:20, directing my eyes down to her curvy calf muscle. Her hair was straight back, lying over the collar of a black and white pinstriped blouse.

She then turned around and told me to give her a minute by holding up her index finger. I walked closer to her desk and noticed a picture frame turned face down. I turned it over and saw that it was a wedding picture of her and her husband. She looked so happy. Then out of nowhere, a neatly manicured hand gently wrapped around mine and tenderly forced it back down. She then took that same hand of hers to turn and pull me close up on her back side. "Mmmmmmm!" softly escaped her mouth. Her perfume was fruity, sweet, and edible. She leaned her neck to the side while still fussing at the recipient on the other end of her phone.

I placed my hand on her barely existent waistline. My nose was now on her neck and I lightly trailed it along her collarbone while inhaling. Buddy sprang to attention when he was reacquainted with the crevice that he snuggled up against and slept in last night. Carolina jumped as she felt me poking her, and turned around smiling.

"No excuses, I need that inspection completed today!" She looked down at Buddy and waved. A couple of seconds later she ended the call. Now with no distractions we looked at each other while awkwardness filled the air. "So how are you?" she asked, breaking the silence.

"Pretty good and you?" I placed both of my hands in my pockets.

"Better, because of my friend." She took two steps towards me. "Thanks for valuing our friendship enough, to stop us from probably doing something we both would've maybe regretted."

Speak for yourself. "Yeah, no problem." I still tried to hide my hard on. "No problem at all."

"Yeah, I can see that." Carolina walked around her desk, but not before grabbing a feel of my bicep. "Can I be honest with you though?"

I took a seat in front of her desk. "Of course, hopefully you will always be."

She looked directly in my eyes before making her next statement. "I wanted to so bad Future. I wanted you...so damn bad." She looked down at some paperwork on her desk. "Still do. This morning before I left your place, I hopped back in your shower, which I absolutely love by the way."

"Thanks."

"You're welcome." She looked up at me and then back down towards her desk. "I had three orgasms," her cheeks instantly turned rosy, "all within five minutes. They all came, thinking about you. You have this...thing about you that is so magnetic. It's kind of scary how easy it is to fantasize about you or how you make me want to spend time with you. I know I said it before, but you are going to make some woman very happy. She started to smile. "When you learn how to be monogamous, that is."

"Monogamous? What's that?" I asked jokingly.

Carolina broke out laughing. "You probably don't know the meaning of it for real. Okay, let's get down to business. You're probably eager to get your keys."

Carolina stacked in front of me what seemed to be an encyclopedia full of papers for me to sign, and when I finished, I received the keys to my first negotiated family investment property.

We finished up and I walked Carolina to her BMW. "So what are you about to get into?" she asked, while putting her briefcase into the trunk.

"Probably swing by my parents and take them to see the house. Then I'm going to the gym. I have a lot of energy to work off right now."

She made the zipper sign and ran it across her lips. "I'm going to be a good girl and leave that alone." I closed her car door after she entered it. She rolled down the window and stared into nothingness. "I'm leaving him," she said out of nowhere, without any emotion.

I stooped down so that my face was on the same level as hers. "You sure?"

"Positive," she answered definitively. "Gave it a lot of thought. At first, I was going to leave clear with no hassle. But since he had no remorse or respect, I figure I'd squeeze him where it hurts the most, his wallet."

I saw the cold look in her eyes and immediately thought of R. Kelly's song and how it was so true. When a woman is fed up, there ain't nothing you can do about it. I leaned over and kissed her on the cheek. "I'll talk to you later Carolina."

"Okay, and good luck on your property. I'll call you if I hear of any other good investments."

"Yeah, you do that," I said, poking out my chest.

"Who knows, in a couple of years you might be ready to step up to the majors."

"Never know, might be before you expect."

Carolina began to inch away in her chariot as she said her last statement of the evening. "I wish I could've introduced you to Angel, you really would have liked her." Then she sped away.

"Angel," I whispered to myself while squinting. I now had a possible name to the voice that I heard filled with so much passion when she orgasmed over the phone. A possible name to the person I longed to talk to and text every day. A possible name to the person I am dying to meet.

While driving in my car I redialed my parents. "Nope, still not here," my dad informed me. I told him that I would go to the gym first, and then I would try again.

I walked up to the gym and inhaled the fresh outdoors air into my lungs. I looked up at the fair blue sky. This is turning out to be a good day. I inhaled deeply again and smiled as I opened the gym door. What a great fucking day!

THE "PRESENT"

Only thirty minutes had passed, and just that quick I was singing a new tune. "Shit, what a weird fucking day!" I whispered to myself. I couldn't believe that She was actually at my fucking gym.

Where did she go? I asked myself, as I stood outside my gym entrance door, the same door that I had entered just a half hour ago. The same door that the woman from the club just stormed out of.

Maybe she received some bad news. Whatever it was made her pretty upset. Today, I was intending to come face to face with her. No more Mr. Nice Guy, and no more Mr. Cool. I wasn't sitting back any longer. Today, she was going to find out how I felt. I didn't really care if I ended up looking like an ass, at least I wouldn't have any regrets.

As soon as I stepped into the parking lot, a speeding Ford Edge almost ran over me. "What the fu...?" It was Her, looking pissed as hell. She was now being held up from getting onto Telegraph Road by the oncoming traffic. The cars were unknowingly assisting me in foiling her getaway.

I thought about walking up to her car. Naw, probably would pull off before I even get to her. I decided to run to my car, that way I could catch her at a red light or something and flag her down. I hopped in Sally and threw her in reverse. Right when I was about to pull up behind her, she sped off. "Shit!"

Johnie Jay

I looked left, not a clear opening in traffic for at least five cars. I looked right and saw that she had driven through the recently changed green light. "Fuck!" When the last car passed, I zoomed into the opening in traffic and switched over to the right lane, then back to the middle and then to the right again. I was driving like an Indy car driver.

There she is. I saw her brake lights come on from the thickening traffic that was in front of her. "Yeah, got you now!" I tightened the grip on my steering wheel when I noticed the green traffic light that was coming up fast suddenly turn amber. I'm running it, I had convinced myself, I'm running it! Or, so I thought until I noticed a policeman filling up his cruiser at the gas station on the corner, right beside me.

I looked at the traffic light, now the color of blood, the color of love, that crazy bitch Kandi's favorite color, the color that causes everyone to stop. Stop acting like a damn fool and calm your ass down. I raced my engine and looked at the officer who now had his lips twisted to the side as if to say, "Go ahead nigga, try it if you want to. I've been waiting to chase someone all day."

I focused my energy back on the stop light while grumbling, "Muthafucka, if I did decide to run it, what I have under this hood, you couldn't catch me if you tried."

The light finally turned green and I slowly crept off the starting line like a tortoise along with all the other drivers noticing the police officer. A couple of seconds later when I no longer saw him in the rearview, I turned back into speed racer. The difference now, there was no sign of Her. I switched lanes and still didn't see my target.

I heard a crackle followed by thunder and five seconds later the sky opened up and cried. I laughed as I pulled over to let up Sally's top. Its funny how quickly sun can turn into rain, figuratively and literally. What started as a good day just didn't seem all that pretty or good anymore. "Damn!"

INEVITABLE ACT II

Stuck In The Middle

Buying your first piece of property, owning your first home, makes you feel so important. I felt like a real American and finally got a piece of the American dream. I was floating on cloud nine. I have my own space. "Hmmmmmm," I sighed as I backed out of my driveway. I couldn't even stand still when Carolina handed me my keys to the condo. I called my parents and told them to meet me here.

Now I don't even feel like going back to the apartment. It shouldn't be too bad though. Only three more days, hopefully it goes by quickly.

I picked my brain to remember if I needed anything to help me finish packing before I reached the apartment.

Buzzzz!

My phone vibrated in the middle console's cup holder. I picked it up, saw who it was and unconsciously rolled my eyes. Why does he still call, better yet, why do I answer?

"What?"

"Damn Angel! Why do you always have to be so cold?" he asked, actually sounding a little hurt.

"I just don't see why you still call me. We don't have anything to talk about," I shot back just as cold.

"I still call you because I still miss you." He had the nerve to sound sincere.

"Oh yeah, well forgive me for not believing a word that

comes out of your mouth."

"You should believe me because it's true. I...I wanna see you."

"You mean you want to fuck me? You can be honest."

He started coughing, probably because he was caught off guard by my bluntness or probably because he was getting blunted. "Well," he answered reluctantly, "yeah...that too. But I do actually want to see you."

"Mmmm hmmm. That's what these calls have been all about huh? You're trying to get back up inside me." Just thinking about my ex's curved dick made the inside of my walls contract.

"Naw...I mean, kinda...but naw." He had now started to stutter.

"You know what? I never would have thought that I would be able to fully get you out of my system. Never would have thought in a million years that I would be able to turn you down for sex. Now, Damien, I can honestly say you no longer mean shit to me. Not even the smallest piece of shit. Therefore, this is going to be the last time that I ever answer my phone when you call. This is going to be the last time we ever speak and I hope that the last time I saw you, will be the last time that I will ever see you. So for the last and final time, goodbye!" With that, I hung up on my ex-lover for the very last time.

Right after drying off from my shower, I was startled by a knock on the door. Wonder who that could be, wasn't expecting any company.

"UPS, I'm looking for an Angel McCloud," the chipper deliveryman announced after I opened the door.

"Yes, that's me." I pulled the belt a little tighter on my robe.

"Sign here. I have another package in the truck." I signed in the provided space on the computer board. "Be right back," he said, before turning and walking back to his truck with a smile still on his face.

I took a couple steps back into the apartment and examined the medium-sized box when I saw the UPS guy walking back towards the door.

"Okay, here you are." He handed me another package. This one was larger, flat, rectangular, and wrapped in brown paper. After thanking him, I brought the second package in and closed the door. After checking and rechecking to see if the name was correct on the label, I started to open the first package. "Might as well see what's in them."

I started with the larger of the two. My mouth instantly dropped open when I saw what was inside. "No...he...didn't!" I could not believe my eyes. It was an original Jonz painting. I couldn't believe it. I knew this was nobody but Juwaun's doing.

Then I fixed my eyes on the other box I sat on the floor a few moments ago and decided to tear into it also. I noticed the return address didn't have a name but it did have a city, Farmington Hills, the city where Juwaun resides. I opened the box and pulled from it a beautiful gold and teal, wrap around the neck maxi dress. This is why he was asking me what size I wore. I held it up to my body. "Damn this is hot, right size too." He got it right without me even telling him. I looked in the bottom of the box, and discovered that there was something else in there wrapped in plastic.

Wow! Somebody was trying to earn major brownie points. It was a pair of matching gold and teal Giuseppe Zanotti sandals. While pulling them out, I noticed a small note card fall to the floor. I picked it up and proceeded to read. Hey beautiful, just thought I would get you something to wear for the party. Hope you like it. P.S. Hope you like the housewarming gift as well.

Wow, I couldn't even wait. Felt like it was Christmas. I tried on my new gifts in front of the mirrored wall. "Wow! Good pick Juwaun, good job," I said, as I twisted and turned while looking at myself. I looked around for my cell phone and remembered that I had left it in my purse. After retrieving it, I called Santa Claus.

"Hello?" I was greeted by Jawaun's baritone.

"Hey J.J.!" I responded with excitement leaping from my voice.

He laughed. "Haven't been called that since high school."

"Um I received a couple of packages today. You wouldn't have anything to do with that would you?" I asked, eager to hear his answer.

"Who me?" was the answer that he came back with. "What kind of packages?" His response was so transparent.

"Well for starters, I received a one of a kind Jonz painting."

"A Jonz original? Somebody spent some cheese."

"Exactly," I agreed. "The second thing I received was a beautiful sundress with a pair of matching sandals."

"Well obviously somebody is digging you."

"Boy, stop playing around," I said, laughing.

"Okay, okay it was me. I hope you liked the gifts."

"I absolutely love them, really I do." I hesitated before making my next statement. "You really didn't have to do this. I mean I almost feel uncomfortable receiving them, because I know I probably will never be able to get you anything that equals to half," I thought about how much the painting must have set him back, "no, a quarter of what you paid for them."

"Whoa, hold up! I don't know who you're used to dealing but when I buy you something your only job is to enjoy it, that's it. I don't want you thinking of ways that you can repay me. I'm in pretty good shape when it comes to materialistic things anyway, but if you did want to give me something," he said pausing for a second, "you could give me you."

I thought about how good life might be if I was his

woman but unfortunately, I wasn't feeling him quite enough to give him the answer that he wanted. "I don't know what to say. I mean I'm really flattered—"

He cut me off as if he could sense the but that was coming on. "Well baby girl, don't say anything. Just enjoy the gifts and prepare to enjoy tomorrow with me. Think you can do that?"

"I think I can do that," I humbly answered.

"Good!"

"Okay Juwaun, but I do have another question. How did you know my size?"

"I don't know if I want to tell you all of my secrets, but that night at the Elysium Lounge when you came up to the VIP one of the girls that was up there sitting near us was my cousin who happens to have her own fashion line. When I pointed you out to her, she already had sized you up." I was speechless. "So, if there is anything you need," he cleared his throat, "fashion wise of course, let a brother know," he said, chuckling.

I tried to contain my excitement. "I'll make sure I keep that in mind."

"You do that."

"Okay Juwaun, thanks again, I really appreciate it."

After hanging up I was happy and scared at the same time. It was great that Juwaun was so generous, but I didn't want to send him the wrong signal, didn't want him to think that I could be bought. I really tried to not put him in a category, but I did know some guys that gave you things early in the relationship to either buy your love or buy their way into your pants.

Now my excitement and energy was through the roof and I thought no better way to utilize it other than the sex I wasn't getting, was to go to the gym and work up a good sweat.

Within thirty minutes, I was out of the apartment and pulling up to my new gym. This was only my second time here since I purchased my new membership. It was only about ten minutes away from my new place. The difference between my old gym and this one, which was in Dearborn, was that this one had more white men. That was actually okay with me, because it meant fewer distractions.

The first half hour at the gym was great. Thoughts of me being treated like a princess by the Prince of Detroit, and the fact that I had officially cut all ties to my piece of an ex-boyfriend had me all bright inside. Yep, all was going good until I saw Him. What the hell was he doing at this gym anyway? Did he have a membership here? Was he visiting? All these questions ran through my head as I sat in my car with it started.

About a minute ago I had stormed out of the gym when my so-called, supposed-to-be-future, whatever you want to call him embarrassed me by giving his attention to an overweight, big booty woman instead of noticing that I was there.

I backed out of my parking spot and sped to exit out onto Telegraph Road. I don't know what I really expected. He don't know me, I don't know him, but it feels like I do—like we do. I don't know what's going on. Maybe I should give up on the idea about this man that's out there for me. Maybe I'm supposed to just settle.

I darted out into the opening in traffic and dialed Tierra.

"Hey girl what's up?"

"Hey Tee, where you at?"

"Still at work. I have to work overtime today and I'm tired as hell. What's the deal?"

"Oh nothing," I said, trying not to sound too overwhelmed. "I was just going to stop by, that's all."

"Oh okay, well I'll probably be off in another hour, come over then."

"Okay girl, call me when you get off." After hanging up, I immediately called Brianna. In doing so, I almost ran the red light.

"Hey Angel."

"Hey Brianna," I replied, this time a little less energetic than when I called Tierra.

"What's wrong baby?" Brianna must have noticed it because she sounded concerned.

I sighed. "Bri, girl, you would not and I repeat, would not believe the day I am having."

"Damn mami! Well where are you right now? Can you come over?" She had answered my question before I had even asked.

"Be there in a few."

Instead of continuing down Telegraph to Ford Road, I turned down Cherry Hill and headed west towards Brianna's house in Garden City. I had begun to notice that the sky was starting to match my mood. That which was a moment ago sunny and bright, had now become grey and gloomy.

Krriiiibooom!

The loud thunder startled me and I rolled my windows up, noticing the sparse raindrops falling on my windshield. Ten minutes later, I pulled up to Brianna's house and stepped out of my air-conditioned car into the humid summer air with my umbrella raised. Damn it's hot out here! I rang Bri's doorbell and when she opened the door, I felt her central air reaching out to give me a hug.

"Hey girl, come on in."

I walked into her family room and into a tantalizing aroma that tickled my nose. "Oh my God, Brianna, what's that smelling so delicious?"

"A little something that I was cooking when you called." She shut the door behind us and started walking back towards the kitchen.

"Please tell me that you do not wear those shorts outside of this house," I said, looking at my friend from behind.

"Why not," she asked, stopping dead in her tracks to take

131

a good look at her shorts. "These are my favorite lounge shorts. I have like five pair."

"Brianna, they barely cover your butt cheeks." Not only were the shorts tight, they were sunk into the crease of her crack. We both started laughing.

"Yeah I know. I rarely go outside with them on, only to get the mail or something. I love looking at the old men breaking their necks to look at my ass though!"

"They can't help it...it's so...big!"

"You sound like the white girl in the "Baby Got Back" song," she said, laughing at me.

"Is it hard? I mean firm or, or is it soft?" Brianna's ass was really that amazing that it made you ask those kinds of questions.

She turned the oven off and turned back to the side. "Touch it and see."

At first, I was a little apprehensive but what the hell, we're best friends. I grabbed her right cheek from behind. "Damn, so soft." Brianna laughed at my amazement. "No, it really is." I moved a little closer and grabbed the other cheek with my left hand. "Wow, now I see why guys and girls be trying to get a piece of this." I sunk my fingers in her huge booty like I was kneading dough. "This thing could be addictive."

"So I've heard," she said, smiling.

Realizing that I've been gripping my best friend's ass way past the uncomfortable limit, and the fact that she was standing up here letting me do so caused me to release my grip. "So," I said moving from behind her and to the side, "you made enough for your girl right?"

"Yes dear!"

"Good, so what are we having?"

"Grilled chicken breast, rice, broccoli, and King Hawaiian rolls."

"Sounds delish!" I said, practically salivating while trying to imitate Rachael Ray.

"Now go and sit down while I make your plate."

"Don't have to tell me twice!"

"Do you want something to drink?" she asked, barely audible from her head being inside of the fridge door.

"Hell yeah, as long as it has alcohol in it," I replied.

"Moscato?"

"Sounds good to me."

A couple of minutes later Brianna came into the dining room carrying our plates. She sat mine down in front of me, then walked around the cherry oak dining table and sat her plate across from me. Then she brought two glasses and filled them with Sutter Homes Moscato, which was actually my wine of choice, and sat the unfinished bottle in the middle of the table.

"Oh, almost forgot." She hopped out of her chair, grabbed a lighter from the kitchen counter and lit the two large candles sitting on the table.

I took a bite of the grilled chicken and savored the taste as it melted in my mouth. "Thanks for letting me crash and eat up all of your food."

"Whatever," she said, raising her voice, "you know that you are welcome over here anytime. You're my nigga, you know that." We both laughed. "So what's up, what happened today that had you sounding so stressed out?"

I took another bite of my chicken followed by a nice size gulp of wine. "You sure you have time?" I asked, making sure she really wanted to lend an ear.

"Girl it's Friday and I don't have to work tomorrow. I have nothing but time."

"Okay, here goes." I then proceeded to tell Brianna everything, from how I really felt when I saw the mystery man for the first time, and how he makes me feel every time I see him. I told her that I think about him every day and especially at night, which usually leads to me touching myself to the point of orgasm.

After seeing that she wasn't looking at me too crazy, I decided to tell her that the guy I accidentally texted wasn't just a one night thing, but it has been a daily occurrence.

I looked at her face. It was expressionless. She took a drink from her glass. I did the same before I continued. I then told her that a guy that my realtor said I should meet and thinks that I'll like a lot, sounds a lot like the guy that I've been texting. Then to top it all off, I explained the situation with Baby Boy. The more I talked and explained, the more embarrassed I became. I really sounded crazy when I actually heard the words instead of just thinking them.

"Can you believe that? These are all different guys that I have either not met, not seen, or haven't spoken to. These are the men in my life. Pathetic huh? Oh, and then there is Juwaun."

"How's that going?" she asked calmly, still sipping.

"I don't know. I mean its going. He's rich, handsome, and generous." I told her about the gifts that were delivered today and her mouth hung wide open. "But I don't know, he just, I don't...I don't think that he's somebody that I want to actually be with right now."

"So don't be with him then," she said, raising her voice. "If he wants to be generous and give you gifts and spend time with you, let him."

"I don't know; I just feel like that would be deceiving him, because he kind of let it be known that he wants to work on building towards something."

Brianna poured the last of the bottle into my glass, and then went to the kitchen to get another. "You're not done drinking are you?" she asked.

"Hell naw!" I took another sip of wine, but this time held it in my mouth for a couple of seconds and let it tickle my sweet and sour glands before swallowing.

"You're going to have to let him know that right now you just want to take things slow. Then if he wants to keep giving you gifts after that, you take them. If you feel guilty, then you give them to me."

"Whatever Bri, you're silly."

We continued drinking wine after finishing our meal but moved our conversation over to the sofa in front of her giant plasma. She couldn't believe when I told her that I had seen the guy from the club today at my new gym.

"I don't know Angel; this really seems kind of weird. If you have feelings for this guy like you say you do and you keep seeing him, I don't know, maybe God is trying to tell you something."

"That's exactly what I've been thinking."

We were nice and buzzed now and I had to go potty. While sitting on the toilet I heard Brianna yelling from the other room. "You know what would be some really weird shit?"

"What's that?" I yelled back, while wiping.

"If the guy from the club, the mystery texter and what's the guy name from the radio?"

I pulled up my panties, then my shorts, and stood stiff as an arrow, scared of what she was going to say next. "Baby Boy?" I reluctantly answered.

"Yeah, Baby Boy...it would be some scary shit if all of them," I stood in the bathroom doorway as she finished her statement, already knowing what she was going to say, "were all the same guy."

I rejoined her on the couch and tried to block the impossibly possible notion from my head. "Wow, somebody's been drinking a little too much," I said, trying to make a joke out of the situation.

"Whatever." Brianna had one leg outstretched on the couch and was playing with a lighter in her hand. I looked around for candles and didn't see any.

"What's up with the lighter? Don't tell me you about to go Fire Starter up in this bitch."

"No sweetheart, I figured since you were stressed out and all, that there is nothing better to take it all away other than a nice tightly rolled J." She reached over to the end table on her side of the couch and picked up a neatly rolled white joint.

"Ooouuu, I'm telling," I said, in my best child impression. Brianna smiled. "Girl you know I haven't put my lips on a joint in over three years."

"Are you serious? I thought you said that Damien smoked all the time."

"Yeah, he did, not me! Most of the time I made him go outside. But I must admit I loved the smell and the contact that I got when he did smoke around me. Guess I didn't want to become a head like him. So how often do you smoke missy?" I asked, trying not to sound judgmental.

"Two to three times a month, if that. I'm going to be honest. I love it. If you are not mentally strong though, it is easy to become a weed head. Just be my smoking partner and you won't have to worry about that."

"Sure."

"So what's up? You smoking, huh, huh, are you smoking? Peeeer pressure!" Brianna lit the joint and took a couple of drags.

"You're crazy you know that? Tonight this ain't peer pressure because I want to get high. Gimme that!" I said, reaching my hand out for the bone. I always seemed to do things that I normally wouldn't do when I was around Brianna. She always seemed to get me to let my guard down.

I choked like any other rookie would on the first couple of puffs, but after the third puff puff give, I became accustomed. The one thing I noticed is that the smaller the joint became the slower everything moved. When you're high things slowed down enough for you to critique and comment on them. Brianna and I became body experts and the fashion police to every music video that we watched.

"Damn LL Cool J looks scrumptious," Brianna said, lighting the second, and from what I could see, the last joint that was on the end table. "He has to be at least forty now, but he still looks like he's in his mid-twenties."

"Yeah, Botox will do that for you," I shot back.

"Botox, girl he is all natural."

"Okay." I took another toke. "You believe that if you want too. That nigga don't have one wrinkle in his face. I mean, don't get me wrong, I would fuck LL in a heartbeat, but I would know in my head that I'm fucking a forty-year-old man."

I passed the joint back to Brianna. "Its funny how having money can really make you look different." As we stared at the TV, BET was flashing pictures of Jay Z and Beyoncé across the screen. "Because I'm sorry, but about four years ago Jay was not doing it for me, but now after marrying Bey and knowing that he's worth almost a billion, he's starting to grow on me a little bit."

I laughed at Brianna and now that I was high, I couldn't stop. She started laughing at me laughing and before you knew it, we both had tears in our eyes. "Bri," I called out, trying to catch my breath, "I think, I think I'm about to turn gay."

She looked me in the eyes. "Bitch don't look at me. I'm not gay, I'm bi. I love dick." We laughed hysterically again.

"I do too but I think I'm giving it up. I'm not getting any right now anyways, so it shouldn't even be that hard." Brianna stood and went over to the DVD player and flipped through what looked to be a binder of movies. "I don't think it'll be that hard to give up," I continued. She selected one of the DVD's and inserted it into the player. "That's one of the problems with us women. We give dick too much credit, too much power!" I watched as she pressed the play button on the DVD player. "I mean dick ain't even all—" I paused as I gawked at the TV, as a chick bent over and a long, thick black dick attached to a beautiful male's body, rammed her from the back, "—that!"

"Mmmm hmmm, ain't all that huh?" I saw Brianna through my peripheral staring at me while smiling. I would've looked back at her, but the sight of dick, fucking, moans, stroking and grabbing had me momentarily enthralled. "I can tell by the look on your face that it ain't all that. Especially with that slobber running out of your mouth."

I instinctively wiped the corners of my mouth. "Shut up Bri, I'm not slobbing." The weed definitely had its grip on me now. She continued laughing, and I continued watching. I felt my juices starting to stir. "Damn his dick looks soooo good."

"Yes it does." Brianna and I both became silent and apparently horny by the way we both couldn't sit still, and squirmed in our chairs every time we saw the dick make a deep plunge. "Ooouuu that looked like it felt good."

I felt my nipples harden and looked down at my tank top to confirm. I ran my hand over my left breast.

"Um Angel, are you cold?"

"Hell naw, but I'm horny," I replied, missing her joke, well right then anyways. I caught it about a minute later and busted out in laughter out of the blue. Even though the weed put me in a better mood, it didn't relieve all of the stress. I grabbed the back of my neck and gently began massaging.

"Come here," Brianna demanded, while patting the space on the couch closest to her. After looking at her with must have been questionable eyes she elaborated. "Come over here so I can work the kinks out."

"Oh okay, thanks." I shook my head at the crazy thoughts I was having. I felt like Smokey on Friday. "But I'm fine."

Brianna called my name again, while holding her arms in the same position. Feeling that she wasn't taking no for an answer, and that I really needed a neck and shoulder massage, I scooted over to her. The instant she put her hands on my neck and squeezed chills ran through my body.

"I can feel knots in your neck." She worked her hands over to my right side trying to get a better position. Then she took her left leg, which was closest to me and stretched it out on the couch behind me. Her massage intensified as she scooted closer to my back.

"Mmmm, feels so good."

"Not too hard?" she asked.

"Not at all." While I sat on the couch, my head was kind of angled towards the wall so I couldn't really see the TV. I shut my eyes and enjoyed the massage and the sounds of the threesome enjoying themselves in the porno. My mind began flashing pictures of Brianna and me taking the place of the two females.

I opened my eyes and tilted my neck a little to see what was causing the one female to call on the name of Jesus. A thick white woman was lying on the edge of the bed spread eagle, and an equally thick black woman stood in between her legs with two fingers inserted in the white woman's pussy, while the thick dick was going in and out of her mouth. The camera panned back and forth from the meticulous finger work to the long fluttering tongue of the black woman on the white woman's pink nipples.

"Damn she has a long tongue." I couldn't believe how far the black girl's tongue hung out of her mouth. "Betcha she can lick a good coochie."

"Humph, no doubt about that," Brianna agreed.

I turned my head back straight so that Brianna's massage could be more efficient. "You sound sure, what you know her or something?" I asked, joking. A couple of seconds later I felt warm breath on my ear, followed by a wet tongue curling around my earlobe. "What the hell?" I jerked forward and stared back at Brianna who was cracking up laughing. She then licked out her tongue and showed me hers was equally, if not longer than that of the woman in the flick.

"The reason I sound so sure is because I know what I can do with mine." She fluttered her tongue like a helicopter propeller, and my clit tightened as if she was actually licking it. My panties were soaked. I tried to play it off as if it had no effect on me. I turned back around hoping that Brianna would continue to massage me with her hands and not her tongue. Didn't know if I could take that again, considering how horny I was at the moment.

I know that I'm not gay and I don't think that I'm bi, but I needed to be touched. And at this moment, it didn't matter who touched me. I leaned back until my head rested on Brianna's left shoulder. She removed her right hand from my neck and continued to squeeze with her left.

I looked up at her face. She looked down at mine. Our lips were now inches apart and our breath was intermingling. I closed my eyes and leaned until I felt softness. "Mmmmm." I pulled back an inch and then leaned in again, and was greeted by the same softness, a softness that I have never before witnessed in a kiss. It felt strange at first, sort of like kissing myself.

I felt Brianna's breath through her nostrils getting heavy. Mine did too. She stuck that long tongue of hers inside of my mouth and I sucked on it like a Laffy Taffy. The mixture of wine and ganja was invigorating. It was an acquired taste that I got used to really fast.

Brianna moaned, I followed with moans of my own, and then she pulled away. I pushed forward because I wanted more. I was curious to see if this feeling got any better. Then I felt a kiss on my forehead. It was a polite stop sign. I opened my eyes to Brianna looking at me.

"I don't want to end up doing something tonight that we'll both end up regretting tomorrow." She rubbed the sides of my face and pecked me on the cheek. "If I didn't think we were just kissing because you are confused right now, I never would've stopped it—stopped us. You are my best friend and I don't want to do anything to jeopardize that. I was always attracted to you, and would never want to just have a one-night stand with you. That would just make me want you even more. So for my sake and yours, I think that we should cool down."

I sat up from her chest and turned so that we were directly in front of each other. She grabbed both of my hands commanding my attention. "And baby if you ever kiss me again, I will show you and your pussy what I can do with this long ass tongue of mine." The both of us busted out laughing. The mood had lightened and we continued watching the porno and analyzing it for another half hour and the entire time, I kept thinking what if...

On the way to my apartment, I thought about my near bi encounter. I smiled, thinking about what Tierra would say if she found out. "Y'all did what?" I could hear her loud ass mouth now. It was now 11P.M. This long day was almost over. I couldn't wait to take a shower and hop in the bed. The weed had taken me to a good high, but now I was on my way down.

After showering, I sat on my bed while rubbing my temples. "What a day." My eyelids felt as if they had giant grains of sand in them. The Sandman was definitely somewhere in the vicinity.

Before turning off the lamp I made sure my phone was on vibrate. There were going to be no distractions from tonight's deep sleep. My phone's screen displayed one text message. My heart skipped, and then pounded hard when I saw who it came from. I couldn't help but to smile as I read his text. **Hey beautiful...this has been one hell of a day for me and for some reason it made me think more about you lol...in a good way of course.** I looked at the user name after the text, don't think I've ever noticed it before. Futur-lux-bryte. How cute. My hard body mystery texter was going to be on my mind as I slept. I briefly thought about responding but the Sandman, with his jealous ass, cock-blocked and put me to sleep.

My alarm clock woke me up at 9:30 the next morning. I fought my hand from pressing the snooze button and knocking the clock off the nightstand all together. I had to get a move on because my hair appointment was in one hour and I had to drive across town to Novi. After finally putting some clothes on, I flipped the TV to channel 42 to check the today's weather before I left out. Eighty-nine and partly cloudy, with a light breeze. Perfect!

Heading west on I-96, the sun was beaming from behind me and was reflecting brightly off my rearview mirror. I pulled my Dior sunglasses down from the visor. After slipping them on, I inserted my Bluetooth into my ear and synced it to my phone. It was now 10:10 and I was pulling up on Novi Road. I had about four hours left. Yesterday Juwaun called me to let me know that he would be picking me up around 2:30. I was actually starting to get a little excited. I figured that there might be some famous or at least wealthy people at the party, which means probably a lot of models on guys' arms. I had to make sure I came with my A-game. I was planning to turn heads with my new sundress.

I held the three down on my key pad to speed dial my mother's cell phone. "Uh hello?" When the other end picked up, I only heard breathing in the phone. Lord please don't ever let me catch my parents in an uncompromising position. Just the thought of my dad having my mom's ass up in the air almost made me vomit.

"Hey baby," My mom answered, sounding winded.

"Ma!" I yelled out loud. "What are you doing?"

"I'm walking baby," more panting, "me and daddy are walking on the track." For their age, my parents were in very good health. They walked the track at Garden City Park faithfully at least four times a week. "What are you up too?"

"Nothing much, I'm on my way to get my hair done now."

142

Johnie Jay

"Okay, are you coming over your aunt's house today?"

"Um, don't know if I'll be able to make it. You know I have a date with Juwaun today."

"Oh yeah! You've been seeing a lot of him lately huh?"

"Please Ma, it's been hardly a lot, three at the most," I responded, rolling my eyes and smiling.

"Is that my baby girl?" I heard my Papa Bear asking in the background. "Tell her to bring me a jersey."

"Did you—?"

"Yeah I heard him," I answered my mother before she asked her question. "Tell him I'll do what I can."

"Well are we ever going to meet the young man?"

"I don't know yet Ma, I mean it's really nothing serious for me at all. We're just friends, so I don't even know if I want him to meet my parents just yet."

"Understandable." My mother's breathing started to taper off a little. "Well, call me later if you can. If not then I'll see you in church tomorrow, right?"

"Huh, what was that? Can't hear you."

"Mmm hmm, anyway, your dad and I have been invited to dinner tomorrow after church."

"Oh yeah with who?"

"The couple I told you about a little while ago. Remember the guy that's from Alabama like your daddy?"

"Well you guys have fun; I'm at the shop now."

"Alright baby, but they invited you too if you want to come. Plus they have a son, who is single by the way, and from the picture I saw, very handsome. Has a strange name though, think it's something like—"

"Ma, please, don't even think about it. No more blind dates, ever!" I thought about the couple of times she tried to hook me up with lame guys from church, who tried to have sex with me in the first three minutes of talking. "I'll call you later."

143

"Bye baby."

I walked inside of Kali's Salounge. She's been doing hair since the age of fifteen, so it was only natural for her to get her own salon. She was really doing well for herself. I absolutely loved coming here. It wasn't your ordinary mom and pop's hair salon—it was a salounge. A salon mixed with the comfort of a lounge, where you can get pampered from head to toe. I've been coming to Kali so long that I now get the VIP treatment. Being the friend that she is, she put me right in despite it being a holiday weekend.

"Hey Angel!" the receptionist greeted me warmly.

"Hey, how are you?" I dared not try to guess her name. She was one of many teenagers who was still in school, and seemed to switch jobs every two weeks. One month ago, there was another receptionist that stood in her exact spot.

"I'll tell Kali that you're here."

A couple seconds later, the tall lean teenager was leading me back to my stylist's room. I saw a woman in a red jumpsuit stand up from her chair to check her freshly inserted weave that fell to the middle of her back. Kali had done her right. If I didn't see the woman in here, I would've sworn that all of that hair was naturally hers.

"See you next week Kali," the woman said, running her hands through her do.

"Okay Kandi, have fun at the party." Kali brushed off the stray strands of hair from her chair, preparing it for me.

"You did your thing on that weave girl," I said, nodding my head toward the exiting lady in red. Something about her looked very familiar, think I've seen her before. Maybe it was here.

"It should look good for how much that hair costs. She only buys the top of the line or shall I say her married boss buys her the best."

"Ooouuu," I whispered really low.

"That's what I said when I first found out." I followed

144

Kali back to the shampoo bowl and sat in the chair. This was my favorite part of coming here. Getting my hair washed was so relaxing, almost orgasmic. "I'm telling you she is a trip," Kali continued, "be talking about him like he's really her husband. Anyways, enough about her, what's up with you? You must have a hot date or something tonight."

Kali directed my head back into the shampoo sink and began to rinse my hair. "Huh, why you say that?" I asked, trying to play it off.

"Is the water too hot?" she asked, while adjusting the temperature.

"Nope, perfect."

"Cool. You must have forgotten that I just saw you last week. And I've been doing your hair since forever, and since forever you've been getting your hair done every other week. Unless that is, you were going on a hot date." I couldn't suppress the smile that forced its way on my face. I was busted. Hairstylists knew their regular customers well. "Mmm hmm, just as I thought. So spill the beans. Who is he and where did you meet him?"

I closed my eyes as the tiny jet streams massaged and tingled every single one of my hair follicles. I thought about the first time I felt Juwaun behind me on the dance floor and inhaled deeply. "I think it's been about three weeks now, but it's nothing serious. We're just friends."

"Mmm hmm, so where are the friends going on their date tonight?"

"Just a little get-together that his brother is giving."

"You go girl, meeting the family already, damn!"

"Shut up Kali, we are just friends."

"So what is this friend's name?" She towel dried my hair and added a generous amount of conditioner while massaging my scalp. I had to fight falling asleep to pay attention to her.

"Juwaun," I answered reluctantly. I didn't want to give

145

away too much info.

"Juwaun huh?" she said, while combing the conditioner in. "What a coincidence, that's my baby daddy's name."

I turned around and looked at her after she placed the shower cap on me. "Baby daddy? Girl what are you talking about, you don't have any kids."

"I know that. Come on, I'm going to have you get your mani and pedi while your conditioner sits. You're getting a fill-in right?"

"Yes."

She continued talking on the way back to the manicurist's station. "Oh and I was talking about my future baby daddy, Juwaun sexy fine ass Jones from the Detroit Lions."

There was no way I was going to tell her that's exactly who I was talking about. If that kind of information got out in a salon, the entire city would know by this evening.

While I sat in the massage chair soaking my feet, the nail tech started on my hands. Even though the time was moving fast, I was still on schedule. By the time Kali was finished with my hair it was 12:45. She had me looking cute as always, and I headed home with a sunny attitude to match the equally bright sunny day.

Juwaun called around 2:00 to inform me that he was on the freeway heading towards my place. By this time, I was almost finished dressing. I sat on my couch and slipped my sandals on, which showed off my perfectly French pedicured toes. I did a test walk to loosen them up a little and to see if these were going to be the kind of shoes that looked good but in about an hour you can barely wiggle your toes. Surprisingly, they were quite comfortable.

I surveyed my closet and decided on a small teal beaded handbag to accent my dress. I turned and twisted in different directions, lifted my arms, sat on the bed, and stood back up all to check how I was going to look in any situation that might occur today. Oh wait, one more. I bent over grabbing the mattress and hiked up my sundress. I smiled, "Yeah, I wish." I smoothed my dress back down and felt no panty line, thanks to my La Perla Mermaids thong.

I went to my nightstand on my way out of the room and opened the top drawer. I stared at the two boxes of condoms that I've had for over three months. I felt my eyebrows rise as I grabbed one of each condom. Never know what kind of mood I'll be in later.

I heard my phone ring in the living room and jogged to it. "Hello!"

"Hey baby, I'm pulling up in front," Juwaun's deep voice resonated back.

"Okay, I'm here." I hung up, sprayed Juicy Couture on all of my pulse points like my mom showed me when I was younger, then lifted my dress and sprayed a couple of sprays toward the pulse point that beats stronger than all of the rest, something that I taught myself over the years. Hey, you never know he might get tired and want to take a nap on my lap, face down. I laughed at my nasty thoughts when there was a knock on the door.

When I opened the door, Juwaun stood there for a couple of seconds with his mouth wide open. "Come in silly." I continued holding on to the door handle.

"Wow Angel, you look magnificent! Where did you get that dress? Damn you have good taste!" He smiled wide, displaying teeth that were white enough to be featured in the next Colgate commercial.

"Thanks, I picked it out all by myself," I said, as I did a turnaround for him.

"Good Lord girl, look at your backside. You get Botox shots in that or something?"

"Shut up!" I playfully pushed him in his muscular, solid as an oak arm. I walked over to the kitchen counter to get my purse when Juwaun called me back.

"Come here for a sec."

I turned around and looked at him with my hands on my hips. "And what do you want?"

He outstretched his arms. "I want you to come over here."

I walked over to him and he spun me around 180 degrees placing my derriere up against his crotch. "Oh now you want to feel up on it. Just a minute ago you were talking about it."

"I was talking about it in a good way though. You know I love your booty." He wrapped his arms around me and pulled me in tighter.

"Don't you think we should be going? You know it's after 2:30." The position we held was starting to feel too good.

"Yeah, guess you're right, maybe we should be leaving but not before you put these on."

As I turned around to face Juwaun, he was taking his hand out of his pocket. He opened a small black velvet box unveiling a pair of earrings, both of them with three diamonds each one hanging under the other in descending size. I tried to get my mouth to close, but it just wouldn't obey. "Wha...what is that?" I asked, pointing to the box that was still in his hand.

"Well this, is a box and if I'm not mistaken, these are called earrings."

"Okay and why are you pulling them out?"

"That's because my dear..." Juwaun closed in on the space between us, "they are yours."

I stood with a blank stare for a few seconds. I'm sure it probably had Juwaun a little confused on why I wasn't jumping around his neck thanking him. "Juwaun, I really don't want to sound unappreciative, but I don't think I feel comfortable taking any more gifts from you right now. I mean after getting all of this yesterday," I looked over my new outfit, "I don't know." I tried to think back on the last gift any of my ex's gave me and drew a blank.

Johnie Jay

"I feel you, really I do, but I don't have any hidden agenda. It's not like I'm giving you gifts so that I can get the booty quicker."

"Quicker?" I asked, looking directly at him not able to mask my smile. "And who said I was giving it to you at all?"

He laughed and shook his head. "Baby I'm just saying I give you things solely because I want to. There was a time where I couldn't buy a woman that I liked anything. Now that I can afford it, don't hurt my feelings by turning my gifts down. Just accept it as a friendship gift." He took another step forward. "We are just friends right?" he asked, with one eyebrow raised.

"Yep!" I answered quickly.

"And that's all you want it to be right?"

"Yep!" This time I answered so quickly that it didn't even sound convincing to me. He was now so close on me that I felt his bulge on my stomach.

"Well then you have nothing to worry about." He placed his index fingers under my chin and raised it until I was looking directly in his eyes. I knew what was coming next and I wasn't going to stop it. I closed my eyes and welcomed him a little more into my world. He kissed me soft, caring, brief. He pulled away and left his sweet aroma around me.

"So, my friend, I would really appreciate if you would take my friendly gift…" he took both earrings from the box and placed the velvet cube back in his pocket. Then he unscrewed the earring backing, gently tugged on my earlobe, inserted one of the earrings into my left ear and screwed the backing on, "… as a token of my friendship." I continued looking at him, still in shock as he did the same to my right ear. Something about him caused me to let my guard down. He stood back and looked at me. I couldn't stop blushing. "Absolutely beautiful, now let's go before we're late."

Juwaun walked to the door, calves bulging from under his linen shorts. As we walked to his car I admired his firm taut rear

149

end. "Damn Juwaun!"

"What's wrong?" he asked, briefly turning around.

"You get Botox shots in that thing?" I asked, pointing to his rear just as he had done to mine earlier.

"Hey, hey! No wise cracks about my butt. That's a sensitive area for me."

"Aw poor baby, I personally don't think there's anything wrong with you having a better ass than your date." I tried to hold in my laughter but just couldn't contain it.

"Oh you got jokes huh?"

The sunrays blinded me as they danced off of Juwaun's brand new radiant white on white, chromed up convertible Jaguar XKR-S. He walked around to the passenger side and opened the door. My car was parked right next to us so I unlocked my car door and removed my sunglasses from the visor. "You sure you don't want to take my car?" I asked, shutting my door and returning to his.

"Um maybe next time." He responded with a smile, as he walked around to the driver's seat. I leaned over to open his door. "Thanks, you want the top up?"

"Naw, I'm good."

"You sure that pretty hair style is going to hold up?" Juwaun checked behind us and then put the chromed feline in reverse.

"Gotta do a little more than put a little wind in my hair to mess it up!" I put my shades on and looked out of the passenger side. "Gonna need some fingers and a little sweat," I said, a little more quiet.

"Mmm, I'll make sure to take note of that," he said softly, making me smile. I ran my fingers through my short-cropped curls to give him a visual teaser.

On the way downtown, we listened to Gary Taylor's The Mood of Midnight. My daddy absolutely loved him some Gary

Taylor. "What you know about this young buck?" He didn't answer, just smiled. I was somewhat impressed at how mature he was for his age.

When we reached Jefferson Avenue, he informed me that it wasn't going to be much longer. I mentally prepared myself for what was to come. I mean this was the first time I had dated anyone famous or with any kind of money. So I really didn't know what to expect from his peers.

I felt my phone vibrate in my handbag. Seeing my caller ID brought a nervous smile to my face. Juwaun instantly turned down the volume to the radio. "You don't mind?"

He waved his hand and shook his head. "Of course not, go ahead."

I answered the call. "Hey girl."

"Hey mami, what's up?"

"Nothing much, on my way to a party with Juwaun."

"Oh yeah, that is today. Well, I didn't want anything. I was just calling to check up on you. Wanted to make sure that you were...um, doing alright."

"Actually I am. I had a nice time." I tried to speak as guarded as I could. I didn't want Juwaun to know of my near bi encounter with my best friend.

"I'm glad you did because I did too. Okay, well call me and let me know how it goes," Brianna said, sounding a little more cheery.

"Bri thanks a lot," I rushed to get in before she hung up.

"For what?" she asked.

"For being my best friend."

"Aw Angel, you don't have to thank me for that. It's my honor to be your best friend. Okay, now I know I'm getting off before you make me cry."

"Girl, you are so crazy. Okay talk to you later."

"Okay Angel, tell Juwaun I said he better take care of my

girl."

I slapped Juwaun on the shoulder. "Hey, hey what I do?" he asked, looking at me while smiling.

"My girl Bri said you better take care of me."

Juwaun laughed and gently stroked the back of my neck. "You tell Bri, that's exactly what I'm planning to do."

"Ooouuuuuu, sounds like somebody is going to have a nice time today and tonight." She busted out laughing. I did the same.

"Bye Bri."

The rest of the drive Juwaun kept his hand gently rubbing the back of my neck. We pulled up in the underground garage and I must admit the butterflies were starting to flutter. We stepped in the elevator and Juwaun pushed the button for the twelfth floor.

"Are you alright?"

"Huh, yeah why do you ask?"

"You just seem a little nervous that's all." I inhaled deeply as he stepped over to me and wrapped his muscular arms around me. All my worries seemed to melt away as he gently squeezed.

Ding!

"Here we go, are you ready?" he asked.

"As ready as I'll ever be."

He grabbed my hand and held it tight, as he took the lead like a real man should. These lofts had to be huge because there were only four doors on the entire floor. The further we walked down the hallway the louder the noises, voices and music became. Juwaun gave a couple of hard knocks when we reached the door with 12-D on it. A couple seconds later the door swung open, allowing the loud noises to spill out.

"What's up cuz!"

"What's up Avery?"

We walked into the loft and I immediately realized that I was correct on my assumption. This place was huge.

"Your brother is in there entertaining of course."

"Of course. Avery, I would like to introduce you to Angel. Angel this is our favorite cousin Avery."

I shook the pleasantly plump cousin's hand while putting on my award-winning smile. "Nice to meet you Avery," I said, over the loud music.

He shook my hand, released it and then took a couple of steps back. "Whewwweeee! Same here. Juwaun, it's about time you met someone that's classy and stopped fooling around with all of those hoodrats."

"Oh you're going to play me like that in front of company. Let's see what you say when I tell my momma," Juwaun said, smiling at his cousin.

"So, you like hoodrats huh?" I joked, nudging him in the arm, causing his cousin to laugh.

"I'll catch up with y'all in a few. I have to go get my drink on. Angel," Avery extended his hand for a second time, "it was nice meeting you."

"Same here. So is everyone going to expose you like that?" I asked, as Juwaun's cousin blended in with the crowd.

"Let's hope not," he responded, then grabbed my hand and walked me into the living room. It wasn't even 3:30 yet and this party was packed to the gills. People were everywhere. And not just people but famous people. I saw players from all of the Detroit sports teams and many people that I have seen on TV, but couldn't place their names at the moment.

Juwaun brother's place was crazy. There were paintings covering the walls. I counted about five flat screens grouped together on another wall. The furniture was chic and there was a cobblestone bar on the far wall, with streams of water running down it. This looked like something that would be in a L.A. nightclub.

We walked towards the large, opened, glass patio doors

and there were just as many people outside as were inside. When we stepped through the doors, our feet were greeted by soft plush green grass. It covered the entire outside area which was about half of the area inside. It really looked like someone's front lawn. There was landscaping, lights, black lava rocks, different kinds of shrubs, another smaller bar and two nice sized, smoking, barbecue pits.

"Wow, your brother went all out for this place," I said, looking around in amazement.

"Yeah he should've, how much he's charging me. This is just one of four of his properties."

"Charging you? What do you mean?"

Juwaun looked at me and questioned, "You mean I didn't tell you? My brother is my agent."

"Oh I see. No you never told me that."

"All of the gifts I told you about, those endorsements were partially because of him. He is good, but I still think he's overcharging his baby brother." I could tell by the huge smile on his face that he really thought whatever the amount that he paid was very well worth it.

"Does he have any more clients besides you?" I asked, being nosey.

"Only two and that's only because he doesn't want any more. He said that the three of us take up too much of his time as it is. He's over my best friend from grade school, who went to U of M with me and was drafted number two, behind me. Also, one of my younger female cousins who went to Michigan State, and was rated the number one player in college. She's going to the WNBA this year and he's already inked a crazy Nike deal for her."

"Keeping it all in the family, sounds pretty good."

"Speaking of the devil. I should've known that he would be somewhere around food." We were now standing in front of one of the grills a couple of feet from a lighter, skinnier version of Juwaun. He was preoccupied talking to the cook.

"Tone Tone!" Juwaun called out for his older brother. They both shared the same Colgate smile and you could see the love they had for each other as they embraced.

"Baby bruh, what's up boy?"

They released their embrace and Juwaun looked over towards me. "This," he extended his arm towards me like he was unveiling a surprise behind the curtains, "is the friend that I've been telling you about, Angel. Angel...Antonio."

His brother extended his hand and I accepted. "I hope it wasn't all bad," I stated, while giving a quick glance over to Juwaun.

"Of course not, nothing but good things. Where is your drink?" Antonio asked.

"I wasn't offered one yet." I knew that Juwaun was about to get in trouble with his big brother.

He started at Juwaun. "That is inexcusable! Somebody should've offered you one."

Juwaun started laughing, looking back and forth between his brother and me. "I don't think I like where this is headed." We all laughed.

"Come on y'all, let's go get some spirits." Antonio led us to the outside bar. What are you having Angel?"

"White wine, preferably Moscato if you have it."

"Same here," Juwaun added.

"I don't think I asked him, did I?" his big brother asked me.

"I didn't hear you ask," I replied.

Juwaun started looking around the patio area. "Where's Tasha? You want to keep treating me like this? I know how to get you in trouble too. Where is your fianceé?"

"Okay, okay crybaby." Antonio handed us both a glass of Moscato and he cracked open a MGD. "Tasha is around here somewhere, networking as usual. Always trying to get customers for her boutique, she just opened not far from here."

I made a mental note of the boutique. The benefits from knowing Juwaun seemed to get better by the day. He came closer to me and placed his hand delicately on the small of my back. I leaned into the crest of his arm to let him know that the teasing was all in good fun.

A couple of seconds later Antonio walked over a tall, slender, caramel brown-skinned woman who could have easily been a professional runway model.

"Hey Juwaun!"

"Hey sis, what's up?"

"Nothing much, just trying to keep these horny women in check. They're trying to get me to hook them up with anybody famous." She gave Juwaun an endearing hug.

"Where were you a few minutes ago when your fiancée and my friend over here were teaming up on me?" Juwaun asked.

She cut her eyes at Antonio. "He better not be messing with my boy."

"Nope not me," Antonio said, with his head tilted.

"Now that's not fair, you're going to just leave me out in the cold like that?" I asked, laughing.

"Sorry," Antonio said, as he patted me on my shoulder. "It was either me or you."

"You see how men are girl? They'll leave you at the first sign of trouble." Antonio's fianceé shook her head.

"I see," I said, smiling. "I'm Angel."

"Angel," she said, grinning while looking at Juwaun. "I think I might have heard your name mentioned a time or two. I'm Tasha, Antonio's fiancée. I love that dress," she said, taking in my entire new gift.

I felt my cheeks tighten. "Thanks, my friend picked it out for me," I said, running my hand across Juwaun's arm.

"Well your friend has good taste." Juwaun stood silent

with his chest poked out proudly.

"Speaking of material goods," Antonio cut in, "you have to make a decision soon on Nike or Reebok, because they keep blowing up my phone."

"Come on Tone, no business talk at least for one day," Juwaun said, shaking his head.

"Yeah baby I agree, no business talk today," Tasha agreed.

"I can't believe that I made you wait to get a better deal and you finally get a superb offer, and you're acting like it doesn't even matter."

"No it matters," Juwaun said. "I just haven't thought about it, that's all."

"How could you not think about it? You know what, you're right," Antonio threw his hands in the air, trying to smooth out his obvious frustrations. "I'll give you today." Juwaun and Tasha threw him daggers with their eyes. "Okay and tomorrow but come Monday morning—"

"He's hopeless," Tasha commented on Antonio, while standing on her tiptoes to kiss him on the forehead. "I'm going to take Angel for a woman talk and introduce her to a few people."

"Okay we'll meet up with you girls in a few," Antonio said returning the kiss.

Juwaun held both of my hands as I pulled backwards. "Promise you'll bring her back to me Tasha."

"Boy please, you need to stop." All four of us started laughing. "Come on Angel."

While walking back inside of the loft, I realized that I had left my drink at the bar. "You mind if we stop by the bar?"

"Of course not, I'm due for another drink," she responded. "Charlie, give us two glasses of the good stuff."

A couple of seconds later, I was taking sips of the "good stuff" and I swear it was the best wine that I have ever tasted. "Wow," was the only word that came to mind.

"I know, good isn't it? Believe it or not, it has vodka mixed in it."

I took another sip. "Mmmm."

"Just wait until the steaks are done. It tastes even better with meat. Remind me to give you a bottle before you leave." I logged that comment into my memory bank. I hoped she wasn't joking, because I was taking her at her word. She excused herself for a second and spoke to a couple, and then returned her attention back to me.

"Okay Angel, it's time to put you up on things since you are new to the scene. I'm sure you've seen all of the athletes and famous people here, well most of them are married."

She took another sip of her drink. I followed suit. "That's not a bad thing is it?" I asked, knowing that there had to be another part to her statement.

"No, actually that's a wonderful thing! Except for the fact that none of the women or men here brought their spouse."

She drank her wine normally, while I almost choked on mine. "What do you mean?" I asked, confused. I mean I heard stories of groupies, but I didn't think that every athlete fell victim to them.

She looked at me directly. "I mean, the people here have wives and husbands, but most of them are here with their other better halves. To make matters worse, many of the wives know about the other women. Almost blew my mind when I first saw how things were in this lifestyle."

"Wow!"

"Yep, like take for instance him over there standing, talking to the two women. He's one of the rare ones. He brings his wife with him to little events like this. That's her on the left."

"They actually look happy together," I added.

"They should," she shot back, "that's the mistress on the right."

"Wow!" I tried to think of another word to use for my excitement but couldn't.

"Yep, don't feel bad for the wife though; she knows about the mistress, in fact they all live together."

"Are you serious? Please tell me you are kidding," I said, looking over at the happy trio.

"Wish I was."

My mind drifted off into the future. Could I even see myself settling if Juwaun and I were together? Would it be easy for him to give in to the temptations of fame? Is it even worth taking that chance? I was already apprehensive about dating him, and now getting a glimpse into what life could be like with him is not making me feel any better.

"So if you don't mind me asking, how do you stay sane knowing that your future husband is working or dealing with people in this lifestyle? Aren't you a tad bit worried?"

She chuckled. "Worried? Not at all. He better be though. He knows the type of person that I am and I don't take any shit. There is always a chance for your man to cheat in any relationship, but I made sure that he knew for certain that I'm not one of those women who will stay married to someone who I know is cheating. Play superstar if you want to, but if I find out about it, I'm out!" I nodded my head in agreement.

"Hey Tasha," a Jill Scott look-a-like called out as she walked by us with her friends.

"Hey girls."

"Nice party."

"Thanks." When Jill Scott's look-a-like walked out of hearing distance, Tasha cut into her as well. "She's dating her sister's man believe it or not."

"You know what? I don't think I can take any more." We both broke out in laughter.

"I feel you girl, it's literally enough to write a book on."

I shook my head. "What ever happened to just liking the person that you are with?"

"That is so nineties," Tasha answered waving her hands. "You must have missed the memo, infidelity is the new monogamy."

"I see," I said, smiling.

"Do you mind if I borrow my friend back for a while?" Juwaun asked, coming up behind us holding two plates of food.

"Well, I guess," Tasha answered apprehensively.

"Cool, I'm going to grab us a couple of seats at that empty table."

"I'll be right over," I told Juwaun as he walked away. "Thanks for putting me up on game Tasha."

"No problem girl! Wish I had someone to do the same for me. Had to find out one day by calling one of the player's wives by the girlfriend's name."

"Oops!"

"Big time! Seriously though, Juwaun is a good guy. He and his brother are cut from a different cloth, so I hope I didn't scare you off."

I smiled. "Not at all. I like to know about my surroundings."

"Yeah, we'll talk before you leave," she said looking around, probably for her future husband after talking about all of these scandalous bitches.

I walked over to Juwaun who was sitting at one of many round draped tables that were set up. I tried to put my feelings and the look that was coming over my face aside when I saw a gorgeous, red-boned woman standing over him. Talking is one thing, but she was being a little too touchy feely for my taste.

I cleared my throat to throw a monkey wrench in their conversation. "Oh hey Angel," Juwaun said, caught a little off guard, "didn't see you there. Angel, this is Angie." I can't believe she had the nerve to have a name similar to mine. "She's one of the dancers in Locamotion, the dance team for the Pistons. We went to high school together."

"I like your name," she said, smiling innocently.

"Likewise," I responded, knowing that I was lying.

"Is this your woman Juwaun?" she asked.

Juwaun sported a look that suggested that he wished she would've asked another question. "Um, naw, we're friends."

What do you mean naw? Don't you see that she's trying to get with you on the sly? What you should've said was yes to keep her off of you. Even though I'm the one who insisted that we be friends, those words just came back to bite me in the butt.

The lady with the similar name continued smiling, probably feeling like she had a better chance on bagging him when I wasn't around. Funny how another woman wanting the guy who wants you, who you didn't even know for sure that you wanted, makes you all of a sudden want him. "Talk to you later," she said, dragging her hand from his left shoulder, around the back of his neck and over to his other shoulder.

Juwaun stood up and pulled out my chair. "So how are you enjoying yourself?" he asked me nervously.

I sat my wine on the table and took a seat. "So far so good." I surveyed all of the goodies that were on my plate, as a server came over to bring us silverware wrapped in a cloth napkin. "So was Angie just a friend in school or was she a friend?" I smiled slightly, not wanting to sound like I was jealous.

"Just a regular friend," he answered, before taking a bite of his steak kabob. I figure I'd drop the subject. We came here to have a good time. Truthfully, I was just Juwaun's friend and that was because of me. So I couldn't get jealous over females jockeying for a position that he tried to offer me. I hope I don't live to regret that decision.

After we finished eating, we moved to one of the available

leather love seats. We had been sitting and talking for a while, when a tall woman that was standing in front of the coffee table dropped her purse. When she bent over, her already super short mini hiked up over her ass, showing all of her goods.

"Wow!" we both said in unison.

"Now that was intentional. Can't even lie about that one," he said, sipping on his wine.

"That's how I'm coming to the next party, assed out. Except, I'm not going to shave." I laughed at the thought of me bending over showing my bush.

"The hell you're not!" Juwaun said, shaking his head smiling.

"Why not? They're doing it."

"Yeah but they're desperate to find a man. You have guys desperate to be with you."

I looked into Juwaun's eyes and felt his sincerity. No doubt he would've gone in for a kiss if people weren't around. The crowd had become a lot thicker in the last hour.

"I'm going to go the restroom." I looked around. "Which is—"

"Right down the hallway first door to your right. If that one is too crowded, then there is another one outside, behind the Jacuzzi. Do you want me to walk you there?"

"No that's okay, I should be fine. Be back in a few."

As soon as I left Juwaun, the vultures started swarming. I saw a couple of females point as he walked toward the kitchen, and overheard another saying how she would literally fuck him blind. I also noticed that I was getting a lot of attention as well from guys that were at the party. They probably were thinking about how well I would fit in with their other girlfriends and wives.

"Hey gorgeous," a tall baldheaded man called out as he exited the restroom, "I'm right here, heard that you were looking for me."

162

Johnie Jay

At a closer look, I realized that the guy was Chauncey Billups, point guard for the Pistons. I heard that he has numerous business dealings and a bunch of family in Detroit, which kept him around frequently. These athletes already look tall on TV but in person, they look like giants. I gave him a polite smile as he and I both were stuck in between the traffic in the narrow hallway.

"I saw you over there sitting with Juwaun earlier. Is that your man?" he asked, now staring at my lips.

"He's my friend," I forced out. I wonder if Juwaun would have felt how I was feeling a moment ago with the lady who shared the similar but knockoff version of my name.

"Friend huh?" He smiled showing off his dimples. "He better hurry up and claim you before somebody else does." The crowd loosened up a little giving us room to move. "I'll see you around," he said, licking his lips before disappearing.

I was next in line for the restroom. By now, I really had to pee but I held my composure pretty well. When the restroom emptied, I locked myself in, laced the seat with a disposable liner, pulled my La Perla's down, and sighed as a seemingly endless brook of urine exited me.

When I left the restroom, I immediately looked for my date in the monstrous crowd and saw everyone but him. I walked back towards the love seat where we were sitting and saw that it was occupied by a couple making out. I turned and saw Tasha walking towards the outside patio. "Tasha!" I called out over the loud music hoping that she would hear me.

She turned around, saw me waving my hand and walked towards me. "Hey what's up?"

"Have you see Juwaun anywhere?"

"Girl whenever you can't find your man just look for a TV that has any type of sports or a game on. I think I just saw him, Antonio, and the fellas over there in front of the TVs." She pointed to the far wall where a bunch of guys were gathered around what looked to be a TV wall with four giant flat screens side by side.

"Thanks!"

"Did you need anything else?"

"No thanks, I think I'm fine." I walked towards the giant TVs and made out Juwaun through the crowd of men. It wasn't really hard to do being that he was one of the only guys wearing white. Another guy that was standing next to him was wearing white as well, but he wore linen pants instead of shorts. I noticed Antonio talking to him for a second and then the two all-white wearing brothers shaking hands. Immediately after, as if he felt me coming closer, the unidentified guy looked in my direction, locking in on my gaze.

Juwaun turned around and scanned the room probably looking for me. He didn't have a homing device and laser lock on targeting like the other guy though. Antonio pointed to something on TV. The mystery guy who probably was an athlete also by the way he was built was less concerned about sports. Apparently, he would much rather watch me. He took a sip from the amber colored concoction in his glass. The V-neck, short-sleeved shirt that he wore hugged his biceps tightly and lay softly over his muscular chest as if it was fresh cream poured over hot black coffee. He held his stare and so did I until...

"Girl, I love your sandals! What brand are they?"

"Thanks, they're Giuseppe's," I answered, uninterested.

"Oh okay, are they comfortable?" the stranger asked, causing two more women to sneak a peek.

"Yes," I replied, trying to be courteous.

"Well I hope you don't get mad at me if you see me out and I have them on, because I'm buying those."

"Of course not, I would do the same." I looked down at her navy blue pumps. They weren't all of that, but I complimented her anyway. "As a matter of fact, don't get mad if you see me with

164

yours. I like those."

She let out a hearty laugh. "These are Jimmy Choo's!" she said, like she had been waiting all night to announce the expensive designer.

"It was nice meeting you," I said, cutting this meeting short.

"You too!"

I continued my journey and regained the stare shared between the man in white and me. The shorter the distance between us became the more familiar he looked. His complexion, his shoulders, his eyes. I slowed my pace. His goatee, yes I've definitely seen him somewhere before. As my brain tried franticly to put the pieces together, my heart had already completed the puzzle.

My pussy instantly became wet, making the passageway to my love, slick and ready for him. I think it wanted him more than my heart did. Why wouldn't it, she had been stroked oh so good, in countless thoughts and dreams for countless nights since first seeing him. He took another sip from his drink and licked his lips slowly, against my objection of course because I wanted to lick his lips for him. I tasted his tongue at that moment. It was sweet, tempting, and dangerous.

He had managed to creep back in the cracks in my life. He was now the crack in my life, my real life drug and I was an addict. No matter how long I went without seeing him, he's still there. I needed to talk to him, went too long already without knowing how his voice sounded or how his skin felt. I had to find out his purpose in my life. But how? How could I get him alone and tell him that I...belonged to him?

I saw Juwaun out of my peripheral smiling and waving me over but I was on a mission. Think! Think! I stopped walking and smiled back. I held my wine glass up and pointed to it. I then held up my index finger signaling I would be right there after I got my refill. He nodded okay and turned back around to talk to his brother.

Our eyes reconnected. He had seen everything that just went down and decoded the secret message. I made a beeline for the large cobblestone inside bar. I turned around to see him excusing himself from the fellas and cutting across the room to meet me at the secret checkpoint.

When I reached the bar, I saw that he had been diverted by someone who looked like the woman I saw at Kali's shop earlier. She wrapped her hands around his right bicep like it was something she had done before. Wonder if they really knew each other, or if she was just another groupie. Something about seeing them two together though seemed a little too familiar. Hmmm, wonder if I saw her somewhere other than The Salounge. They exchanged a few more words and he continued towards his destination, me!

I turned my back and slightly leaned on the bar. I had to get my face together and my feelings in check. The way I was feeling at this moment, I had to make sure that I don't embarrass him, Juwaun, or myself by jumping him right here and now.

I felt him drawing near. I saw his shadow as He came up from behind me. I smelled his familiar cologne as it reintroduced itself to my nose hairs. I took a sip of my wine and closed my eyes as I felt his left hand come around my waist and slide to the middle of my thigh. He firmed his grip. He was very bold, very brave, and I was crazy. Crazy to be letting this happen right now but I couldn't stop it. His front was on my back. As he leaned over, I felt his breath near my ear. It made my pussy and abs tighten at the same time. I laid my head back on his chest.

"You miss me?" he asked, over the loud noises.

"Of course I do," I said, trying not to sound too disappointed.

"Don't leave me like that again. Had me all worried and

166

shit."

"Mmm hmmm. I'm sure you had someone to keep you busy."

"Not who I wanted," Juwaun shot back, quick and convincing.

I turned around loosening Juwaun's grip on me purposely, to discreetly see what went wrong with the previous game of cat and mouse. He passed along side of us and headed towards the outside patio. It took everything in me to keep my head looking forward, focused on Juwaun while he was talking. I wanted so bad to scream out, "Wait!" and run after him. But I did what seemed to be the best thing at the time, suppressed it and tucked it away.

"You want to get out of here?" Juwaun asked, looking directly into my eyes.

"If you want to. What's wrong, not having a good time?" I asked, to see where his head was at, both of them.

"Actually I am I just figured that since it's so lovely out, maybe we could ride out for a while and catch some of this sunshine before it leaves."

"That sounds good." I mean I might as well get out of here before I get into trouble.

"Let's go tell Tone and Tasha that we are about to leave," Juwaun said. I was kind of hoping that he was going to tell them himself, that way I could've disappeared for a few. But I see that's not going to be happening.

We found the two lovebirds in the kitchen hugged up, exchanging smooches. As we said our goodbyes, I reminded Tasha about my wine and she proved that she was a woman of her word. She already had the bottle on the counter ready for me. She and I made an unofficial date to go shopping, while Antonio tried to sneak talks about Nike again. I did a three-second glance over to spot Him in the midst of people. I spotted my target like I had GPS tracking. It probably was only for half a second, but that was all the fix I needed. I did this while still talking to Tasha, without looking obvious.

Juwaun and I cruised downtown for a while grabbing up all kinds of attention. People were pointing at him and pointing at his car. Women seemed like they were trying to find out who the woman on the passenger side of the car was and wondering why it wasn't them.

"Want to go back to my place?" Juwaun said out of the blue. I looked over at him sporting a huge smile. "What? It's not even like that. I just wanted to know if you would like to see my new place that's all."

"You sure that's all?" I couldn't help but to smile. Juwaun was indeed a perfect gentleman, but I knew that if the mood and time was right he would make a move. I glanced at his muscular forearms as he gripped the steering wheel, then at his thick strawberry chocolate lips and imagined how they would feel on mine. My eyes lingered down to his lap. His linen shorts were doing a horrible job at hiding what he really had in mind.

Maybe I should stop playing so hard to get and give into what he and I both wanted. He wanted me...I wanted sex. More from another individual than him, but at this point I think that I may have to settle. "Let's go see this place of yours," I said, adjusting my sunglasses as we drove into the soon-to-be setting, warm, orange and red sun. Who knows if everything goes right I might just want to see much more.

A fluffy white cloud slowly passed over, temporarily blocking the sun's rays and immediately reminded me of my White Ranger. A sly grin brushed its way across my face. He always seems to find a way to put my mind back on Him.

Interception

Saturday morning, the first full day of my shutdown vacation. I opened one of my eyes and looked at the clock on my nightstand. "Damn!" 11:30 already. I had intended wake up at 9:00. Must've forgotten to set the clock last night before I turned in. Last night was a rare one for me. It was a Friday night and I didn't even go out to party, nor did I have a freak in my bedroom.

Caesar called me yesterday evening and said some people from work were hooking back up at some bar, but I've seen enough of them. Didn't feel like making a case to any of the girls I've fucked about why I haven't called, or why I haven't tried to hook back up. I had a ton of missed calls from past flings and one-night stands. I even received a call from Ricka, but I didn't answer.

Yesterday I finally came to the conclusion that I'd been living a lie. All this time I've been mistreating and dogging women, hopping from one to the other, acting like being a dog is the thing to be, was really me searching for something. My heart was really looking for someone.

I stood in my walk-in closet to decide what I was going to wear to the party today. I often dressed by the mood that I was in, and today after some well-deserved sleep, I was feeling pretty good. As my eyes scanned the closet from left to right, I caught sight of a pure white linen set that I purchased on clearance last fall, but never wore. I then browsed over the two shoe shelves that ran along the walls of my closet under my clothes.

"Yeah these will do." I removed a pair of camel colored sandals and matched them up with a camel colored Hermes leather belt. After hanging my outfit on the outside of the closet door, I grabbed a pair of basketball shorts, a cutoff, and my Jordan's and got ready to go get my hair cut. I had to be super tight for this party. No telling who was going to be up in there. I still wasn't sure if I wanted to try the settle down thing. Until then, I still loved women and no telling who I might pick up and bring back to my floor.

I stayed at the barbershop for about an hour and it proved to be very therapeutic. I actually told Keith about some of the weird things that have been going on in the last month. It felt better actually getting it out of my system. I tried my best not to think about Her, but the more I spoke with Halo from the show, and the more I texted my latest obsession, made me think about her even more.

I turned onto my street and noticed a line waiting to get into the underground parking structure. Must be for the party. I drove alongside of the visitor's line and noticed numerous beautiful women that hopefully would be attending the get-together. I felt my pulse start to quicken as I thought about possible hook ups. I was addicted to the female species.

I stepped inside of the bat cave and started to get ready for the party. After dressing, I looked in the full sized mirror wall that was perpendicular to the closet entrance. I nodded in approval at the way I filled out my V-neck linen shirt. The contrast of the pure white on my dark skin was a good look. I opened my watchcase and decided to go a little flashy, selecting my 2.5 carat diamond bezel Breitling. While placing the watch on my left wrist I noticed that it was almost 3:30. The party was officially underway.

I made myself a glass of Hennessy and apple juice. I didn't want to waste any time trying to get my buzz on when I got there. I finished half of my drink and placed the remainder in the fridge.

"I'll come back for you later." It was time to get this show on the road. I grabbed my phone, no missed calls, no missed texts.

I couldn't believe I was going to this party by myself. I think I would rather have a stunner on my side. Men with women get way more attention than a man who was by himself.

All of my freaks that I called up to invite to the party were either going out of town for the holiday, attending a family picnic, or didn't have anything to wear. The latter group did make sure to tell me that if for some reason they did find something to wear, or if someone was nice enough to buy them an outfit that they would be glad to go. Needless to say, I'm at the elevator right now by myself, waiting to go to the party...by myself. I only bought gifts for a select few. Those women who received gifts from me definitely were showering me with gifts.

I stepped in the elevator, pressed twelve and mentally prepared myself. I didn't want to be acting all starstruck if some VIP's were up in there. The elevator stopped on the twelfth floor. Left hand in my left pocket, I smoothly walked towards the crowd in the hallway. Shit, today I feel like the superstar.

"Invitations please!" the pudgy man asked the anxious partygoers who stood outside. I took my invitation out of my back pocket and stepped to the doorway. "Make yourself at home, the bar is in the far corner," he said, while taking my invite.

Now that's what I'm talking about. Time to get my drink on. It is a good thing that I grabbed me a bite to eat on my way home from the barbershop. Now I didn't have to waste any time filling my belly before I drank.

While walking over to the bar, I noticed all of the differences between Antonio's loft and mine. When I first came to check out the lofts, the manager asked if I wanted to see the ones for thirty thousand dollars more. At that time, it wasn't even an option, so I didn't want to waste their time nor mine. Now I see where the extra money goes. Wow! It has more space and a lot of it. The ceilings are higher, there is a landscaped patio, and a beautiful bar, equipped with a pebble-backed waterfall wall, and that's just from what I can see.

While being temporarily mesmerized by the bar, the bartender broke my stare. "What will it be sir?"

"Let me have a Hennessy and... do you have apple juice?"

"Sure do, coming right up."

I leaned back on the bar and checked out the scenery. Definitely nice. There were many couples here, but a lot of these guys' women were staring me down. One even excused herself, came over to the bar, and snuck me her business card.

I noticed what looked to be four 62-inch flat screens on the far wall, and started to make my way over. I tried to look for a lady who was on my level, a normal down to earth woman but so far no luck.

"Hey handsome!"

Mmm, may have spoken too soon. "Hey yourself."

"You look familiar," she said, looking me over slowly.

"I was thinking the same thing," I said, admiring her strong oriental features.

She snapped her fingers as if a light bulb turned on in her head. "I know, I think I saw you when they had the mixer outside on the yard this spring."

I looked at her as she did a slight turn to the side, unknowingly giving me a glimpse of her healthy derriere, reaffirming that she was indeed the woman that Antonio and I were speaking about in the elevator. "Yeah, okay, that must be it."

She took a sip from her glass, still looking me over. "I love it when dark-skinned men wear white. Makes your skin look so rich and smooth."

I held out my arms. "Hmm, I never noticed."

"That's because you're supposed to leave the noticing up to me." She picked an imaginary piece of lint from my chest.

Johnie Jay

"Mmm, nice; you work out I see."

"A little bit," I responded, looking directly into her chinky eyes.

She opened up her purse and pulled out a bright yellow business card. While handing it to me, she announced her name. "I'm Canary."

"Canary huh? Nice name. I'm Future."

She smiled back. "Future huh? Nice name. You should call me sometime."

I looked over her card. "Caterer?"

"Yep, know how to cook a brother a nice hot meal," she said with a smile. Canary was auditioning for this position pretty hard.

"Is that so, even soul food?" I had to know if she could cook what I liked to eat.

"Of course, my dad is Japanese, but my mom is a sista, therefore, all of this rump!" She lightly slapped her butt causing it to ripple. "Trust me, this is one woman who knows how to cook. I have a restaurant opening up a couple of blocks from here later on this year. I'll finally be able to do what I love, and give up the flight attendant gig that I'm doing now."

My mind was still processing the way her booty moved from that slap. "Sounds lovely." Now when I get hungry and want something good to eat—"

"Then you call mama." She licked her lips. "I'll definitely feed you something good."

"I'll keep that in mind, because I love to eat," I said, while rubbing my goatee.

She blushed. "You make sure you do that." She then turned and walked away, showing off what she inherited from her mother's side of the family. Gotdamn!

Then out of nowhere, "Future!" I heard my name being called and was momentarily disappointed, because my attention

173

was distracted from the bouncing booty cheeks now fading into the crowd. I turned around and saw Antonio, the host of the party, beckoning me over. I did the reverse nod, raised my glass, and walked towards him and the wall of flat screens.

"What's up man, nice party!" I said, giving Antonio a pound.

"Thanks, glad that you could make it. You know its food outside right? Better get your grub on; you know how fast food disappears around black folk."

"Yeah, I hear you." We both laughed. There were a handful of guys standing around watching SportsCenter on the TV's. Stuart Scott had just announced that they would be back after the commercial break. A Lamborghini commercial came on, and I felt the Hennessy in my gut start to separate from my stomach acid. I instantly became a little nauseous when I saw Juwaun Jones driving, and then getting out of a new Lamborghini Sesto Elemento. I looked on quietly, but the other guys seemed to be overly excited, especially Antonio.

"Damn that car is beautiful," Antonio whispered.

"Yeah, it's cool," I agreed, not wanting to ruin the obviously cheery mood.

"Uh oh, there's the man of the hour right there," Antonio said, now raising his voice. I looked at Juwaun's fake ass smile on the television. "Yeah, who got you that deal huh?"

I looked around to see who Antonio was talking too.

"You did, almighty big brother sir!"

"Future, I'd like you to meet my baby bro, Juwaun."

You've got to be fucking kidding me, brothers?

Juwaun looked at me. "What's up?"

"What's up man?" I replied, shaking his extended hand.

"Future is one of my neighbors. He lives a couple of floors up."

"Oh okay, you look familiar," Juwaun said. "Think I've

174

seen you somewhere before."

I shook my head. "Naw, probably not me."

"I think it may have been at another get-together or a party or something, anyways are you enjoying yourself?"

"Yeah this is live," I said, looking at all of the partygoers.

"Lots of females," he said, looking around. "I have to be on my best behavior today. I brought a friend with me."

"Aw man you're good. If it's just a friend you can network a little," I joked.

He smiled. "True, but this one is special and I'm trying my best to change that friend status." Time slowed down as I realized who this female friend might very well be. Impossible, she couldn't be here. "Speaking of which, I better be finding her; she may be lost."

He turned and started looking at about the same time I felt a force in the room. Something was definitely about to happen. My Spidey senses were going crazy. I felt a strong electric current and navigated to find its source. And there She was, standing in the midst of everyone glowing like an angel.

I saw Juwaun waving her over. I took a sip of my drink. She saw me, I saw her. She knew it, I felt it, we felt it. She pointed to her empty glass. Juwaun nodded. I acknowledged what she was implying, without saying a word. She didn't come over because we were supposed to meet without the added company. Juwaun turned back around towards the fellas and the TV's.

"You find her?" big brother asked Juwaun.

"Yeah, she's getting a refill."

He obviously missed the signal that I received, and it's a good thing that he did. This was my cue. I downed what was left of my drink. "Be back fellas, I have to get me another drink."

"Go ahead," Antonio insisted, "I'm sure you remember where the bar is."

"That's the first thing that I logged into my memory!" I

said jokingly. I walked away, first calm and then more brisk. The faster I walked the more interference the crowd ran. They were like defensive linemen. I had turned into Juwaun the football player after receiving the ball, stiff-arming, jab stepping, and juking. They were good but I was better. The end zone, my prize, was eyeing me telling me to come and score. She had beaten me to the bar. I sped up even faster and was blocked by a defensive back with a nice backside.

"Kandi?"

"Hey baby! You missed me?" Just like that, I was tackled.

"Hey!" That was my answer.

"I've been calling and texting. You're too busy for me?" She caressed my shoulders.

"Yeah I've been a little busy," I answered, looking around. I was starting to wonder if this chick was stalking me, but I threw that out of the window when I thought of all of the possible people that she could've known here. "Do you know Antonio?"

"Um no, don't think so. I came with one of my girls who knew someone that was coming." I looked over at the bar. She had her back turned now. Her posture showed that she was waiting, not frustrated yet. I still had a chance. "Well I see you are in a hurry, so I was thinking that since you live just a few floors up maybe we could—"

"I'll let you know," escaped my mouth and before I knew it, I had started the second down.

"You do that!" I heard fading in the background with all of the other noises. My target had looked back briefly again and located my gaze. I was only twenty feet away, less than seven yards from the end zone and then, tackled again but this time by a much larger DB. The fucking Lions had switched Juwaun from offense to defense. He was five steps ahead of me and had walked up behind Her and stolen my potential spot. I smoothly detoured to the left and headed through the patio doors. I passed the two lovers, friends, pals, whatever the fuck they were. We caught eyes, she looked as if she saw my determination, and my nostrils caught her scent. My heartbeat began to come back down to normal.

Over the next twenty minutes I ate, met many of my neighbors, and discreetly looked around for Her. I caught a glimpse of Juwaun walking around in the kitchen, and then saw Her receiving a bottle of wine from a woman standing by Juwaun and Antonio. I had let another chance slide right through my fingers. I know that she wants me the way I want her. I don't know why she's with that bum. She must be bored or maybe it's because I took so long making a move. I watched as he left with my prize, Her hand in his. I shook my head, disgusted with myself. Even though there were women galore at this party, they didn't seem that interesting any more.

I think it was time for me to say my goodbyes as well. I walked towards the kitchen where I saw Antonio.

"Great party man."

"You leaving already?" Antonio asked.

"Yeah, wish that I could stay a little longer but I have a couple of things to do."

He patted the woman standing by him on the backside. "Oh by the way this is my fiancée, Tasha."

"Nice to meet you."

"Same here," she responded, before sashaying away.

"Man whatever you do in life, make sure finding you a good woman is one of them. I'm talking about a really down female who will have your back no matter what. I mean look at all of these females here." We both looked at the view. "Ninety percent of these women will leave you at the first sign of broke. There is no greater feeling than knowing that you are with someone while you're feeling like it's you against the world."

"I feel you man. You're one of the lucky ones. We're all trying to get on your level."

He smiled. "Definitely lucky. Well you know where I live if you need anything." He took out a business card and handed it to me.

"Thanks again for the invite," I said, on my way out.

On my way to the elevator, the image of my mystery woman popped back up in my head. There were a couple of people in the hallway getting their game on but I had tunnel vision. I took a deep breath as I stepped into the empty elevator and pressed the white circular button marked 15. The elevator door started to close and with it, I hoped, the constant thoughts of a woman that I've continuously failed to connect with.

I guess someone had other intentions, because just before the door closed a hand came in between the doors, causing it to reopen. Not just any hand, but a female hand equipped with blood red polished fingernails. With my back resting on the back wall I watched as the door opened completely and Kandi stepped in. She licked her lips like an animal in the wild, ready to feast, and quietly pressed the button to close the door.

I didn't say a word. I was too emotionally drained and a little too tired. I looked past her intensely staring at me and saw the thirteenth floor light up. Just two more to go, please hurry up! Then all of a sudden, my body shifted from the elevator suddenly stopping. Kandi had her hand on the red emergency stop button, but that didn't stop the lust or the passion that I saw elevating in her eyes. She stepped towards me. I slowly shook my head knowing full well that I should be verbally saying no. Shit, I shouldn't even be close to this crazy bitch right now, but Buddy definitely wasn't thinking the way that I was.

"Wanted to taste your dick as soon as I saw you today." She continued talking barely above a whisper. "Wanted you inside of me." She squatted down like a professional stripper, heels and all without losing her balance and undid my belt buckle. I could feel Buddy trying to help her with the zipper as he forcefully pressed up

178

against it.

"Mmm, I miss you too!" she said, while rubbing her face up against my extra hard dick. "Do you miss me Future?" She looked up at me with sex in her eyes. I shook my head no, hoping that she would believe me. Hell, I was hoping that I would believe myself.

"Well, let's just see about that," Kandi said, right before taking me in her mouth. With her hands on my thighs, she held her balance and rolled her head from side to side sliding her tongue over my head. She moved with the smoothness of a cobra, slithery and just as deadly. She kept her eyes on me the entire time. I love getting hands-free head. Most women tried to jack you off and end up halfway breaking your dick off in the process, but not Kandi. She let her mouth reap all of the praise. She had me.

I tried my best to keep my knees from buckling, tried hard not to lock my fingers in her long hair that flowed down the sides of her face. I guess I didn't try hard enough. I grabbed the back of Kandi's head and slowly maneuvered her so that her mouth sucked me back and forth to a slow rhythm.

She moaned, made gagging sounds which I absolutely love, and gripped my thighs tighter telling me how good my dick tasted. "I want to swallow you daddy! I want your hot cum all down my throat." Damn she had a slick mouth. Kandi knew how to talk and keep a man aroused. I knew that I shouldn't be fucking with her anymore, but she was addictive. I was hooked from that first time that I saw her squirt. It was as if her pussy had spewed a magical mist on me. I was lost in passion as she continued sucking me.

Sperm goes through three stages before a man has an orgasm. The problem is that most guys cum too quick to realize it. I felt my cum entering into stage one. At the first stage, the dick does a quick jerk as the sperm enters the back of the dick from the balls, which is what I just felt. I didn't want it to get to the tingle, which was stage two. The tingle was too close to stage three, the point of no return where your entire body tingles. In stage three, the more you stroke, the more intense and better the tingling becomes, and who doesn't want that.

Well, actually I didn't, because if you fall into that temptation, the actual act of fucking or sucking would soon be over, at least for a while. I actually enjoyed the act more than the inevitable outcome. I enjoyed fucking and pleasing women, more than I enjoyed cumming.

I grabbed her up from her stooped position and tasted her tongue. She shivered and placed my fingers in between her folds. Just as I suspected, she was warm and dripping fucking wet. I placed my finger in my mouth and sucked her from me. She grabbed my hand and stole her flavor from my other fingers.

I wrapped both of my hands around her luscious ass cheeks and felt no sign of lingerie. I moved my index finger towards her ass crack and felt a slither of satin that had to be a G-string.

"Fuck me baby. Take your pussy. Take me daddy!" It's something about that daddy word. I turned her around and moved her hair from the back of her neck. My tongue traced circles on her neck as if I was trying to draw the Audi logo.

She leaned over and braced herself on the wall. "Take your pussy daddy!" she repeated, while spreading her legs. I inched closer to her with my pants now around my ankles. She looked back at me as I stroked my dick.

I was fighting with the thought that I shouldn't be here. Only inches away from her moist love spot, and the little devil on my left shoulder reminded me of how good the last time was. "Mmm it will definitely be better this time. No restrictions, unprotected, uncovered, mmm yeah, it will definitely be better!"

The angel on my right opened her mouth to speak, but I hunched her ass off and entered Kandi. She looked back at me moaning, while biting on her bottom lip. I grabbed her arms as I did short strokes trying to prepare her walls for my thickness. She was so fucking wet.

"Give it...give it to me baby." I braced myself with one arm on the wall, the other on her voluptuous chest and in one slow steady motion I gave her all of me. I pushed into her until I disappeared. She was so hot. Kandi immediately made her pussy walls contract, grabbing a tight hold on me.

I began stroking her slow and deep, but she didn't want to get reacquainted nor did she want to be romanced. She wanted to be fucked! Kandi reached behind me and gripped my ass. She pulled me into her at the pace that best suited her. With all the nasty talking that she kept doing, I doubled the pace that she had set.

Her pussy started making noises and talking to me telling me that it was having a nice time, that it was glad to feel me again.

I wrapped her hair around my fist and started fucking her caveman style. "This what you want? Huh, is this how you want me to fuck you?" I asked, pounding away.

"Yes daddy, take your pussy...ooouuu shit you're fucking me...so, so good."

"You want this dick?"

"Yes!"

"Tell me that you want it then, fucking tell me." I quickened my pace with force. My pelvis was smacking up against her ass. "Yes daddy yes! I want it, don't stop!" Kandi's legs started to shiver and then all of a sudden...

"Is everything okay in there?" the voice from the intercom on the wall asked.

I caught my breath and cleared my throat before answering. "Um yeah, the elevator just seemed to...stop on us." I pulled out of Kandi and pulled my pants up from my ankles. Kandi adjusted her G-string before straightening up her dress.

"Someone may have leaned up against the emergency stop

button. Check the red button on the side of the door," the security suggested.

After straightening ourselves up, I pulled the emergency button out to the dismay of Kandi, and the elevator restarted its acceleration.

"You weren't finished with me were you?" Kandi asked, still looking horny as hell.

"I think that we should finish this later...at another time." That was the nicest way that I could think of to tell her that I had made a mistake, and didn't plan on doing so ever again.

"Later? What do you mean, later? You get me all wet, pussy all throbbing and you want to finish this later? Naw fuck that!" She walked towards me and reached for my dick. "We're going to finish this now."

"Kandi please I..."

Ding! The elevator sounded as it reached the fifteenth floor.

Kandi came a few steps closer to me. "Baby, I don't see why you just can't take me to your place and—"

I stepped from the back of the wall and moved in between the door. "Kandi, I just have a lot of stuff to do. I'll call you."

She put her hands up to calm herself down. "You know what? You do that." The look in her eyes had turned from passion to rage. I think that I may have seen a little steam coming from her ears, but I had to end this charade.

I backed out of the elevator door and watched as Kandi intensely stared into my eyes as the door closed. I hope that this will be the last time that I see her. Somehow, I highly doubt it.

I walked into my door and sunk into my couch, accepting its soft hug and embrace. I aimed the remote at my flat screen and watched it come to life. I wonder if Caesar found something to get into. I took out my cell and dialed his number.

As I put the phone to my ear, I caught a whiff of Kandi's

sweetness still lingering on my fingers. I inhaled deeply. So sweet. But thinking of her recent psychotic behavior immediately made my mood sour. I stood up and walked toward the bathroom. Had to get her off me, out of my life, off my skin. I had to wash myself free of Kandi.

Caesar's phone rang four times before going to voicemail but I didn't leave one. I knew when he saw the missed call he would call back. I started my shower and threw my soiled clothes in the hamper. Just as I did, I heard my phone's ringtone.

"What up doe?"

"What up Future? I was drying off my truck when you called. I don't hear any noise, is the party over already?"

"Naw it's still going on. I just needed a breather. I ran into Kandi."

"Kandi...Kandi? Wait a minute, you mean Red Dress? Oh shit, how was she looking?" Caesar asked with excitement.

"Good as hell," I answered, chuckling. "But I'm telling you the bitch is crazy."

"Why is it always the pretty ones?"

"Seems that way huh?" I walked back into the living room to switch the TV off. "I can't believe I just fucked her in the elevator."

"Hold on, you what...in the where?" Caesar busted out in laughter. "She must not be too crazy."

I turned on the sound system from the living room, selected a Jay Z playlist, and synchronized it to the bathroom. "Trust me, she is. She reminds me of the chick in Thin Line Between Love and Hate." I heard my phone beep and looked at the screen. "Shit, speaking of the devil."

"Kandi?" Caesar asked, already knowing the answer.

"Yep," I answered reluctantly.

Caesar started laughing harder. "Man you have fucked up and met a real live stalker!"

"Whatever, so what's going on with you? You have a hot date or something?"

"Naw, no date. Probably hitting up a club so that I can up my roster." He said with a great deal of confidence.

"Cool, that sounds...hold up Cease." I took a couple steps toward my door. I thought that I heard a knock and then my phone beeped again. It was Kandi on the other line, followed by more faint knocks on the door. "Aye yo Cease, let me hit you back," I said quietly. I hung up the phone while creeping a little closer to the door.

"Future! I know that you're in there!"

"Is she fucking serious?" I whispered to myself. I crouched down low like she had x-ray vision and could see me through the door. Sounds crazy, but I wouldn't put it past her.

"Future!" She continued knocking, and then about ten seconds later...nothing.

I hit my palm over my forehead. Why did I fuck her again? Stupid! Stupid! Stupid! Damn it! I almost forgot that I had my shower running. My phone vibrated again with a text message. I was reluctant to read it, but did so anyway. FUCK YOU. Please let this mean that you're done with me.

As the steamy hot water ran from my head to my feet, I thought about my personal life. I really had no one but Caesar and my parents to talk too. There was no woman I could trust with my feelings or lean on if I had a bad day. It would be nice to have a real female companion. I rambled off names of women that I had been with, none of whom made me want to bring them home to meet my mom. None that made me want to do anything besides have sex with them. And to think that She started all of this crazy thinking. She made me want more. With the bar of soap in my hand I washed Kandi off me and out of my life, and wondered instead how my life would be if I had Her and only Her in it.

Johnie Jay

It All Boils Down To This

"Thanks for calling in Meagan from Cleveland."

Meagan cut Michael off before she was disconnected, "Okay Michael but before I go," can I speak to Baby Boy for a quick second?"

"Uh oh Baby Boy, this is not one of your exes is it?"

"Naw Mike, not from Ohio. Not after how those Buckeyes have been manhandling my Wolverines for the last couple of years." The two men started laughing.

"Baby Boy, I'm coming to Michael's Masquerade Ball this weekend, and I was just wondering if I could get a dance with you. My girlfriend saw you at the party last year and said that you were foine!"

"Foine? What's foine?" Mike asked, teasing the caller.

She proceeded to break it down for him. "Foine is when you say fine with a frown on your face. Means he looks so good that he makes your face ugly." We all laughed, I had to remember that one.

"I think that I'll be able to pull off a dance with you," Baby Boy said, "but how am I going to know that it's you if you're wearing a mask baby?"

"Oh, I'll have on a lime green dress with lime green hair," she responded.

"Lime green hair?" I could imagine Baby Boy laughing hysterically inside, but he did a good job holding it in. "Yeah uh, I'll make sure that I keep an eye out for you."

"Wow, looks like you have a fan club huh Baby Boy?" Mike asked while chuckling.

"Looks like it."

"So what do you think Halo? Do you agree with Meagan on the topic?" Michael asked after disconnecting the caller. "Do you think that dirty hands and fingernails on a guy is something that really turns you off when you're out?"

"I definitely agree with her. I don't think men understand. They are so homophobic that they end up missing out on things that they should be doing, like getting a manicure. That's something I think every man should do regularly. They don't necessarily have to go to the nail salon, but they should at least take care of their nails themselves. I mean every woman loves a hardworking man, and I don't think that we want their hands to be softer than ours, but you have to take care of them. You can tell a good lover, I believe, by how good he takes care of his hands. That's the kind of man that grabs you, rubs you, and enters you with his fingers."

"Whoa, whoa, this is a damn family show young lady," Mike joked.

"I'm serious though. If you're at the bar and you step to me with hands looking all rough and ashy, fingernails all ragged and dirty, and you think that you are going to put those things on my chest or in between these legs, no sir! That's one of the differences between a guy who just has sex and a passionate lover."

"Okay, I hear you. Baby Boy, do you agree with her and do you get manicures?"

"Of course I do and I do agree with her on that one." Baby Boy's baritone voice resonated through the phone and performed foreplay on my eardrums. "I think men try to be so hard, thinking that being rough makes them more masculine. Women like a man who takes care of himself. It lets them know that he's also capable of taking care of them. I work at an automotive plant during the week, so I know all about hands getting oily and rough and fingernails getting grimy, but before I go out I make sure that my hands and everything else looks good."

"Good to know," I said, cutting in. "So do you always wear gloves...while you are working?"

"Of course, I wouldn't handle the part...without protecting myself." We both laughed. He caught my wittiness. I loved that.

"See now, y'all are acting up. Don't think that I don't know what y'all are talking about. Gloves, protecting, y'all are just nasty. Okay Baby Boy, I have to ask you now. I let the ladies have the majority of the show, now it's the fellas turn."

"Oh Lord!" I had gotten used to my role on the show. I was to play the role of the strong-willed woman, putting the boys in check when they got out of line. Going against most of the things that Baby Boy said and flirting without seeming to enjoy it too much. Now that was the hard part. I really enjoyed flirting with him. I enjoyed it even more when he flirted with me. I have gone home plenty of nights and masturbated to things that I thought he would do to me if given the chance.

Michael Baisden continued his questioning. "Tell me something that really ticks you off that you see while you're out at the bar or at the club."

"Well Mike, it's gonna be kind of hard narrowing it down to one thing women do to piss me off but I'll try," Baby Boy responded.

"You are a mess," I threw in on cue.

"I hate it when I'm at the club where there is a lot of dancing going on and people are actually on the dance floor...dancing. You go to the dance floor where you see a young lady dancing—"

"Uh oh, I know where you are going with this one," Michael over-excitedly shouted. I felt the corners of my mouth curl upward as I felt where Baby Boy was taking us also.

"You come up behind her, she's grinding away to the song that's playing, shaking the booty everywhere, when she looks back and stiffens up like the Statue of Liberty. 'Naw I'm good!' What the hell is that about?"

"Maybe she didn't like what she saw," I threw in for good measure.

"I doubt that," he rebutted.

"You are so cocky!"

"Not at all, it's just no way that she couldn't like what she was seeing." Baby Boy laughed as if he was twenty percent joking and eighty percent telling the truth. "Even if that were the case, you are not on the dance floor looking for your husband or your next baby daddy, well at least I hope not. So if a guy comes up to you ladies and you're on the dance floor, even if it's for a little while, dance with him. It's really not that serious. Or here's an idea, if you don't think that you feel like dancing, stand your narrow behind in the aisle somewhere. Get off of the dance floor where people actually want to dance, with other people." Michael and I laughed out loud. "But here's the real kicker, a lot of the women who turn you down are not all of that themselves. They're the women that you are only dancing with because all of the tight women are currently taken."

"Wow!" was my response.

"What are you wowing at woman?"

"What if they just wanted to dance by themselves? Is that a crime?" I asked, smiling over the phone.

"Dance by themselves huh? Get dressed up, hair done up, makeup on, smelling all good, wearing too tight clothes, and uncomfortable shoes. You do all of that to come to the club, get on the dance floor and dance by yourself? Come on Halo!"

I laughed at that one. Women will wear some shoes that'll make their toes feel like they're going to fall off as long as they look cute.

"Look, I'm not saying that I agree with that. If I come to the club looking cute that don't mean that I want to bring someone home. Personally, if I'm on the dance floor, I'm going to shake my booty and I don't like dancing alone. My girls are cool but I'm not going to dance with them all night either." I prepared to spice things up. "But, in their defense, plenty of women don't feel like being groped and grabbed and have their booties smacked. And a lot of them, me included, don't want to feel y'all, how shall I say, not being able to control your members."

Both of the guys had to laugh at that one. "Wait a minute, wait a minute Halo. No you didn't say control y'all members." Michael could barely get out his statement.

"Well, I'm trying to keep it clean," I protested.

"I feel you girl."

After the laughter died down, Baby Boy continued to defend his position. "How do you expect us to control our members when women show up to the club half naked with your chest all out and your booty hanging? Then when you do dance with us, you grind your big booties up on us. Gyrating and thrusting on our crotches. And you mean to tell me that you're going to be shocked when we get aroused, come on Mike."

"Oh I'm there with you Baby Boy, I totally agree."

"I agree as well. As long as I feel something of a nice size I'm not complaining at all," I added.

"Halo, you are something else. Well that's all the time we have today people. Guys remember to check those hands and fingernails before you go out and ladies keep your butts off of the dance floor if you're not planning on dancing...with a guy." All three of us shared a laugh. "And remember, I'll see everybody in Detroit this Saturday for MBMB, Michael Baisden's Masquerade Ball. Make sure you go to Ticketmaster if you haven't done so. They are running out really fast. Or, you can continue listening to the radio to win you a pair of tickets. Whatever you do, don't miss out. Both of you guys are going right?"

"Of course!" Baby Boy responded.

"Yes," I added on.

"So, have you two decided on if you are going together?" Michael asked.

"This is your last chance Halo, my last offer."

"Very tempting, but I'll stick to our original plan. We'll meet up there."

"Well, till next time...keep it sexy!" After a couple seconds of silence I heard Michael's voice come back in. "Okay guys remember, just give them your names at the door and they'll give y'all the all-inclusive pass. Halo, have you found a dress yet?"

"Picking it up tomorrow. My girls and I finished our masks though. I must say we did a pretty good job."

"What about you Baby Boy, you good?"

"Have to pick up my suit from the tailor and I found a little novelty shop the other day for my mask. So um Halo, how am I gonna know who you are with the mask on and all?"

"It's going to be up to you to find me," I said stringing him along, "but I'll give you a hint, I'll be wearing all white."

"Okay guys I have to get going. See you on Saturday." With that, Michael ended the call.

I flipped my cell phone closed and felt the same excitement that I felt when I was preparing for my prom. I couldn't wait to finally see Baby Boy. I was also thinking about telling my secret texter to meet me at the same event. I figured that meeting there would be safe just in case he didn't turn out to be what I expected. We agreed not to trade face pictures, not knowing who knew whose people and to insure he wouldn't load my pictures up on YouTube or something. He didn't have a face for all of those body and ass pictures so if someone asked, it ain't me!

I was pretty much settled into my new condo a month

after closing. It was so much better than my old apartment. I have my own attached garage, two floors, a basement, and my very own lawn. Owning your own property is very rewarding. I felt much sexier now. When I backed out of my driveway and looked at my place there was no way that anybody could tell me that I wasn't the shit. It did take some time getting used to though, because I remember pulling up to my old apartment a couple of times after going out.

I walked by the painting that Juwaun gave to me for a housewarming gift. He had been really generous, always giving me something. I ended up accepting the earrings, the painting, and the outfit, but when he picked me up for a date and had a black rectangular box on the passenger seat that contained what looked to be at least a four-karat diamond tennis bracelet, I had to turn him down. I even refused the diamond watch he tried to give me while taking me out to lunch one day. The truth is, I couldn't let myself feel like I was being bought and I told him so. I didn't want to feel obligated to any man especially for something that he purchased for me.

I heard Jim Jones' "Ballin" come from my phone, the ringtone that I had set for Juwaun. Speaking of the devil. "Hello!" I chimed, while running my hand over the cherry wood picture frame that housed my newest painting.

"Wow, you sound very enthused. Were you thinking about me before I called?"

"Mmm, maybe."

"Maybe? I can't get a yeah?"

"Maybe is better than no," I said.

"I guess," he said, a little deflated. "So what are you up to over there?"

"Nothing much, about to hop on the computer to check my emails before I go to the gym." It was true that I was going to use my computer, but my reasons were not just about email. Naw, my eyes were on the clock. I was waiting for an hour past the time that I last saw Him at the gym exercising so I wouldn't run into him again. I'd been doing this to avoid Him for a while now, and so far it has worked. Even though I saw Him at Juwaun's brother's party and wanted to take him right at that moment, I'm coming to the realization that maybe I was a little hasty about Him being in my life, or that we were meant to meet.

Now I'm starting to think the opposite. Maybe our paths crossing was a mistake. Maybe all of the obstacles that kept coming up were God's way of stopping something that wasn't supposed to happen. I shook my head as I tried to convince myself of this for the umpteenth time.

I still think about Him every day. Whenever my girls and I go out, I still look for Him. After not seeing Him for nearly a month, I thought my desire would have cooled down but it didn't. Even with my mind occupied by Juwaun, Baby Boy, and the texter. All of them combined don't add up to the zeal that I have for Him.

"Well, I was calling you to say don't make plans for this weekend," Juwaun continued, breaking me out of my trance.

I felt my face start to tighten as my eyebrows rose. "Wow, that's pretty demanding of you."

"Okay Angel, could you please not make plans for this weekend?"

"Sorry boo, already made plans. I'm going out with the girls."

"Again?" he asked, with a bit of agitation in his voice.

I had to let his question sink in for a minute. He had caught me off guard with that one. "Excuse me? Again?"

"I mean it seems like I get dissed for your girls every time that I try to spend time with you."

Now I had my hand on my hip. "Juwaun, I've known you for how long now?"

"I don't know, a little over two months. Why do you ask?"

193

"Because, I've known my girls for four years, and you mean to tell me that you expect me to start dissing them for you?"

"No! But you could start spending a little more time with the guy that one day is going to be your man. When we are in a relationship, how are you going to split the time between us?"

"Who said...?" Okay, Angel, take a deep breath and calm down. I inhaled deeply, trying to lower my rapidly rising blood pressure. I tried to speak in a calmer tone. "Who said that you were going to be my man? I thought we were going slow, figuring each other out while we had fun. I told you numerous times that I wasn't looking to be in a relationship right now."

"So you're telling me that you're planning on being friends forever?" he asked sarcastically.

"Certainly longer than a month!" I shot back.

"Do you honestly think that I would have bought all of those gifts for a woman who I thought was just going to be my friend?

"Are you serious?" I switched the phone to my left ear and my right hand was now on my right hip.

"Wait, I...I didn't mean it like—"

I cut Juwaun off in mid-sentence. "Now we finally get down to the real deal. What were you trying to do, buy me or something?"

"That's not what I...what I mean—"

"Now you see why I was turning down your gifts. A nigga buys you something and the next thing you know, he's acting like you're his wife." Now I was stomping around my family room. "You know what, come and get everything, everything that you've given me. I can't be bought."

"But baby?"

Click! Can't believe this shit. "Damn it!" As soon as I let my guard down. I scrolled through my phone log and dialed Tierra.

"What's up girl, you ready for—"

Johnie Jay

I cut her off. "Can you believe this nigga?"

"What? Believe who?" Tierra asked sounding dumbfounded. "Who are you—?"

I barged in again. "He acted like he couldn't understand why I couldn't cancel Saturday with y'all to spend it with him."

"Well what's so bad about that? A guy trying to spend time with you these days is priceless."

I exhaled. "He couldn't understand why I couldn't cancel Saturday, especially after all of the expensive gifts that he bought me."

"What? Are you serious? Did he actually say that?"

I knew that I had added a little, but it was still on the right track. "Serious as a fucking heart attack." I felt my heart beating fast as if I was preparing for a fight.

"Wow, and to think, I'm up here believing he was one of the good ones," Tierra said.

"Shit, you and I both. I'm done with his ass!" I shouted, still heated over the incident.

"Whoa let's not be so hasty. Now I can see making him suffer for a bit, maybe withhold the ass."

I stood staring at my ceiling. "We haven't done anything yet."

"So you've been getting those gifts without giving up anything. Even better Angel. You have to stay with him!"

"What, are you crazy?" I asked, looking at my phone while taking it from my face.

"Hear me out. I think that you have just scratched the surface. You can get much more than you did. He's going to really be throwing out the gifts now, knowing that you are upset." Leave it to Tee to give me the typical hood response. Instead of her having my back, she was trying to capitalize on material things. I have to love her though.

"Um okay Tierra, thanks for the advice. I'll...I'll um holla

195

at you a little later."

She had excitement in her voice now while thinking of her master plan. "Okay girl, but remember, keep him around for a while. It will be good for all of us." Which was her main reason from the jump for me getting with him.

"Yeah, I'll do that." I hung up and dialed Brianna.

I came on her with the same opening statement, but she had a slightly different opinion than Tierra. "Well I think it's pretty obvious, you have to leave him alone." That's my girl. "If he's thinking that way already, how will he be later on? It will only get worse."

I smiled while thinking about how different my two friends were. "I just got off of the phone with Tierra. Guess what she told me to do."

"Please, I don't even have to guess. 'Stay with him and get everything that you can.' Am I right?" she asked, already knowing that she was.

"You've got it. I mean I see what she is saying to an extent, but there comes a point where you can't compromise your integrity for a pair of earrings. I don't ever want guys to think that I'm obligated to them." I heard a beep and looked at my phone's screen. It was a text message. "Hold on Bri."

I went into the message inbox and read my new text. **Hey, are you busy?** It was from Mr. Mystery.

I texted back, **Give me one sec!**

Ok

"Hey Brianna, I'll call you back in a few."

"Okay baby, nice show by the way."

"Thanks, I do my best." We said our goodbyes, and I walked to my bedroom and sat on my semi-soft mattress. I continued doing what I had started a minute ago. Hey are you still there, I pressed send and patiently waited.

Fifteen seconds later, I received my response. **Of course**

196

I'm here. What are you up too?
> **Nothing, relaxing...thinking about you!**

Is that so? I imagined his eyebrows rising on the other end of the phone. And what are you thinking about?

I read his text and smiled as I texted back. **I was thinking...when was I going to see that thick dick of yours...in person?** I figured that would throw him for a loop.

> **Um, am I reading this right? Thought the deal was to keep this over the phone?**
> **R U scared or is your face that unattractive?**
> **Lol, if I remember correctly baby, I was always game for actually meeting up, but I fell back to make you more comfortable.**

Mmm hmm! I was trying to put some of the blame on him but it was me who wanted to keep our relationship over the phone. In some strange way, this made me feel safe. It kept me in more control of the situation. After this last month or so, the mystery texter and I have grown quite close. So close that I'm actually contemplating breaking one of the main rules.

You've been a good boy and I figured that we should meet and see how good our personal chemistry is. I couldn't believe that I was actually doing this. I shook my head as I pressed send.

My phone alerted me quickly of his response. **Now you're talking my language Gabrielle. So when are you thinking that this little meeting should go down?**

My fingers were moving like little butterfly wings over my phone's screen. Before my rendezvous with him started, I didn't even know that I could text this fast. I felt like a damn court reporter. **I'm thinking that you should get a ticket to Michael Baisden Masquerade Ball this Saturday...that way if your face is really ugly, lol, you can cover it up with a mask.**

Lol, I see you got jokes. Well my dear, I don't have to go out and get tickets because I already have them. I'm already going to the ball.

I looked at the words on my screen and held my breath as my heart skipped a beat. My phone alerted me of another incoming message. **Seems like we were meant to meet. Probably would've danced together and wouldn't have even known.**

Looks like it, I texted back.

Check your picture mail, he instructed.

I went into my picture mail and opened the newly sent pictures. My eyes focused in as that gorgeous ass dick that I have become so accustomed to seeing popped up on the screen. I licked my lips as I imagined that fathead resting on them.

Hope that gets you over until you actually see it in person.

I instantly rubbed my nipples as I felt them harden. I unenthusiastically removed my hand so that I could reply. **So what if I want to see it Saturday?**

As in...actually at the ball? he asked.

There...or afterwards, I nervously texted back.

Then we'll make it happen.

Mmm hmm sure you will. Send.

Trust me, I wouldn't say it if I didn't mean it. My heart sped up as I thought of actually seeing it in person what has made me play with my pussy and orgasm so many times. **If you want to see it then you will see it.** I believed every word. I loved when he talked to me with his cocky attitude. The same way I loved when Baby Boy did it.

I might just hold you to that!

If you're going to hold it baby...you might have to use both hands.

I looked at that picture again. At least eight inches and super thick, I thought to myself. I looked at my tiny hands. "Damn, he might be right," I whispered. **What are you doing over there**, I texted and sent.

Driving.

Driving? How did you take that picture?

Lol, I pulled over to a side street, pulled it out and...snap!

U R A freak! And it turned me on so much.

He texted back, **And proud of it.**

So where are you headed?

Home, from the gym...wanna cum with?

Mmm would love to cum with, I texted back, **pussy is puckering as I'm typing.** I patted Kitty as I pressed send.

I waited anxiously for my phone to vibrate with his response. Taste it for me.

Taste it? I was a little confused.

Yes!

Now? I typed with a question on my face and on the screen.

Yes, with your fingers. I want you to taste yourself.

He was so nasty. It drove me crazy. I never had anyone talk to me the way that he did. I gave in to what he wanted me to do, although he didn't have to push me very hard. **Mmmm, tastes like honey,** I texted after I sucked my index finger.

I bet it does. How many fingers did you use?

One.

Use two, I want you to really taste my pussy for me. Kitty must've liked this game because at that moment I felt her supplying plenty more honey for me to taste.

I held the phone down toward the bed as I spread my legs wide and inserted my middle and ring finger, slow and deep in my moist slit. I arched my back as my Kitty adjusted to its new neighbors. I felt the phone vibrate in my free hand and read the new message.

199

I'm pulling over to a side street. I'm going to tell you exactly what I want. Instead of typing words just type "..." we'll make that be your words, your response.

I texted back, trying not to get my sticky juices all over my phone. **Okay, but it feels soooo good!**

Lol, pull them out, slowly and use both of them to play with your clit. Put it between both fingers. Imagine that your fingers are my lips.

I did as he instructed and placed my clit in between my two fingers sending tingles through my pelvic bone.

... I replied.

How does that feel baby? Is it wet?

...

Very wet?

...

I want you so bad baby, right now! You ready for me, for this dick?

...

Reading his words had the same effect on me as if he were right here saying it in my ear. I felt my O nearing from deep in my womb.

Put them back in baby, both of them. I did. **Faster, fuck that pussy faster.** My orgasm was now halfway down. My pussy was making smacking noises from being soaking wet. **Put another finger in,** he demanded.

...

I struggled to put in the third finger and imagined the three of them together being close to his girth.

Do you feel me baby, do you feel me stretching those walls...squeeze that pussy on me mami...cum baby...cum for daddy!

.... I held the period on my phone as I closed my eyes

200

and released my orgasm. I looked at my phone and his last remark, after a couple of seconds of trying to catch my breath.

I can't wait to see you Saturday, and to tell you personally what I want to do to you, until then...!

Thanks to my secret texter, the rest of my evening was wonderful. I went to the gym, had a good workout without seeing any distractions, well, at least not the one that mattered. I did see a nice piece of meat running next to me on the treadmill and thought about putting the moves on him. But I am going to be more than occupied in a few days. Don't need any more complications right now.

I came two more times playing with myself thinking about how good my nut was earlier that night before going to bed.

The next day while at work I decided to have my girls over for a couple of drinks and to try on our dresses for the upcoming ball. The first to arrive at my place was Tierra. "Hey Tee!"

"Fuck the small talk; I need a drink. These bitches damn near drove me crazy at work today."

I closed the door. "Well damn, hello to you too." Outsiders that heard Tierra speak would probably say that she's rude, but everyone who knew her knew that this is just who she was.

She walked over to my couch and sat down. "I mean they got all moody because I came back a little late from lunch."

Okay, I figured that I would bite. "A little late Tee? How late is a little late?"

"Just an hour," she said casually.

"An hour," I shouted. I looked at her and even she had to laugh. "You are a mess. Is that your dress?" I asked, pointing to the garment bag that she brought in with her.

"Sure is! That's my baller-getter."

"Whatever, what do you want to drink?"

"What you got?" she asked, turning around on the couch

looking at me.

"Wine, vodka, Patron, but they were supposed to be for the daiquiris that I'm making later."

"Why do we have to wait?" she asked, sucking her teeth.

"Because, our other friend hasn't come yet and I'm still waiting for the pizza." While we waited for Brianna, I poured Tee a glass of wine and listened to another one of her great dick capers.

"You should've seen it. I lost track of how many times I came...we fucked for like four hours." Yep, it was the same ole story. About ten minutes later, there was a knock at my front door.

"Hey girl!"

"Hey mami," Brianna answered, and wrapped her arms around me, giving me a hug. I did the same and we both released our embrace uncomfortably quick. "Hey Tee." Brianna walked over towards Tierra and draped her dress over the arm of the couch.

"Do you want something to drink?" I asked her.

"Of course, that's why we're here?"

"And here I am thinking that you guys were coming to see me," I said, moping to the kitchen to fix Brianna a drink.

"We did Angel, of course we came to see you," Brianna assured me. "Just as long as you keep supplying the drinks." My two friends gave each other high fives.

"Whatever. Forget y'all."

My girls and I chilled out, drank, and enjoyed Jet's pizza. I'm really glad they're in my life and I enjoyed every moment that I spent with them.

Tierra was the first one to show off her dress for tomorrow. Brianna and I tried to wait patiently for her to come out of the guest room.

"Okay girls, feast your eyes..." Tierra came from the hallway and stood in front of us.

"I thought that you were going to put the dress on. Where

202

is the rest of it?" I teased.

"Shut up Angel. It isn't that tiny." She rubbed her hand over the short black satin and sequined dress.

"The hell it isn't." Brianna agreed with me and we both laughed. Tierra strutted in front of the couch and struck a couple of poses. Her dress, although short, was very cute. It was strapless and came to her upper thigh. Her DD's snuggled in nicely without looking smashed. She already had her long, human hair ponytail in and ready for tomorrow.

"I should've brought my shoes. I'm telling y'all I'm going to be fly as hell up in that bitch!" She had her hands on her hips now, acting like she was posing for the paparazzi.

Next up was Brianna. Tierra had changed back into her clothes and was now sitting on the couch with me. We were all on our third daiquiris

"Okay, I'm letting y'all know right now, I'm not taking any booty jokes," Brianna said, as she stepped into the living room to show off her gown.

"Gotdamn girl, are you smuggling something back there?" Tierra stood up to get a closer look at Brianna's donk.

"Shut up Tee. Angel what do you think?"

I looked at her gold form-fitting, hip hugging, ankle length gown. "I love it. For real, that dress is beautiful. But your ass," I said cracking up laughing, "is so damn big!"

"But does it look good?" she asked.

"I just said it does," I said, standing up and looking the dress over.

"No, my ass. Does my ass look good?"

"Of course it does," I answered, now feeling the effects of the Patron in my margaritas. "You know your ass always look good." I gave Brianna a light pat on the ass. She gave me a smirk that suggested she wanted me to do it again. Tierra was obviously too tipsy to notice. "I can already see the trail of guys following up behind you."

"On the real Bri, that dress is fire," Tierra said, walking around and getting a panoramic view.

"Okay girls, guess it's my turn. Looks like we've saved the best for last." I teased.

"Whatever, just put the damn dress on."

I went into my master bedroom and slipped my dress on. I loved it from the moment I laid eyes on it two weeks ago at Neiman Marcus. It came down to my ankles and had a deep split up to my thigh up in the front. I looked in my closet mirror before going back downstairs. I smiled in approval at myself as I left the room.

"Here I come," I announced. I paused at the bottom of the stairs, holding on to the banister with one hand. Brianna started whistling and clapping like I was the recipient of an Academy Award.

"What the hell? Are we going to a wedding or something? This chick looks like a damn bride," was Tierra's reaction.

I released the banister and walked closer to my friends. "Please, wedding gowns are nowhere near this fly." I modeled in front of my girls feeling like a superstar.

Tierra ran her hands over the soft satin and lace on my gown. "Girl, I can't even front, this dress is crazy. Shows off the cleavage, hips, and the ass and gives you a peek at the legs while you walk. It's perfect!"

"Aw, thanks Tierra. You're about to make me cry." Tierra giving a compliment was such a rare thing I was thinking that I should've recorded her comments on Brianna and I.

After modeling our dresses for each other, we all sat on the couch and watched The Real Housewives of Atlanta marathon.

"You better be taking notes Angel, this might be you one day," Tierra said.

"Me? Yeah right. I don't think I'm cut out for that lifestyle.

Seeing my husband one or two days out of the week, and him going to different cities without me is not my idea of a healthy relationship. I don't think I could do it. You feel me Bri?"

"Mmm hmm," Brianna answered softly, sipping on her drink.

"Well I could," Tierra threw in.

"No shit! I never would've thought."

"Shut up Angel," Tierra had to laugh at that. "So what time are we leaving tomorrow and who's driving?"

"Um okay, yeah, about tomorrow...um." Both of my friends looked at each other and then fixed their stares on me. "I think I might meet y'all at the ball."

"Meet us? Why is that?" Brianna asked, looking a little shocked.

"Um, I'm supposed to be meeting someone there and if everything goes right, no telling where I might end up later that night." I blushed a little, hearing reality spill from my lips.

"Whahhh, look at you trying to pre-order a booty call. So who are you supposed to be meeting?"

Even though I didn't actually tell Brianna about meeting the mystery texter, she was looking at me like she already knew. I thought for a couple of seconds before spilling the beans. I told my girls everything about my text-capades from the first night up until now. Tierra sported a huge look of shock.

"My girl is a fucking freak! The same guy that sent you the picture of the pretty dick? Bri, you knew about this?" Tierra asked.

"I mean she mentioned it, but I didn't know all of the details. So you're finally going to meet up huh?"

"Yes, I'm so anxious. I hope he's not short. It doesn't look like it from the pictures."

"Let me make sure I'm getting all of this," Tierra said, still trying to put it all together. "You've been texting this guy ever since you sent us the dick pics?"

"Yep, I can't wait to actually meet Baby Boy either."

"Me neither," Brianna chimed in. "Everybody says he looks good."

"That's what I hear," I said, smiling.

"Wait, wait, who the hell is Baby Boy?" Tierra asked, waving her arms.

"Damn Tee, where have you been? That's the guy who calls in on The Michael Baisden Show who debates...with...me." I slowed down my words, realizing that I haven't been filling my girl in to the events of my personal life. Since I was in the tell-all mood, I figured I would tell her all about the show and Baby Boy, and also inform her that's how we received the VIP hookup for the masquerade ball.

"And here I am thinking that you were just the sixth caller or something. I'm going to have to change my stations up so I can hear my girl. Dang you're a star up in this bitch, and I didn't even know it." Brianna and I started laughing.

"Okay now that I've caught you guys up and have come clean it's your turn to do the same. Time to come clean on something that you have been holding back from the sisterhood."

"She must be talking to you," Brianna said looking at Tee, "because I tell my girls everything!"

"Me too," Tierra said, looking away.

"See, y'all are not playing fair," I said, crossing my arms and pouting like an infant.

"Okay you big baby, dang!" Brianna let out a big sigh. She took a sip from her margarita. "For the last month, I've been dating Joe, and I think we may be getting a little, well, exclusive."

Tierra and I looked at each other like who the hell is Joe? The name did sound somewhat familiar. And then after clearing the haze off my brain that the alcohol was providing, "Wait Joe, Joe? Isn't that the white guy from the club, the quarterback?"

"The one from the Lions?" Tierra asked. Brianna shook

her head yes while looking down towards the floor. "Damn Bri, you've had a case of Jungle Fever all of this time and didn't even tell us?"

"Well technically it's not Jungle Fever. She's damn near white herself."

"Shut up Angel! Anyways, I think I really like him. He is so nice. Hope he's not putting on a front like Juwaun, but he hasn't tried to buy me any gifts. He just takes me out a lot and spends time with me." She was smiling from ear to ear.

"Look at you, all gushing. Haven't seen you this happy in a while," I said.

"I know I really am happy though. I know it's still early, but so far so good."

I walked over and gave my girl a big hug. "I'm so happy for you." I turned around and looked at Tierra who looked like she was sporting a little attitude. "Your turn!"

She looked at me rubbing her temple with one hand and waving me off with the other. "I'm not joining in this shit. I don't have anything to tell anyway."

"Why are you getting so feisty Tee? I'm sure your ass has some stories you haven't told."

"For real," I said, and high fived Brianna. "You sure you don't want to tell us about another five hour fuck fest?"

"Or a guy that you've met with a fifteen-inch dick?" Brianna added. The liquor had us loose lipped now. The things that Brianna and I usually said to each other, we were now saying in front of Tierra.

"I'm saying, can you spare some of those super dick dudes for your girl? Here I am starving for stiff dick, and my girl over here is fucking all the guys with the best stuff."

"I'm just glad that she's not bi, she probably would take all the chicks with the wettest pussies too." Brianna was now laughing so hard that she was holding her stomach.

In the midst of us laughing, I happened to look over at Tierra, who now had her head hung down and what appeared to be tears were running down her face.

"Tee?" I stood up and cautiously walked over to my girl. "Tee, are...you okay?"

"Tierra, oh my God! I'm so sorry baby, I was only joking I didn't mean to—"

Tierra cut Brianna off in the middle of her statement. "No, don't be sorry. It's not your fault. It's mine." She raised her head and revealed her red eyes and tear soaked face. "I let him...I let him strip me of everything."

"Who? Did someone hurt you?" I asked, gently rubbing her back.

"My first crush in high school. I liked him so much." She sniffed and wiped her face. Brianna pulled some tissue from her purse and handed it to her. "Would've done anything for him. He actually asked me to fuck him and his boys. I couldn't believe it and when I refused, he forced himself on me. When he finished, he let his boys have their way. The first guy who I thought I was in love with took advantage of me."

"I am so sorry Tee. I never knew." I tried to apologize for my recent childish behavior.

"It's not your fault. I never told you. Never told anyone. I think because of that I started looking for love from anyone who would show me that they were interested, even if it was just sexually. It's easy for you two to find someone; you guys are so pretty. When I'm with you, I dress revealing to ensure me getting any attention, but most of the time the result is I end up getting noticed by someone who don't really care for me."

I was really feeling bad now. Brianna and I were sitting on both sides of Tierra's feet crying harder than she was. Tierra blew her nose on the tissue and let out a laugh. "I guess that's coming clean for your ass huh? Oh and for the record, the big dick and forever fuck stories were exaggerated too. Instead of looking like a slut to my girls, I figured that I would make the guys as perfect as possible to try to make y'all envious of me like I was of you two."

"Tierra, you make it sound like you're not pretty. I think that you are very attractive," Brianna said.

"Whatever, you don't have to butter me up. I know I'm the least attractive out of the group," she said, giggling. "I just don't like feeling like I can't compete."

"That's the thing baby," I said cutting in, "with your girls, your sisters, you never have to compete. Now with other chicks, maybe, but we should never feel uncomfortable around each other. So from now on, if there is something bothering us we're going to let it out. Deal?"

"Deal!" they both chimed in. We gave each other a group hug and finished our drinks. We chatted for a little while longer, and I let my girls know that I had an early hair appointment and that I had to get my beauty sleep. I offered for them to spend the night, but both of them chose to go to their own beds. While lying in bed, I thought how blessed I was to have two best friends.

The next day at Kali's Salounge, I sat on the plush microfiber couch and looked at the clock on the wall, as the long arm went twenty minutes past my appointment time.

"Kali will see you now," the upbeat receptionist informed me.

"Thanks." I walked back to Kali's personal room and saw a lady standing in the mirror admiring her do.

"Thanks Kali, you always do me right girl. I have to look good just in case I run into my boo today," she said, before turning to face Kali.

"What, are you going into work today?" Kali asked, laughing.

"No, not him," she responded smiling, "even though he did leave me an urgent message saying that he need to talk to me. I was talking about the guy that I met at the club. You know, the one that's starting to play hard to get."

"Oh, I remember, you're talking about Mr. Irresistible?" Kali replied.

"Yes, mmm girl you should see him. Making me horny just thinking about him."

Kali waved as she noticed me in the room. "Hey girl," she said, nodding me to come over. "Well Kandi if he looks as good as you say he does, ask him if he has a brother."

"Will do," she said, walking by me flashing a courteous smile.

Kali waited a couple of seconds before going to her door and closing it. "Girl, whew! She is a mess. Do you remember when I told you about her situation with the boss? Well now, she's on this other guy something crazy. Talking about he's playing hard to get. Puhh! From the things that she told me, it sounds like he just don't want her."

I laughed at my beautician. Gossip was a natural part of the beauty shop. "You are something else."

"So what are we doing today?"

"I just want a wrap. I'm going to wear it straight for the ball."

"Oh speaking of the ball," Kali said, tapping me on the shoulder, "that's what she was getting her hair done for. And get this, her boo that she was talking about seeing, she don't even know for sure if he's going to be there. She said that chances are that he will because he goes to all of the live events. Going to surprise him I guess. Can anyone say stalker?" She started moving her fist up and down as if she was stabbing someone.

"Wow!" I think that I was starting to see a little too much of this woman.

"So why are we doing a wrap, that's a little boring for a ball isn't it?"

"Well kind of, but I'm wearing a little gold beaded Egyptian hairnet to go with my gold mask."

"Ooouuu that sounds cute. Make sure you take pictures."

"I will." For the next forty minutes, Kali filled me in on the latest gossip around the shop while washing and styling my mane. I loved getting pampered. Getting your hair done made a woman feel like a new person.

On my way home, I got a car wash, checked on my parents, and stopped by Bob Evans to get a chicken Wildfire salad to go for my lunch. Think that I'm going to eat light today, I don't want to be too stuffed when it comes to this evening.

At 3:00, I called my girls to see how their day was coming along. Tierra was at the nail shop getting her mani and pedi, while Brianna was at lunch with Joey. I can't wait until I'm able to go to lunch with someone that I genuinely like.

Unlike the rest of the week, today was going exceptionally slow. I tried to do little things around the house to take my mind off of the event, but failed miserably.

I watched TV from 6:00 to 8:00 and it felt like four hours instead of two. My girls and I agreed to meet at MGM at 10pm, which meant that I had to be leaving out of here at 9:30. I figured I'd take a nice relaxing bath with a glass of wine to knock off a big chunk of the remaining time.

Sitting in my tub, suds up to my neck, I let Beyoncé serenade me while I enjoyed sipping on my Moscato. I have a good feeling about tonight, I thought to myself as I placed my glass on the tub and grabbed my loofah. I thought about the first night that I saw the man I thought would be an important part of my life, as I gently lathered my breasts.

As my fingers ran over my nipples, I giggled at the fact that I really had an orgasm from just thinking about Him sucking on my titties. I fought with myself over going there again. I really wanted to masturbate, but I had to get him out of my head. I didn't want to give him any more power over me than he already had.

Before getting out of the tub, I put the sweaty wine glass to my lips one last time to finish off my drink. After getting out, I towel dried and oiled myself with Oil of Olay shimmer lotion. While selecting a pair of black thongs from my lingerie drawer, I heard my phone ring.

"Hello?"

"What's up girl!"

"Hey Bri, I'm just about to start getting dressed."

"Same here. I just got off the phone with Tierra, and she said that she's getting ready also. Aye, that's crazy what went down last night, right?"

"I know, I've known Tierra for almost five years and I never knew that she had been raped." I held my hand to my heart feeling a fraction of the pain that she must've felt.

"I felt like a complete asshole when I saw her crying." I heard the remorse in Brianna's voice.

"We have to make sure that we are there for her if she needs us."

"I totally agree. Okay on a lighter note," she said, now with excitement in her voice, "I'm getting really excited about tonight. I heard it's going to be a lot of celebrities there, but everyone is going to be semi-disguised, so you could be talking or dancing with anyone."

"Yeah I'm excited too, can't wait."

"So you and Baby Boy are finally going to meet huh? And make sure you tell him to take off his mask, so we can see how he looks."

"Yeah, I'm definitely going to figure out a way to see his face, I might take him out in the hallway or something." We both laughed.

"Alright Angel, give me a buzz when you leave out."

"Will do!" I hung up and started preparing for my night. I

walked around my place switching between two pairs of shoes, trying to decide which ones would be most comfortable for tonight. I decided on the gold pumps. Next on the agenda was my hair. While standing in the bathroom mirror, I placed the gold beaded hairnet over my wrap, and secured it in place with four tiny hairpins. I tested it out by shaking my head from side to side. "Nooooo, stop it! I am not the most beautiful woman that you have ever seen," I said, out loud to the imaginary guy complimenting me. "A goddess, me?" I held my mask up to my face and smiled as a true resemblance of Nefertiti stared back at me. I placed the mask in my gold beaded clutch that I had selected to carry, and looked myself over one last time in my full-length mirror. "Okay Angel, let's give'em hell!"

Ten minutes after leaving my house, I cut the dancing in my car short to call my friends. "What's up Bri?"

"Hey, have you left yet? And turn the damn radio down," Brianna yelled over the phone.

"I can't, this is my jam. They're playing the hits tonight. I'm ready to go get my groove on," I said, nodding my head to the radio. "I guess I'll turn it down a little. Where are you?"

"About to hop on the freeway."

"Same here. Hold on," I said, checking my caller ID. I clicked over when I saw Tierra's name flash across the screen. "What's up bitch!"

Tierra laughed. "Hey hoe, where are you?"

"Just about to hop on the freeway and you?"

"I just got on. Have you talked to Brianna?"

"Yep, she's on the other line now."

"Okay well when you pull up to the casino call me. Tell Bri to do the same."

"Okay," I said, before clicking back over. "That was Tee, she said to call her when you get there."

"I'll make sure to do that. You go ahead and get back to

213

your dancing. I'll talk to you shortly."

I laid the phone on the seat, and went back to enjoying the lively mix music playing on the radio, until I exited off the freeway and headed towards MGM Grand.

When I saw my phone light up, I thought it was one of my girls telling me that they had arrived, but when I picked it up I saw that I had a new text message. I opened it and began to read. R we still on? My heart sped up as the reality set in that we really were going to meet tonight.

I texted him back, **Of course we are, unless you're chickening out.**

My phone vibrated in my hand alerting me to his response. **I wouldn't dare...can't wait to see you!**

I smiled. **Same here.**

I'll text you when I get there.

 I'll be waiting! I inhaled and exhaled deeply as I pulled up to the front of the casino. The line was getting thick but after about five minutes, it was finally my turn. "Ma'am," the valet said as he opened my door. He handed me a ticket and instructed me to give it to any of the attendants when I was ready for my car.

Immediately after entering the casino, I heard a woman instructing guests to go to the second floor for the Michael Baisden party. I called my girls while I took a seat on a plush love seat in the lounge area near the casino's entrance. Tierra was already in the valet line and Brianna was just pulling up. I looked on as more masqueraders showed up for the ball. A few were tacky, but for the most part, everyone that I saw looked quite grown and sexy.

While admiring everyone else's masks, I was reminded that I hadn't put mine on yet. Guess I'll step in the ladies room before my girls showed up. From the looks of things, I wasn't the only one with that idea because every mirror was currently taken; women were lined up placing or straightening their decorative masks. This really did remind me of Eyes Wide Shut.

Johnie Jay

I took my place at the mirror just as someone was leaving. "Like that dress," I said, as the women in the flowing fire red dress passed me.

"Thanks, love yours too," she responded. When she turned around, I saw that she was wearing a mask that was graced with red feathers.

I moved to the vacant mirror and placed the mask's elastic band under the hair at my nape and the beaded net. The mask only came to my nose, so I still had to make sure that my lips looked kissable.

I felt my phone vibrating in my handbag and retrieved it. It was Tierra. "Hey, I'm in the ladies room to the right, as soon as you come in." A couple seconds later, my girls come into the ladies room.

"What's up y'all!"

"Damn it's packed in here," Tierra said, nudging me over from the mirror. "Let me get in here and put my mask on."

"Hurry up, I have to put mine on too," Brianna said. We all had the same mask, but we colored and decorated them to match our dresses.

We took the elevator up to the second floor and waited in line to enter the ballroom.

"Do you see all of these good looking men?" Tierra said, looking around the waiting area. Many of the men had not put their masks on, and I'm sure a few probably wouldn't since it wasn't necessarily a requirement. "I'm going to remember what they got on so if I see them with masks on, I'll already know who I want."

"You are a mess," I said, as we stepped to the door. I gave my name and they gave us three VIP passes and pointed us in the direction of Michael Baisden's white tent in the far corner of the ballroom. "You guys ready?" I asked my girls, but I really was asking myself.

Brianna held up both of her hands while walking into the

215

music and the crowd. "Let's get our party on!"
Here goes nothing!

Finally

This party was off the hook. Michael definitely did it big this time. I've been to a couple of his other parties, but none of them were like this. There were so many women, but I think the most exciting part of it all is that you really could meet someone famous, and not really know it.

"I'm so glad that you scored these tickets dawg. I would hate if I would've heard about this party afterwards," Caesar said, looking around the crowded venue.

"I feel you. Let's head over to the VIP tent and see who's up in there." I only had one person that I really wanted to see, well two. Halo was first on my short list. I had also told my little texter friend that I'll hit her up when I made it here. The truth was that I was already here when I texted her. I had to make sure that I checked out the scenery first and if everything went well with Halo, I might not get back to that text.

"Mike B!" I yelled to the man of the hour who had his mask in his hand.

"Future, that's you?"

I laughed. "The one and only."

"I couldn't tell; you look so much better with that mask on." We gave each other a pound and a half-hug.

"You're going to play your boy like that huh? Aye, this is my ace, Caesar." I watched as they gave each other the man's customary handshake.

"Please tell me that you're not anything like him?" Michael said, teasing Cease.

"Of course not," Caesar replied, shaking his head looking in my direction.

"So are y'all enjoying the view?"

"Definitely, you've outdone yourself tonight, man." My attention was momentarily distracted as a woman with a huge ass walked right in front of us.

"You know," Mike put his fingers to his temple while focusing on the same woman, "I might just have to agree with you on that one. Man, y'all better get your drink on. The bars under both tents are open bars, so help yourselves."

"Sounds good to me," I said, looking at Caesar who seemed to agree.

"Mr. Baisden, they have that microphone working for you now," a young lady who looked barely legal cut in.

"Thanks, you remember Future don't you, and this is his boy Caesar."

"Wait a minute, are you the same person who helped me out at the last event when they couldn't find my name on the list?"

The young lady's smile reached from ear to ear. "Jada, nice to meet you again," she said, arm extended.

"Same here," I said, shaking her hand. "Okay Mike, guess I'll meet up with you later. We're about to go get our buzz on."

"Alright Future. Oh," he said, holding a finger up and stepping a little closer, "I haven't seen your girl Halo yet, but I got my eye out for her."

"Damn, almost forgot that she was coming," I said, trying to suppress my smile.

"Yeah, I bet. I'll let you know if I see her."

Caesar was close by trying to spit game to a female that had just passed by. I gave him the sign, letting him know that I was headed to the bar. By the time I reached my destination, he was right behind me.

"Yo, I think I'm going to really enjoy this party," my boy said smiling. We both ordered our usual and Caesar ordered an extra martini. "Now this I don't mind, getting a drink for a chick that I don't have to pay for is alright with me."

We both laughed. "I feel you."

"I'm about to go holla at ole girl for a few," he informed.

"Okay, we'll hook back up in a few. I'm about to go see who I can see." I walked around for a little while, sipping on my drink, looking at everyone partying and discreetly looking for my angel in white.

After not seeing anyone who matched what I thought Halo would look like I decided to go on to option number two. I pulled out my phone and texted, **Hey are you here yet?**

A couple of seconds later, the response I was looking for came through my phone. **Yep, what are you wearing, where are you?**

I looked at my surrounding and texted back. **I'm in the back near the ivory columns, navy blue suit.**

Okay, I'm about to come and find you.

Okay, I texted back. I must admit that I was a little excited to meet the woman who damn near every night has had Buddy hard with anticipation to read her words on my phone. God please don't let her be ugly.

I took a couple of steps forward and scanned the room for Halo. There was no sign of that white dress of hers, the only clue that I had to find her tonight. Then I looked up towards the front of the ballroom at Michael's tent and saw a stunning princess with crazy curves dressed in a white dress. I couldn't get a read on her face from this distance because of the mask and the sea of people. I started walking in her direction to cut her off from wherever she was headed before stopping in my tracks. Damn it, I had forgotten about my texter who was on her way back here to meet me.

INEVITABLE ACT II

"Hmmmmm," I sighed, thinking which decision I should go with. Okay Future, just go with your heart. I bobbed and weaved through the crowd to get the woman in white, who seemed to be calling me towards her without even opening her mouth.

It's Him

"Nice to finally meet you," I said, shaking Michael Baisden's hand. "Crazy party by the way." I then turned to my girls. "I'd like you to meet my two best friends, Tierra and Brianna."

"Now I know this is a masquerade ball ladies, but I'm the host damn it, and I want to see some faces, especially yours," he said, pointing at me. We all giggled as we removed our masks. I had almost forgotten that I had one on. "Wow, friends of a feather. You women are beautiful. What was your name again?"

"Tierra?"

"Tierra," he repeated, looking her up and down. "Very nice, and Halo, do you want me to call you by your real name or—"

"Halo is fine," I said, cutting him off. "Don't know if I want people to know who I am just yet."

"Perfectly understandable," he said nodding his head. The girls and I put our masks back on. "Man, Baby Boy is going to go crazy when he actually sees you."

"Is he here yet?" I asked, looking around.

"Yep, as a matter of fact, he just left the tent a little while ago, and he was asking about you."

"Yeah I'm sure. With all of these women here he's definitely not pressed about me." I was hoping that I was wrong.

"Somehow, I doubt that," he said, chuckling. "Oh well, I don't want to keep you ladies from the party. Halo, I have a couple of people from the show that I want to introduce you to later. Until then, ladies please make yourselves at home, and please get your drink on. The open bar is over there. And if you need anything, especially you darling," he said, looking at Tierra, "you let me know."

"I think somebody has a crush on Tierra," Brianna said, as we made our way to the bar.

"Girl please, he's a little too old for me. But he does have money and he is cute," Tierra said, looking back in the direction of the white tent.

I removed my vibrating phone from my purse and read the new text message. Hey are you here yet? Reality was starting to set in now. I mean I never thought from that first wrong text that I would still be in contact with him and especially not planning to meet.

I nervously texted him back to find out where he was. It was time to show and prove. "Okay y'all, get me a wine."

"Where do you think you're going missy?" Brianna asked.

"I'm about to go see how this guy really looks."

"Do you want us to go with you?"

"Hell naw, because if his face don't match up with those pictures he sent, y'all are not going to be dogging me." They laughed. "I'll be right back."

I started walking towards the back of the ballroom, headed for the big set of ivory columns. On the way, the wolves were eyeing me up and down.

"Aye yo!"

"Damn mami!"

Guys had no clue on how to treat a lady. I mean all they had to do was be mature and say something like—

"Hey beautiful, I've been looking all over for you. May I have this dance?" Wow! Yeah, something like that. He took the words right out of my mouth. I guess he really wasn't asking, because he already had me in his arms and my body synced with his swaying to the music. "So Halo, we meet at last."

I had no doubt in my mind that this was the infamous Baby Boy. I would recognize that voice of his anywhere. "And how do you know that I am this...this Halo woman that you're speaking of?" I asked, trying to contain my smile.

"You have to be. I told you on the show that I could tell by your voice that you were beautiful. Tonight you are absolutely the most beautiful woman in here, even with the mask on. Plus the hairs on my neck and arms are standing up." He smiled wide.

Damn! I hope the guys around here were taking notes. Now that's how you talk to a lady. "You are laying it on kind of thick aren't you?" My hands were on his chest and arms. He felt like a carved out piece of stone under the softness of his navy blue pinstriped suit.

I looked at the part of his face that was exposed from his mask. His lips looked deliciously familiar. He must've noticed me looking, because he gave them a nice slow licking. Felt good in his embrace. Reminded me of dancing with Juwaun, but better.

"So I'm taking it that you didn't come with your man."

"Nope, don't have one. And you?" I asked, looking up towards his face.

"Nope, don't swing that way."

I laughed. "Well that's good to know, but I was talking about a woman."

"Same answer," he said, not taking his eyes off mine since swooping me up.

"Come on, I know you're doing at least three of these women up in here. I mean you're Baby Boy!"

He flashed a brilliant smile and let out a hearty laugh. "I know what you must think about me from the show, but I'm not that bad. Baby Boy is kind of a façade. I'm actually a nice guy when you get to know me."

"Mmm hmm."

"Let me see your face," he demanded.

"No," I teased, turning my head away but still holding him tight. "You haven't earned that privilege yet." I think we may have danced to about three songs by now, and I forgot all about my drink and my texter. I owed it to myself to at least try to find out what he actually looked like. I definitely wasn't going to let Baby Boy get too far out of my sight. My hands struggled to detach themselves from the curves that they had settled in. "I need a drink."

"Cool; let's go get one," he said, as he paused our dancing.

"Actually I already have one on standby with my girls. Thanks to you, they're probably worried about me."

"Look, I have to be honest. I've wanted to see you ever since the first time that I heard your voice. So I don't know what you have to do, but you need to come back." He brought his face closer to mine. "I need you to come and meet me here...really soon."

I was stunned by his bluntness and it seemed like an eternity as we stared in each other's eyes. He smiled and warmed my heart.

"Okay, how about we meet back here in ten minutes."

"Eight," he tried negotiating.

"Ten."

"Ten? Right here?" he asked, with a serious look on his face.

I laughed at how eager he seemed. There was no way that this was the infamous Baby Boy from the radio. "Yes silly! Right here."

"Okay, I'm setting my watch. And then maybe you can show me your face."

"Maybe," I said, walking into the crowd. God, this guy had me where it was hard for me to breathe. His aura was so dense, you

224

could tell that it would take you over if you let it. I looked back and made sure he didn't see me when I changed directions and went back to my original destination, the columns. Now it was time for a little acting. I pulled my phone from my handbag and began texting. **Hey, where are you? I've been back here by the columns and I don't see anybody that's tall and handsome. I** nervously pressed send and waited for a response.

Lol and I didn't see a drop dead gorgeous woman that looked like she was looking for me so I went looking for her. Where are you now?

Still back here, I texted as I reached the meeting point.

Good, I'm coming for you!

I stood anxiously waiting for guy number two. He's got his work cut out for him, I thought as my mind drifted back to Baby Boy.

No Way No How

Okay, I don't know where this guy is, but I've been waiting for like five minutes now and I have to meet back up with Baby Boy in a few. To top that all off, my buzz is on zero.

I looked around again for a guy who looked like he might fit the bill. Judging by all of these beer bellies that I'm seeing, none of these guys could possibly be him...I hope. Plus all of these guys are gawking, but none of them are stepping to speak to me. Let me go check on my girls.

On the way towards the VIP tent, I noticed a little commotion in the crowd. I couldn't really tell what it was about or who it involved because of the thick crowd of people in here. Whatever it was, I was too fly tonight to get caught up in it and possibly wreck my dress.

"Damn nigga, where have you been?" I heard Tierra's big mouth ask over the loud music.

"Looking for y'all," I lied. "Where is my drink?"

"Girl that was about a half hour ago. I drunk that and I'm in need of another one," Brianna said, laughing.

"Good, come on girls; I need one bad. Aye look, there he is," I said pointing forward to Michael Baisden's tent.

"What...who?" Brianna asked.

"Baby Boy," I answered. I saw him talking to another guy pointing to the middle of the floor where I saw the commotion going on a little while ago.

"Where? How can you spot anyone in this crowd?"

"Forget it. I'll just introduce you to him later. Let's go get that drink." And that's what we did. We drank, laughed, talked about what people were wearing, and drank some more. What really got us going is when we saw a plus size woman, in a lime green dress with lime green hair to match. I wondered if she was the caller from the show that was all on Baby Boy to get a dance.

As my girls continued clowning the Jolly Green Giant, I received another text from the guy that I haven't met yet informing me to meet him in the lobby. I lied to Tierra and Brianna when I told them that I was headed to the restroom and would be right back. I left the party, stepped into the lobby, and looked from left to right. I didn't see any sign of anyone looking for me.

"Hey!" Guess I was wrong. I turned around and saw Baby Boy leaning on the wall behind me. "I know that you are not leaving already," he said, now standing tall. "Not when you're supposed to be meeting me on the dance floor for another dance."

Damn he looked good, but I didn't want him to see me out here meeting some other guy. "Naw I'm not leaving, just waiting for one of my friends. And what are you doing out here?"

"Same as you," he answered with a sly grin. "Waiting on a friend."

"Mmm hmm." Okay where is this guy? Baby Boy and I both looked around nervously. There were about thirty seconds of uncomfortable silence. I took a couple more steps away from him and began texting. I'm here. I pressed send and waited.

At that moment, I heard the same text message alert that I had on my phone, come from someone else's. I turned around to see Baby Boy looking at his phone, which happened to be the same kind of phone that I had. He looked at me for a brief second, and then swept the area from left to right. Something wasn't right. My heart started to speed up when he began texting on his phone. "Naw," I whispered, "couldn't be." He looked at me again, still holding his phone.

My phone chimed out loud. I can't believe this. Baby Boy walked closer towards me.

"Halo?" he asked softly.

"Yes," I answered, barely loud enough to hear myself.

"Gabrielle?" he asked, louder than his first question.

I dropped my head in disbelief, shock, and embarrassment, as I thought of all of the conversations and the pictures that I've sent. This guy who I've wanted to meet from the show knows exactly how every part of my body looked. "How did this...how did we?" I let out a long sigh. My mystery texter was Baby Boy.

He lifted my chin up with his index finger. By now I was in dream world. I rubbed my temple and realized that I still had my mask on. He knew how everything else looked on me, might as well show him my face. "Well I guess you probably want to know my name," I said, as I began to remove my mask.

He laughed. "Yeah, that would be..." He abruptly stopped his sentence as my face and identity finally were revealed.

"I'm Angel."

He took a couple of steps back with his mouth wide open. "I can't believe...Angel...all of this time...it's you?"

"What is it?" I asked, confused. I knew I looked good tonight, but I would have never expected the reaction that he was giving at the moment.

"I'm...I'm Future."

I laughed. "Future? Are you serious, that's your real name? This is so weird," I said, shaking my head.

"Yep, real name."

"Okay so...are you going to show me your face?"

He started looking serious. "Are you sure?"

"Damn is it that bad?" I asked, laughing nervously.

He removed his mask and every bit of breath that I had in my body left me in that moment. I mean it really felt as if someone had balled up their fist, and punched me as hard as they could in the gut. This had to be a trick.

"You!" That's the only word that I could manage to get out. Now I was scared. I mean this was really scary. "I...I can't." Okay, let me try to make some sense of this. The guy, my guy from the club just happened to be Baby Boy, who just happened to be the guy that I mistakenly texted, and have been in constant communication with ever since.

I looked around for hidden cameras. I started getting dizzy. I needed fresh air before I fainted. Before I knew it, I was running into the nearby ladies room. I splashed cold water on my face and tried to awaken from this strange dream but it wasn't working. The restroom was packed and noisy and I couldn't think. I had to get out of here at least for a second. I had to get outside. What if he was still waiting for me outside of the ladies room? No matter, just ignore him don't say anything and keep walking.

I raced out of the ladies room and rushed into the awaiting elevator doors. When it reached the first floor, I quickly went through the revolving doors. I had finally got outside and didn't know what to do next. While looking both ways before crossing the valet pickup, I caught a glimpse of a woman in a red dress cursing up a storm as she hopped in her red Range Rover.

I stopped to catch my breath and my composure. "Angel, wait please!" I turned around half-stooped over and saw Baby Boy...Future, whatever his name was, waving for me. Then I heard a car engine revving really high. "I love you!"

Right at that moment, everything moved in slow motion. The red Range Rover raced in Future's direction. I saw his eyes, the sincerity and the truth. I saw her eyes, the hate and the rage. She was yelling and pointing and even though her windows were up, I knew what she was saying was smothered with expletives.

Her vehicle drew nearer to him. I closed my eyes and screamed, "Future!" When I opened them, he was lying in the middle of the road and the Range Rover sped away. I ran over and held him in my arms. Women were screaming and the guys from valet were just standing around with their mouths wide open. "Call 911, please!" I screamed to the top of my lungs. He was bleeding from the top of his head and his body felt like it weighed a ton. I was sitting on the ground, white dress and all, with his head on my lap. My dress now resembled a candy cane. I heard familiar voices through all of the bystanders.

"Oh my God, Angel! Are you okay?" Brianna asked, with Tierra in tow. I couldn't answer them. Not at this moment. My voice was temporarily loaned out to Future.

I continued whispering in his ear, "It's going to be okay. Don't you dare leave me, you can't leave me."

Future squeezed my hand tight. "I need you," he mouthed, before passing out in my arms. The casino's medic and security removed me from him against my will and the paramedics placed him on a stretcher before loading him into the ambulance. Caesar, who I remembered from dancing with the first night I encountered Future, convinced the medics to let him ride in the ambulance.

Brianna found out where they were taking him and shortly after we were in her car going to be near his side. "Where is Tee?" I asked, while reclined all the way back in the passenger seat.

"She's driving your car, right behind us."

"Bri, nothing can happen to him."

"He's going to be fine, I'm sure."

"No, you don't understand. We're supposed to be together and we haven't even spent any time together yet. He can't leave me like this. Not like this."

We pulled up to the hospital and joined Caesar in the lobby. He hung his head and his eyes were red with worry. "His parents will be here shortly," he managed to inform us. I sat by him and placed my hand on his shoulder. I haven't really prayed in I don't know how long but right then and there I did. I prayed and prayed some more. Please God, you do this one favor for me and I promise I will start going back to church.

"Caesar, what happened?" The couple entering the lobby had to be Future's parents. He looked like them both. Caesar rose to meet them and followed them both to the check-in desk. I looked at them fade into the bright lights of the hospital, and prayed that Future wasn't doing the same.

I was awakened by a soft nudge. I immediately looked at my watch. I'd been asleep for about an hour and a half. I looked to my left at my girls who were both asleep, propping each other up as they sat in the chairs. When I looked to my right, I saw the woman who came in earlier with her husband. This was no doubt Future's mom. "Come with me dear," she said, reaching her hand out for mine. I gave it to her and we walked for what seemed an eternity down the hallway towards...the light.

All or Nothing

I called out Angel's name as she ran into the ladies room with shock in her face. I mean I'm just as shocked. The same woman that's been driving me crazy ever since I saw her in the club, is the same woman who has tickled my fancy during the talk show, and from texting over the phone. Now I know that she's supposed to be in my life, and tonight I'm going to let her know so, even if it kills me.

My phone rang and I eagerly answered it thinking that it was Angel calling from the ladies room wanting to talk. I had to look at the caller ID when I answered to make sure that I was hearing correctly. "Carolina?" At first she said nothing, just sobbed. "Carolina, are you okay?" Damn I really didn't need any more drama right now. I turned my back from the ladies room while moving a couple of steps away from the door.

"He's...he's in the hospital."

"What?" I asked, plugging up one of my ears to try to hear her over all of the noise. "Who's in the hospital?"

"Franklin, he's...in the hospital," she repeated.

Oh Lord, I hope she didn't try to kill him. "Did you—"

She cut me off. "No...it's not what you think, we...actually made up. He told me about the entire affair and we both decided to work it out." More sobbing. "She...I told him that she had to go. He had to fire her. The next thing I know he called me and said that he had been stabbed and she left him for dead."

I couldn't believe what I was hearing. "When did this happen?" I asked.

"Tonight around nine. I'm at the hospital right now."

"Is he going to be okay?"

"Yeah, I think so. It was so scary when I didn't know..."

"So...where is the woman, the secretary?"

"I don't know. He told me that she was dressed up and was headed out to some ball before the altercation."

"Ball?" I questioned looking around for...I didn't know what.

"Yeah...I think...Michael Baisden's thing."

This is some freaky shit, I thought to myself. "Did you call the cops?"

"Not at first, but after getting him checked in and the doctors asking all of these questions, they informed me that it would probably be a wise idea. I was just so scared and confused that I didn't even think. I just thought about him being alright." My mind was still stuck on the fact that this crazy bitch was probably at the same event that I was attending. "I knew that she was bad news the first day I heard that name."

This was the second time that I've heard her talk about this chick's name. "What is it? What's her name?" I asked, ear pressing hard into the phone.

"Fyre."

"Fire?" I asked to make sure.

"Yes, with a y. Crazy huh?" I repeated her name in my head. Sounded familiar, even though I didn't know anyone by that name. "Probably why she's always wearing all of that red," she proceeded to say more to herself than me.

I stopped breathing. Could it be? Then my mind went back to the night that Carolina spent the night with me, and the rant that Kandi went on through text when she found out that I wasn't going to let her come over. I think she said something to the

233

fact that if you play with fire you'll get burned. I remember thinking that she mistakenly misspelled fire, when in reality she was referring to her real name. Shit! I was right, that bitch is really crazy.

I saw someone come out of the ladies room out of the corner of my eye. "It's Her!"

"What, who?" Carolina asked.

"Um...Angel," I answered reluctantly.

"Angel? Not the Angel—"

"Yep, that's the one," I said, cutting in. "I'll explain later." I watched as she disappeared into the elevator heading downward before I could reach her. I hurriedly entered the waiting elevator next to the one she took, and pressed the star button to go to the main floor.

There she is. She was exiting the casino through the large revolving doors. I looked from left to right when I exited the building. I saw her standing right across the valet aisle from me. All of the feelings that I had for her that were bottled up inside of me began to boil and bubble up to the surface. "Angel, wait, please!" I thought about if I really wanted to say what I was about to say, and realized that it wasn't a matter of what I wanted, but what I needed to say. "I love you!" I yelled as I stepped into the street.

That's when I saw what had to be a hallucination. A red Range Rover, driven by a woman wearing a red mask and a red dress headed right towards me. That's the last thing that I remembered before seeing my entire life, the good, the bad, and all of the ugly, flash right before my eyes.

Angel's Future

September was the best month of the year, well for me anyways. Not just because it was my birthday month, but also because it's the month that begins the cool down from the summer. Just when things get a little too hot here comes September to calm it down.

These first two weeks were busy ones for me. My actual birthday is next weekend and my first official housewarming was going on today. I couldn't have asked for better weather. It was sunny all day, just a hint of a breeze and a mild seventy-five degrees for the high.

My girls had helped me prepare most of the food the day before, so there wasn't that much for me to do except play hostess, which was actually a tall feat in itself. I had friends and family out in the backyard earlier during the day, but as the sun went down the party migrated towards the house.

Like most get-together's in the black community the elders come out early, but now that it was getting late the real party was about to begin. I walked around my new home asking people if they needed anything, picking up empty dishes, and laughing, mostly at Tierra acting silly as always. Her new man was just as crazy as she was. They made a perfect couple. She told me yesterday that she was going to be bringing someone by. She told me that I knew him and that they had been talking secretly for the last month. When she walked in with my unofficial boss, Michael

Baisden, I almost fell out from shock. For the first time since knowing her, she seemed to be truly happy.

In the living room, people were playing spades at the card table. Brianna and her boo, Joey, were tearing holes in everyone's asses. "How many games straight is that now?" I asked.

"Ten and counting," Joey answered, smiling.

"That's right baby and we're going to win ten more." Brianna and her boyfriend slash card partner high fived. Even though he was white, Joey meshed in very well with all of us. He was very comfortable. Brianna gave me a wink and asked me if I could bring her another glass of wine.

My friends were happy and I was happy for them. Life was good for everyone. I opened the fridge and removed the bottle of Moscato to fill Brianna's glass. "Oh my God!" I said jumping, seeing someone standing right in front of me as I closed the refrigerator. "You scared me!"

"My bad," he said laughing. "I didn't mean to startle you. Tierra just let me in. I rang the doorbell though."

"I didn't hear anything with all of this noise in here. I was wondering if you were going to be able to make it." I pulled out the cork and poured my girl and me a glass of wine. "I was waiting for you to call."

"I did, three times," he said, smiling. "When was the last time you checked your phone? Bet it's on silent."

I pulled my phone from my back pocket and it was on silent. I had three missed calls and one missed text. I opened up the text message and began to smile even before I began to read. **I have something for you tonight...something good!** He knew how to get my motor revved up.

"What's wrong with you, why are you smiling so hard?"

"Oh no reason," I replied, blushing. I turned around, leaned back on the counter, and recorded the sight before me. Mmmm, this guy was something good. Body was tight, hard, solid.

Face was ruggedly handsome and his voice melted my soul every time he spoke.

"Mind going out for a little fresh air?"

"Actually, I think that would do me good right now." I walked to the living room and handed Brianna her glass of wine. I told Tierra to keep everything under control and that I was only stepping out for a minute as I headed out of the back patio door. "Damn, only a minute, that's all he got? You better find you someone else girl," Tierra joked, causing everyone around to erupt in laughter.

"Get your mind out of the gutter girl," I said blushing, and closed the patio door behind me. We walked toward the lit up lake that was in walking distance from my townhouse. I took a seat on one of the benches that surrounded the lake and looked at the moon's reflection as it bounced off of it.

I looked up at him. "Are you going to sit down? And what was this "something" that you have for me?" I asked, with a sly grin. He smiled and leaned his crutches on the side of the bench. Then all of a sudden, he lost his balance and fell to his knee. "Oh my God, baby...are you alright?" I asked, about to grab his arm to help him up.

"Yeah...yeah I think I'm okay." He raised his head and looked directly into my eyes, "But I think that I would be better if..." he placed his hand in his pants pocket, removed a velvet box and opened it revealing a dazzling two carat solitaire platinum engagement ring, "...you would marry me."

I couldn't believe it. Tears started pouring from my eyes as I screamed yes from the top of my lungs.

Future and I have been inseparable ever since he went to the hospital the night of the accident. I remember when his mother came and got me from the waiting area and brought me into his room. He was very fortunate to only have a small fracture in his leg. She told me that right before the meds relaxed him into sleep, he'd told her that for the first time he was in love. She told me that she thought it was the medication talking at first, but from the look in his eyes when he said it, there was no denying that he was indeed telling the truth.

We've been open and honest about everything. He has told me about his past with the plethora of females that he was dealing with, including the woman who tried to take him out. He told me that he would understand if it were too much for me to handle, and I told him that I could handle anything as long as he was honest and continued to be.

We walked back to the house and as soon as I stepped on the patio, I yelled and waved my diamond rock around, letting everyone know of my new situation. I was indeed happy and my Future...looked very, very bright.